The Girl
Who Never
Came Home

BOOKS BY NICOLE TROPE

My Daughter's Secret
The Boy in the Photo
The Nowhere Girl
The Life She Left Behind

The Girl
Who Never
Came Home

NICOLE TROPE

bookouture

Published by Bookouture in 2020

An imprint of Storyfire Ltd.
Carmelite House
50 Victoria Embankment
London EC4Y 0DZ

www.bookouture.com

ISBN: 978-1-83888-971-5
eBook ISBN: 978-1-83888-970-8

For D.M.I.J.

PROLOGUE

They find her body after twenty-three hours of searching.

She is lying at the bottom of a small outcrop of grey-brown rock. The rock is covered in a slippery green moss and one of the searchers, a woman named Adelaide, almost loses her footing as she peers over the edge despite being a resident of the mountains and a keen hiker. She attributes her near slip to the tears clouding her view. It is a terrible thing to see. The girl lies with one leg slightly angled and her arms above her head, her eyes closed and her blonde hair tangled around her face, a sprinkling of freckles across her cheeks. Her phone is lying in one open hand, the screen unbroken.

Unlike her.

She could just be sleeping were it not for the halo of dried blood that surrounds her head.

They find her just as the sun is beginning to rise, as cockatoos squawk to welcome the day.

Adelaide had been sceptical about finding anything in the early-morning spring mist, but the search had begun at dawn, a new group of searchers keen to get going. Some volunteers had looked through the night despite the cold and the danger of walking through the bush in the dark, where snakes twist in dense foliage and foxes hunt their prey. Those shining their torch beams at every skittering noise had taken some comfort from the hooting of owls even as they ducked to avoid swooping wings seeking dinner. There had been little conversation for the few people searching in the dark. Everyone was tired, and only the occasional radio check had interrupted the sounds of the night-time bush. Adelaide had left to go home and get some rest, knowing that she would be up before the sun rose to return, hoping that she would receive a message that all was well and the girl had been found. Her sleep had been light and restless as she listened for a text telling her she was not needed.

This morning, with the passing of nearly twenty-four hours, more people arrived to help.

A missing child spurs everyone on.

It was a flash of colour, a bright neon pink that caught Adelaide's eye. She had been looking for pink.

The description of the missing girl began with pink.

Zoe was last seen wearing a bright pink parka and blue jeans with silver sneakers. She has blonde hair and green eyes. Height: 5ft 3. Weight: approx. 52 kilos.

Zoe's mother had objected to the parka, believing it would not be warm enough for overnight camping in the Blue Mountains, but Zoe had apparently insisted.

Adelaide would not have been able to spot a grey or green or brown jacket, as the wearer lies amongst the overgrown bush and creeping ferns. It's lucky it is pink.

Adelaide calls for help and she leans over to see better, taking a step or two forward, her foot slipping on the moss. 'Oh, baby,' she says, tears spilling over. Adelaide lives in a small house in the Australian town of Leura with three cats and a budgie. She never married or had children but she is a favourite aunt to her six nephews and nieces. The youngest, Peta, is sixteen, and for a moment, Adelaide sees Peta lying still in amongst the bush. She cannot help more tears as she watches the SES volunteer, who arrives quickly and rappels down the side of the rock.

It is only a few metres off the ground and, were it not for the slippery moss and the instruction to wait, Adelaide would have climbed down herself.

Zoe didn't fall far and would probably have had a story to tell as she healed in hospital from a broken leg or arm had she landed differently. As it was, her head hit a small buried chunk of rock with only its point sticking out of the ground.

As it was, she didn't survive.

CHAPTER ONE

The Day After the Accident

Lydia – The Mother

The news filters through the search parties via mobile phones and walkie-talkies with lightning speed. When her phone buzzes at the same time as the walkie-talkie of the SES volunteer she is with, a woman named Irene, Lydia feels her heart lift because it can only be news that they have found her, they have found Zoe. Her tense body is flooded with relief and she imagines herself berating her daughter: 'You gave us a real scare, Zoe. How could you have done that?' She has a vision of her arms around her child, of how tightly she will hug her as she thanks God that she has been found.

As she swipes her screen to answer the call, she watches Irene's face fall, watches the woman put a hand to her mouth. Earlier, as the morning began, Lydia took comfort in Irene's obvious knowledge of the bush, her broad capable shoulders, face weathered by the sun and her quick smile. 'Kids, eh?' she said and Lydia nodded and it only seemed possible that this would one day be a story told at dinner parties – that time when Zoe disappeared from school camp.

Lydia's whole body was buzzing with adrenalin at five this morning, her hands numb with cold despite her gloves. She had only returned from searching overnight for an hour before she was ready to go again.

'You should stay here and rest. You've been out all night,' Irene said to her when she arrived to take over from other helpers.

'Would you?' Lydia replied.

Irene began to nod but then moved her head to shake it instead. 'No, no, I wouldn't.'

Lydia sipped her coffee, hot and bitter, while Irene checked her pack for everything she might need. 'I've lived in the mountains all my life. There's no place I haven't been to. We'll find her,' she said. 'Only last week we found those tourists who had been missing for four days.'

Lydia recalled the story from the news, remembering that it was a couple of Chinese tourists who had gone missing. They had been found after four days, dehydrated and suffering from hypothermia but very much alive and still cheerful despite their ordeal. The thought immediately gave Lydia hope. Zoe could easily survive a day and a night in the bush. Easily. They would find her today, and tonight she would be home safe, tucked up in her bed. Lydia passed the hour she had been walking with Irene planning Zoe's favourite meal for tonight: spaghetti carbonara with garlic bread and lemon cake for dessert. She tried to mentally go through her fridge for the ingredients, finding that listing the number of eggs she would need and wondering if she had enough Parmesan cheese kept her heart beating steadily instead of allowing it to gallop and pound as it had done all night.

'Zoe!'

'Zoe!'

'Zoe!' echoed all over the mountains.

Lydia was quiet, her voice hoarse from a whole night of shouting her daughter's name.

Zoe, could you please not leave your towel on the bathroom floor?

Zoe, have you finished your homework?

Zoe, do you want to help me make some cookies?

Zoe, it's time for bed, night, love you.

Zoe.

Zoe.

Zoe.

'Any minute now,' she comforted herself. 'Any minute now.'

Now, as she watches Irene and answers her own phone, Lydia knows, and it feels as though the knowledge has always been there, that she has always known that this is how it would end. Irene's shoulders slump; defeat bows her body. Zoe has been found but she is not just dehydrated and suffering from hypothermia. She is not just hurt. If she was any of those things, Irene would be rushing Lydia to where Zoe has been found. If she was simply hurt, there would be some cause for celebration, and Lydia is sure that she would hear the immediate roar of the rescue helicopter that she knows is waiting on a nearby field. There would be movement and panic and voices calling through the trees, but there is nothing like that. Just silence and sadness and Irene's pale face.

Zoe is not just hurt. It has only been a day and a night but she is not just dehydrated and suffering from hypothermia and maybe a broken bone or two.

This will not be a dinner table story. This will not be something Lydia shares a wry laugh with friends about. This will be the end of something, of everything. The unthinkable has happened. Her little girl is gone. For a moment she thinks about not answering her phone because then she will not have to hear the truth. But she can see tears shine in Irene's eyes and she feels a flash of sympathy for the woman because she is the one walking with the mother of the child they have been searching for. *I am the mother of the child.* She understands that she cannot turn back this time, cannot erase this moment.

It is Gabriel calling her. Her husband, Zoe's stepfather, has somehow heard the news first, and she feels that this is wrong. She should have heard the news first. It's her daughter.

'Oh God, Liddy, I'm… oh God,' he says. If he were here standing right next to her, he would put his arms around her, would take her weight as she feels her body sag. But she sent him off with someone else, wanting the people who love Zoe to be spread out, to be covering more of the dense bush, where thickly abundant tree roots poke up through the ground, waiting for unsuspecting walkers.

'I know,' she croaks. 'I know.' And then she hangs up.

Her thoughts flash on Zoe's father, Eli, on his exhortations that she 'take care of their babies' as he took his last breaths. She has failed her late husband. She has failed her elder daughter Jessie, and mostly she has failed Zoe, who is gone. She called her phone many, many times after she got the call from the school at 8.30 a.m. yesterday. She had anticipated Saturday morning breakfast with the paper, maybe a short walk with Walter, although the old dog prefers sleeping these days, and perhaps an afternoon movie if she and Gabriel felt like it.

But her mobile had trilled at 8.30 a.m., startling her from her contemplation of the garden. The time is seared on her brain. She will never be able to see that time again without linking it to her daughter's death. Was she still alive at 8.30 a.m. yesterday? When did she take her last breath? Her first breath was an indignant howl at being disturbed from the safe world of the womb. What did her last breath sound like?

Was she still alive when the phone call disturbed Lydia's peaceful Saturday morning plan?

'Is this Lydia Bloom?'

'Lydia Lawson but yes, I was Lydia Bloom.'

'Zoe Bloom's mother, correct?'

'Yes,' she replied, more irritated in that moment than anything else by the interruption to her day.

'I'm afraid it's Paula Fitzsimmons from the year eleven camp.'

'Yes,' she said, slowly, carefully. Zoe had left for camp on Friday and Lydia expected her home on Sunday. As she replays the conversation with the teacher, Lydia remembers that her first thought was, *What has that child done now?*

'I'm really sorry to tell you this, but Zoe is missing.'

'What?'

'She's missing. We know she was in her cabin last night but we can't find her this morning.'

'That's… just ridiculous. What do you mean you can't find her? Have you looked for her?'

'We have, Mrs Lawson, and I'm really… I'm so sorry but we can't seem to find her. We have people out searching and we have called the police. They will be arriving shortly.'

'But I don't understand. How can she be missing? She's at camp with you and everyone else. How can she be missing?'

'I am so sorry, Mrs Lawson. I understand this is hard to hear but your daughter is missing and the police have been called.'

'Have you called her? Does she have her phone with her?'

'We have but she's not answering. We assume she has it with her as it's not in the cabin. I have to go now. We are all helping to search. I needed to tell you in case you wanted to come up here.'

'Obviously, I'm coming up there,' Lydia spat, fury replacing bewilderment.

'Good, you have the information on where it is?'

'Yes… yes, go and find her, just go and find my child.'

'We're trying, Mrs Lawson, we're all trying. I'm so—'

Lydia abruptly ended the call, her heart racing. *How can she be missing? She's at camp. Children don't go missing from camp.*

The minute she hung up on the teacher, she called Zoe's phone. It went straight to voicemail. 'Hi, you've reached Zoe. Leave a message and I may just get back to you.'

'Zoe, where are you?' she barked into the phone.

Over the next few hours, she called her daughter continually, leaving a message each time she heard her voicemail.

'Zoe call me.'

'Zoe, please let me know you're okay.'

'Zoe, people are looking for you!'

'Zoe, where are you?'

She couldn't help thinking that her daughter would answer her call. Whatever had happened, she would answer a call from her mother. Eventually, Lydia gave up, accepting that it was switched off or the battery had run flat, meaning the police couldn't pinpoint the signal, meaning she was missing a whole day and a whole night.

They found her. They found her. They found her.

She thinks about the last words Zoe said to her as she got out of the car to climb onto the bus leaving for camp. 'Why do you have to be such an uptight bitch?'

'You're the bitch,' Lydia replied. Not something she had ever said before and not something she had ever imagined she would say. The words had darted out of her mouth, pointed and poisonous, and she had instantly regretted them. A good mother shouldn't speak to her child that way. A good mother shouldn't lose her temper with her teenage daughter. A good mother should understand that her child is in a transition phase, that her body is governed by hormones and confusion. Lydia has always considered herself a good mother, or a reasonable mother at least. She had shocked herself with her words and had instantly felt her stomach twist.

Zoe was spoilt. There is no doubt about that. Lydia always indulged her younger daughter, allowing her to get away with things that her older sister, Jessie, would never have been allowed to get away with. But lately Lydia found herself putting her foot down, saying no and stopping Zoe from doing exactly what she wanted to do. She was turning – or trying to turn – Zoe's behaviour around, trying to make up for the fact that she had been so lax with her. She could feel her daughter slipping away from her and into a life that could – that did – result in tragic consequences. She was too interested in boys, too fascinated with drugs and alcohol, too keen to be allowed to travel by herself. She answered 'nothing' and 'no one' and 'just out' to Lydia's questions when she left the house. She ate her dinner in front of her laptop or the television. She breezed past her mother without even acknowledging her when she arrived home from school. She was distant and angry. She was sixteen. She was.

'Time to start putting my foot down,' she said to Gabriel only a couple of months ago, and he agreed, but Zoe chafed at the new rules and hated her for them. And now she is gone.

Lydia texted her afterwards, sent her a message as soon as she got home and the regret of angry words settled in.

I hate it when we fight. I didn't mean what I said to you and I hope you have a good time at camp.

Zoe didn't reply and Lydia imagined her stewing in anger. She knew her daughter would tell her best friends Shayna and Becca that her mother was uptight and neurotic and bent on keeping her from ever having any fun.

'No,' she had told Zoe when she asked if she could attend a rave in the middle of the bush with Shayna and Becca the weekend after school camp. 'You're too young. It's too dangerous. No.' She had already denied this request but her daughter didn't give up easily. She was patient and would wear Lydia down to get what she wanted.

'No,' Lydia had said to Zoe about getting a smartphone when she was fourteen but Zoe hadn't let up. She'd argued that all her friends had one. She'd left phone plans on Lydia's desk. She'd pouted. She'd cried. She'd said she was being ostracised for not having one, and finally Lydia had given in and got her daughter a phone.

But Lydia was determined to not give in on this. The word 'rave' only conjured up images of drunk or high teenagers and the stories that inevitably appeared in the media once or twice a year, with a devastated parent: 'She had never taken drugs before and now she's gone.' Lydia never wanted to be one of those parents.

So, she had said no.

'I'm capable and intelligent and I've never done anything stupid and you're still trying to keep me tied to the house. Why can't you let me live my life? I don't want to be stuck at home like you every Saturday night. I want to be able to go out and meet people. You're always so difficult about anything that might be just a small bit of fun for me. Why do you hate me?'

Lydia had sighed, knowing that there were probably quite a few things that her daughter had done that she would consider stupid.

'I don't know why you've chosen this morning to have this conversation, Zoe. I don't hate you. I need to keep you safe since you seem incapable of making good decisions for yourself.'

That's when Zoe had called her a bitch and she had replied the same way. And now she is gone.

They found her. They found her. They found her.

A hideous irony. She was at a school camp, under the supervision of her teachers, far away from anything dangerous, supposedly. She would have been safer at the rave.

Her phone rings: Gabriel again. For some reason he doesn't seem to think she has understood what he was trying to say and so he repeats the news. 'Lydia, they've found her and she's… It's not… She's… gone.'

Again, she hangs up. She feels her body sink onto the wet, muddy ground, the moisture quickly soaking through her jeans, chilling her whole body. All around her birds call to each other and crickets chirp, hidden in bushes. There is a smell of damp earth and, surprisingly, lemon from the white flannel flowers that are everywhere. She stares ahead of her, feeling the clusters of leaves on the bushes in front of her closing in.

Irene hunches down next to her. 'Oh, love,' she says, 'I'm so sorry.'

Lydia nods. 'Yes,' she agrees. Sorry is the right word because inside her sorrow has begun to spread through her veins, thick and dark. She feels heavier, colder. She understands that she will never feel any different. She understands this instantly.

Zoe was sixteen. Zoe was beautiful, precocious, flirtatious, clever, funny, angry, defiant. Zoe was her baby and her baby is gone.

CHAPTER TWO

Monday – Two Days Since the Accident

Shayna – The Best Friend

My mother left my lunch outside my door. I waited until I heard her footsteps going back down the stairs to open up and take the tray inside. I didn't feel like a whole discussion and I didn't want to have to deal with her looking at me in that concerned way, like she's afraid I might off myself at a moment's notice. 'I'm here for you sweetheart,' she's said about 500 times since it happened. I mean, I like that she cares and that she just wants me to know that I can talk to her, but right now, I feel like everything I'm feeling or thinking is kind of stuck inside me, stuck inside and covered in glue so I can't really explain it all.

Lunch is chicken schnitzel with roast potatoes, peas and a green salad so it's more like dinner food but she knows I didn't eat breakfast so maybe she's hoping to tempt me with this. It's one of my all-time favourite meals and one that I haven't allowed myself to eat for a long time. I know she made it specially for me. My brother, Jason hates chicken and so when she makes it for dinner, she has to make another meal for him. He's so spoilt. If I was his mother, I would just tell him to eat what's put in front of him, but Mum is such a softie with us. You'd think that would have made us a little wild because she's a bit of a pushover, but if I think about doing something wrong, I think about Mum's disappointed face.

Her blue eyes get so sad and her mouth frowns and she looks like she's going to cry and she says, 'Oh, Shayna, how could you?' It's the best form of discipline if you ask me because I have never done anything wrong – at least not until now – but I don't want to think about that. And even though Jason is only thirteen, he's so busy topping all his classes and being the head of the chess team and the cricket team that he'll never have time to do anything wrong.

I look down at the meal and feel like I want to cry because Mum's put some peas on the plate in the shape of a smile just like she used to do when I was five years old – but I feel like I may never be able to smile again.

An image flashes in my head. A moment in class at the end of last year. I was upset because I had just gotten the worst mark for my history exam. I was sitting next to Zoe, trying not to cry. I knew I should have studied harder but it was on the same day as the maths exam and I had concentrated on that. I was squeezing my nails into my palm because I thought the pain would stop the tears.

'Don't worry about it,' Zoe said to me. 'It's over and your mum will understand.'

'But I didn't even manage a B, Zoe,' I said and then a few tears spilled down my cheeks and I blushed because I could feel everyone starting to look at me.

Zoe grabbed the exam paper away from me. 'I said don't worry about it. It's one exam in a lifetime of exams.' And then she drew smiley faces all over the paper in different colours. 'See, now it's a happy paper,' she said and I started laughing and for a few minutes I didn't feel bad about the mark.

I push away the memory. I want to resist the food, to simply slide the tray back outside my room and return to lying on my bed and scrolling through the endless posts on Instagram about Zoe with all the hashtags – #beautifulgirl #gonetoosoon #missyouforever – but I'm starving. I've been starving since they found her yesterday, at six in the morning when we were all fast asleep. I thought we would wake up to the news that they had found her and she was fine. I hadn't slept well. I zipped and unzipped my sleeping bag again and again, feeling trapped and hot one minute and cold and exposed the next. I listened to her name echoing all over the mountains as the search parties tramped through the night under thousands of stars. 'Zoe, Zoe, Zoe.' I hoped, I prayed that in the morning it would all be okay. I hoped, I prayed that I would never have to think about Friday night again.

But it wasn't okay. It isn't okay and Friday night will haunt me forever.

My stomach is a tangled mess, and for some reason the only thing that seems to calm me down is eating. I put the tray on my bed and turn around to stare at myself in the full- length mirror, hoping that the sight of my heinous body will stop me from eating. I lift my long blonde hair up above my head and angle my face, staring into my own blue eyes and pouting my lips. Zoe always loved my lips.

'You look like you've had fillers,' she said.

I haven't. I'm just lucky.

'But then you look like you've had fillers on your butt as well,' she said right afterwards and then she giggled and punched me lightly on the shoulder. 'Only joking.' But she wasn't joking. Zoe could be a complete bitch but she always told the truth. My butt is enormous.

'Shayna, you're a size eight,' my mum says when I complain about my weight. 'How much smaller could you be?'

The answer is 'a lot smaller' but I don't tell my mum that. I don't need her dragging me off to see a psychologist about my eating.

I would like to be a size six, like Zoe is. Like Zoe was.

I sit down on my bed as I realise once again that she's actually gone, actually dead. People our age aren't supposed to die. Zoe wasn't supposed to die. Without thinking about it, I begin to eat my food, using my hands and chewing and swallowing fast.

Zoe is dead.

At some point on Friday night, she got up out of her sleeping bag, walked out of our horrible cabin and into the dark. Then she fell down and hit her head and died. It sounds like a joke. No one heard her leave the cabin. No one knew she was gone until she didn't come to breakfast on Saturday morning. We thought she was in the bathroom on the other side of the campsite, the one that was only supposed to be for the teachers, the one that she told us she was going to use. 'They won't catch me, I'll go early. It's in much better shape and it has its own hot water system. No way am I having a cold shower because you bitches use all the hot water on this side of the campsite.'

'She will so get caught,' Becca said and I nodded, almost hoping that she would. She thinks she's better than anyone else, that the rules don't apply to her and that she can do whatever she wants. She *thought* she *was* better than anyone else. I have to keep reminding myself that she's dead.

Once we realised she was missing, once someone had been sent to check the other bathroom and we had all gone around the campsite looking for her, Becca and I had to work out what she would be wearing so that the police could be told. I got kind of scared when Ms Fischer told us she was calling the police. Before that I wasn't really worried. I just thought Zoe was being a bit of a dick and hiding or something, but when Ms Fischer mentioned the police, everything changed. Zoe would know not to take things that far. If she had just been hiding, she wouldn't have allowed Ms Fischer to call the cops. I had sent her like a million texts.

Where are you?
Everyone is worried.
We're all looking for you.

The police have been called.
Stop messing around now!
Where are you?

Ms Fischer and Mrs Fitzsimmons also called her phone and messaged her as well.

'It's probably run out of battery,' Mrs Fitzsimmons said after she had tried a few times.

I looked at Becca when she said that and Becca looked down at her shoes. Zoe had forgotten her charger at home and she was going to use Becca's when her phone was done charging. But… I don't want to think about that.

When I think about Saturday morning and about how Mrs Fitzsimmons started to panic even as she said, 'Now, girls, don't panic,' I imagine Zoe coming from behind a bush or a tree and saying, 'What's all the fuss about?'

Ms Fischer would have been so mad but I think Mrs Fitzsimmons would have been so relieved she would have cried. She looked like she was going to cry.

But that didn't happen and in like twenty minutes the campsite was filled with police. And then all these State Emergency Service volunteers dressed in their orange jumpsuits arrived and a whole lot of people who lived in the Blue Mountains as well. Everyone was carrying backpacks and walkie-talkies. The sky was so perfectly blue it almost hurt our eyes, and the early-morning spring air was crisp and sharp. The smell of wood-burning fires from the houses in the mountains was everywhere, even that early in the morning, and it felt like the perfect day for a hike. It was the perfect day to be on a camp in the Blue Mountains, but instead the whole campsite was flooded with adults shaking their heads and whispering to each other. It happened so quickly; it was like they'd all just been waiting for Ms Fischer to call the police, like they all just sat around passing the time until someone went missing in the mountains. It's usually tourists who go missing. The Blue Mountains look like they're filled with easy trails for people to just wander along but just a few steps in the wrong direction and it's easy to get lost. The dark green leaves of the trees blend in with the shades of green of the bush, and it all disappears into the mulchy brown of the undergrowth. Everything looks the same for hundreds and hundreds of metres. It feels nice and familiar when you start walking but suddenly people look around them and realise that they're actually in the middle of overgrown bush, lost in the middle of nowhere.

Becca and I had to go through her stuff, which was really weird because it felt like we were snooping. She didn't have anything interesting in her bag anyway. Her phone was with her and that's where the interesting stuff would be, just like with all of us. I worry now what's on that phone. There are so many private text conversations and so many things Zoe, Becca and I wouldn't want anyone to see. Her phone was still in her hand when they found her. That's what I heard anyway.

We managed to work out that she would be wearing her jeans, her pink parka and her silver sneakers. She didn't have anything else except clothes and toiletries in her bag, nothing that could tell us where she'd gone or anything.

I wish I could cry. I did cry when they told us. They didn't say anything until we were back on the bus on Sunday.

We spent most of Saturday searching, walking with the SES volunteers in small groups, calling her name. It felt kind of dramatic, and I wouldn't say this to anyone, but I'm sure that if Zoe knew about all the trouble she was causing, she would kind of like it. She liked to be the centre of attention.

'Zoe, Zoe, Zoe,' echoed all over the mountains. It seemed impossible that she wouldn't just answer us. There were at least a hundred people looking for her. At least.

On Saturday night we were all sent to our cabins early. At dinner everyone talked in whispers, and most girls didn't eat much. It was some kind of beef casserole and it was pretty gross anyway.

We didn't mind going to bed early. I felt like I'd walked a thousand miles looking for her, and I nearly stood on a brown snake that slithered away as I picked up my foot. It freaked me out completely.

It was quiet in our cabin with her empty sleeping bag there reminding us that she was somewhere else. *See?* it seemed to say to me. *See what you did?*

'I hope she's not too cold,' Becca said.

'I would be so scared,' said Leeanne.

'I think she's just hiding, giving everyone a scare,' I said because I thought that Zoe was capable of doing something like that. Becca and Leeanne didn't say anything but I heard Becca take a deep breath, like she couldn't believe I'd said it. 'I don't mean that,' I said quickly. 'I'm sure she just got lost and they'll find her soon.'

I felt really bad afterwards. But then I got a little irritated thinking about how much attention she would get when she was found. I just knew it would be all over Instagram for days. It's the kind of thing that goes viral. As I lay in my sleeping bag on Saturday night, I thought that this was just the kind of attention Zoe would like, that we all would like if I'm honest. I'm a really bad friend. I feel like I'm the worst friend in the world. But not just for thinking that.

She has gone viral but she won't get to appreciate it at all.

On Sunday morning they told us all to pack up our stuff and get back on the bus that had arrived. At that point we all thought that they had found Zoe, and we were mostly pissed off that we were being sent back from camp early because she had chosen to take a walk by herself and get lost.

I don't know why we thought they had found her and she was fine. Why did we think that?

Sunday night on the school trip is usually the best night because we're allowed to go into the local town, Leura, and have dinner. The year eleven boys from St John's are also on camp at the same time but at a different campsite, and they are also allowed to go into town on Sunday night. So for a few hours at least, it's amazing to be at camp.

The rest of the time it's horrible. The food is disgusting because you can't make spaghetti for forty girls, leave it sitting around for hours and expect it to taste like anything except sludge. And the cabins are basically tin sheds with bunk beds in them, and the mattresses are gross and I'm sure that there must be a billion bugs living in them. They take us on these hideously long walks where some boring dude goes on and on about the native vegetation in the Blue Mountains until you feel like you want to fling yourself off the side of the actual mountain.

But still, everyone was always keen to go on camp because of Sunday night. I had bought a new pair of jeans and a tight, sleeveless black top even though I knew it would be too cold to wear it, but I planned to wear my parka over it until we were inside.

There are twin boys in year eleven at St John's, identical twin boys who are both on the swim team and both just gorgeous with black hair and dark brown eyes. Their names are Nicholas and Michael, and Becca and I had agreed that we were going to get to know them a lot better on Sunday night. We hadn't told Zoe we like them. That was always a bad idea. Zoe liked the attention she could get from boys – even boys she had no real interest in.

'I can't imagine anything more boring than a year eleven boy,' Zoe said when we were discussing camp.

'Maybe you could ask Callum to drive up on Sunday night,' Becca said. 'We'll cover for you if you want to see him.'

Zoe's boyfriend Callum is in year twelve at St John's so he wouldn't be on the camp. Everyone thinks he is amazing but I think he looks like a Ken doll with his square jaw and perfectly styled brown hair.

Becca and I were kind of surprised when she started going out with Callum. The whole of last year she was obsessed with Maddox Donaldson. He's one of those boys who got blessed with everything. He has honey-brown hair and big dark eyes. He's the biggest rugby player on the team at St John's because he's tall and buff and he's smart. Zoe really, really liked him. She would go through his Instagram photos over and over again, liking everything and sending him cute emojis, but Maddox never responded. He never seemed interested… and then all of a sudden, he was.

About two months into this year when it was still hot enough for us to pretend it wasn't autumn, Zoe came to school bubbling with happiness.

'Ooh, you have news,' laughed Becca.

'I do,' she sang. 'Last night Maddox Donaldson finally, finally messaged me, and he and I started talking – *really* talking – and he is everything I thought he would be. He wants to meet this weekend.'

All three of us jumped up and down because we knew how much she liked him. Sometimes we were so close that it felt like when something happened to one of us – good or bad – it happened to all of us. Becca and I were so happy for Zoe that we couldn't stop smiling. 'I'll make sure that when we start dating, he brings along some friends for you guys. All of the boys on the rugby team are cute.'

She was floating with happiness for two days and then, just like that, everything was over. When she texted me the news, I asked her:

But why? What could have happened?

I don't know. I've asked him and he won't tell me. He won't respond to any messages. He's ghosting me!!!!

She was angry for days and we were angry for her. Then she started talking to Callum, Maddox's best friend. And it wasn't long before they were going out.

'What does Maddox think about you dating his best friend?' Becca asked her after she and Callum had been going out for a month.

'He hates it, I'm sure,' she smirked.

Zoe and Callum seemed really happy but Zoe just rolled her eyes when Becca suggested she get Callum to drive to camp, as though she couldn't think of anything worse. Something had obviously changed.

Becca texted me later:

I wonder what's going on there.

I replied:

I don't know. It's weird that she hasn't said anything. Do you think they had a fight or broke up or something?

On the Thursday before camp we had a meeting with the teachers, who gave us the rules and behavioural expectations. We didn't really listen – no one ever does. We were all too busy texting back and forth about where to go for dinner on Sunday night in Leura.

I don't know why we even discussed it since every year eleven group always ends up at Mario's Pizzeria. It's the only restaurant big enough to accommodate large groups, and the pizza they serve is made on a sourdough crust: crispy and chewy at the same time.

'Where do you want to go?' I asked Zoe, and she smiled and said, 'Maybe I won't go.' And then she winked at me.

I knew she wanted me to ask her what she was talking about but I was too busy thinking about the pizza at Mario's and a few hours of freedom on Sunday night.

I know a few of the other girls also had their eyes on the boys from St John's. There was a rumour that one of them had already stashed some alcohol in a park next to the restaurant. We were all really looking forward to Sunday night.

So, of course, everyone was completely pissed when we were told that we were going back early. Girls kept stopping by our cabin while we were getting our stuff together to tell us how annoyed they were. I don't know what they expected me and Becca to say because, okay, I get that she's our best friend, but it's not like we control her. No one controls Zoe.

It was only when we were all sitting on the bus, moaning about having to leave because Zoe had broken the rules, that Ms Fischer told us. 'I have some dreadful news, girls. After many hours of searching, Zoe Bloom's body was located this morning.'

Leeanne put up her hand. 'Is she okay?' she called, and it was only when Ms Fischer looked at her like she was crazy that we all realised what she'd said. They found her body. Not her. Her body. I burst into tears and then Becca started crying and soon the whole bus was just a bunch of sniffing, sobbing girls. By the time we got back to Sydney, the news had gone viral.

I get up off my bed, away from my empty plate, feeling full and sick. I stand in front of the pinboard on my wall. It's covered in pictures of me and Zoe. I take down a picture of the three of us, of Zoe and me and Becca, and stare at it.

It was taken last summer after a day at the beach. The three of us look so happy, so… alive, that it's impossible to believe one of us is gone. All three of us have blonde hair, although Becca dyes hers and her roots always seem to be showing their natural brown. We're all sunburned and pouting at the camera. Zoe is the smallest of the three of us. She's delicate and tiny in her green bikini that matches her eyes, but she has a perfectly curved waist and nice boobs. Her stomach is pancake-flat. Becca is wearing a full swimsuit in silver. Her skin is olive-brown and only her cheeks are red. Her eyes are an almond colour and she has long black eyelashes. I don't think anyone could argue: Becca is the best-looking out of the three of us. I'm just ordinary. Blue eyes and blonde hair that never lies flat the way I want it to and an okay face.

'Rubbish, Shayna,' Mum always says, 'you're beautiful.' She has to say that though.

I remember that after Mum took the picture, we all jumped into the pool to get the sticky sand feeling off, and then we dressed in our pyjamas, even though it was only five o'clock, and Mum ordered Chinese food. It was a good day. We laughed a lot. We don't laugh as much now. I'm not sure exactly why that is.

Maybe it started when she became really into doing stuff that would freak our parents out.

'I'm happy to wait and go clubbing when I get to eighteen,' Becca said and I thought the same thing.

'Rubbish, why wait? I promise you that Callum will get you the best fake IDs. It will be amazing.'

But I didn't want a fake ID. I didn't want to spend the whole night in a club waiting for someone to tap me on the shoulder and throw me out, and Becca felt the same. But Zoe thought we were ridiculous. I hate that we had started to drift apart. I hate that.

I pin the picture of us back up on the pinboard, looking at how small and light Zoe was. She looked like a fairy, like she could fly. But she couldn't, she didn't.

CHAPTER THREE

Bernadette – The Teacher

'All right, Bernadette – is it okay if I call you Bernadette?'

I nod even though I would like to inform the young detective that it's not okay. I am Ms Fischer, but I am aware that now is not the time to get pedantic.

'Bernadette, can you go over the events that led up to you discovering that Zoe Bloom was missing?'

I take a deep breath and pat my hair even though I know it is still in place. I am liberal with hairspray in the mornings. I wonder how old this young man with his mop of brown curls thinks I am. I know from looking in the mirror this morning that I look well beyond my sixty-two years. It's because I don't dye my hair and also, I'm sure, because I eschew all those ridiculous face creams on the market. They're all complete rubbish.

I am no longer a young woman and I believe I have settled into middle age quite comfortably. Menopause brought with it the relief of not caring that my figure is too square, that men don't look at me as I walk down the street. It seems that overnight all those concerns evaporated. I was delighted. I hated looking at myself each night, comparing myself to women in magazines and on television and even the girls that I teach, finding my eyes too small and my lips too thin. When I was a child my father explained to me that I was 'plain' and that it would do me good to find a use for my brain because I was also 'very clever'. I am sure there are those who, today, would call him cruel but I believe he thought he was doing his best for me. The only regret that I have is it took me so many years to simply give up trying to appeal to the opposite sex. No one thinks to ask me about marriage and boyfriends anymore, though I recall that family gatherings were excruciating because of the endless pointed questions about my love life. Many of my relatives are long gone now, and the rest are not really worth my time and energy.

The only things people ask me about these days are my job and my beloved dog Oliver, who is a Maltese–schnauzer mix and the light of my life. Every day he and I take a morning walk and then he waits patiently in the flat for me to return from work. I leave the television on for him. He seems to like the weather channel. He is always delighted to see me, and that's as good a reason as any I've heard for coming home at night. My work is my other joy. It has been for decades as I have watched young minds blossom and grow and change. There is nothing more wonderful than a teenager learning and embracing a new idea. It is so special to see a connection being made and a thought formed. I return home from work energised most days rather than depleted.

When I see how terribly sad Henry from next door is after losing his wife of fifty years, I'm not sure I mind that I never married. Henry is seventy and alone and I am sixty- two and alone but I'm better at it than he is. He fills his days with unnecessary activities in order to escape what he calls the 'dreadful silence', but I have always been very happy in my own company. All in all, I live a very contented life.

I wish I didn't have to be here. I feel a little more tired than usual. I, of course, spent the whole of Saturday night walking with the volunteers in the Blue Mountains and I didn't sleep well last night either. I have been dreading this interview, dreading what I may inadvertently reveal. I am on my guard as I sit here, my body upright and stiff with tension.

I would have liked to have refused to speak to the police again but I'm aware that would be the first signal that they need to be suspicious of me.

I will return to school on Wednesday with the rest of the year elevens, so it's best I get this done now, although they could have called me at a more decent hour than seven this morning to schedule an interview for this afternoon.

As the detective waits for my answer, I reflect on what has happened, on the surrealness of it all. I have never not returned all my charges home safe from camp. Not once in forty years, even in my first few years of teaching when I taught at a boys' school that was filled with the most rambunctious students – I still got them all home safely. I remember being terrified on my first camp. I kept doing headcounts and yelling each time I couldn't find all the boys, but after a few years I learned to relax. Most students are pleased to be away from the classroom and out in nature and their behaviour is usually quite good. Usually.

'I did the rounds of the cabins at the campsite at around nine on Friday night,' I explain to the detective. 'I looked into each of the ten cabins and checked all the girls off the list.'

'And, sorry, did you say how many girls were in each cabin?'

'No, but there were four. Zoe was in a cabin with her best friends Shayna and Becca.'

'That's only three.'

'Leeanne was in there too. She's not close to the other three but then she's not close to any other students either and there was space in that cabin.'

I have a bit of a soft spot for Leeanne, for how awkward the poor girl is, with her perpetually hunched shoulders and the glasses that slip to the tip of her nose as soon as she moves her head, for how dreadful her skin is, for how she makes me see myself at sixteen. Leeanne is, as I was, the smartest girl in the year. She is planning to study law and I have often told her that as long as she sticks with her dream, she will one day be able to look back at her school years and see them as a growth opportunity rather than a trial to be endured. Teenage girls can be terribly cruel. Leeanne would have made more friends if she wasn't so opinionated, so certain of her judgement and so apt to take over in class. It is where she is superior to everyone else but she is resented for her aptitude rather than praised. When her hand goes up, I've heard the other girls sigh with distaste as she waves her arm frantically in front of me, desperate to prove she has the correct answer. I understand that – at sixteen, I was the same way. It was a cruelty for Leeanne to have to be in the same cabin with Zoe and Shayna and Becca, who seem created to appear on an Instagram feed, but there was nothing to be done. It was the only cabin with a spare bed.

'Right, so you checked in on them at around nine and did a roll call.'

'Yes. I gave all the girls the same instructions. They were not to leave the cabins for any reason other than to use the bathroom until the next morning, when they were expected at breakfast at seven.'

'And Zoe was definitely there when you checked on the girls?'

'Yes, definitely. She asked if they would still be allowed to go to dinner in Leura on Sunday night.'

'Dinner in Leura?'

'Yes, it's part of the tradition of the year eleven camp. We feel that the girls have reached an age of responsibility and therefore they are given a few hours of freedom on Sunday night. There had been… some difficulties earlier in the day… so the girls were all concerned that the Sunday night treat would be taken away. I got asked the same question at virtually every cabin.'

'Difficulties?' asks the detective with a quick nod. This is what the dark-eyed young man has been waiting for: an explanation of the difficulties that occurred on Friday afternoon. I, obviously, explained what had happened to the constable as soon as the police were called in so I don't see why I should have to go through it all again.

'The girls were specifically instructed not to bring any contraband on camp. We understand that they will bring junk food but we will not, under any circumstances, tolerate any alcohol, cigarettes or illicit drugs. It shouldn't even be something we have to put in an email, but every year we do and every year the girls are aware that their bags will be searched before they are allowed to go to their cabins.'

I purse my lips as I remember at least three emails from parents who expressed concern about their children's rights being violated. One father had written in protest:

You are treating my child like some common criminal by forcing her to submit to a bag search.

I had replied:

Your daughter is free to make the choice not to attend camp.

That had been the end of the matter. St Anne's is a private school and the rules are the rules.

Without thinking, I rub my hand on the sofa I am sitting on and I am utterly horrified to find it slightly sticky. I have no idea why I was asked to come into the police station. Surely they could have come to me? Although I am grateful that at least I am not sitting in one of those stark police interview rooms I have seen on television.

I suppose the police have assumed I will be more comfortable in this small room with its sticky brown sofa and the sad, dying potted plant whose leaves curl and brown at the edges.

'You're overwatering that plant,' I inform the detective but he doesn't even turn around in his chair to look at the poor thing. I take a deep breath and my nose twitches at the stale smell of old cigarettes. It must be years since smoking was allowed in the police station and yet the smell lingers in the enclosed room with no avenue for fresh air.

'Shouldn't there be two of you here to interview me?' I ask as images of every police procedural show I have ever seen flash through my head. I am a great fan of television crime series. I pride myself on my ability to untangle the clues before on-screen detectives, knowing long before the end who is guilty. I gaze at the young man in front of me and I wonder at his skills. Will he look at me and find guilt there? I sit up even straighter, determined to give him nothing but inconsequential facts.

Detective Gold smiles at me, an even, white smile. I can imagine he thinks of himself rather highly. He is a good-looking man but I can only see him as a little boy with a big job.

'That's usually the case, Bernadette, but we only have two detectives working on this, and my colleague, Detective Holland, is conducting other interviews.' The way he keeps using my name grates on my nerves.

'Yes, well, I just thought it was usually done in pairs.'

'Usually, yes. Can we continue? Can you tell me about what happened on Friday afternoon?'

I rub my hand on my grey wool pants, hoping to get the stickiness off, knowing that I will immediately wash everything I am wearing as soon as I get home. But my hand remains disgusting.

'I wasn't actually in charge of searching the bags. I leave that to Mrs Fitzsimmons.'

'Mrs Fitzsimmons is the other teacher who was supervising the camp with you?'

'Yes, and because she's… well, she's younger and the students seem more familiar with her so I decided to leave it to her.'

'Right, so what happened once she started searching the bags?'

'I'm sorry but would it be possible for me to get a glass of water? I'm finding my mouth very dry.'

Detective Gold smiles at me again. 'Of course, give me a moment.' He gets up and I wonder why he would leave a suspect alone in an unlocked room and then I have to remind myself that I'm not a suspect and that I, very definitely, have done nothing wrong.

No one thinks of me as a suspect. No one suspects me of anything beyond a failure of a duty of care, but even this is a galling thought. I am sure that once they know more about Zoe Bloom, they will understand that it was not possible to control the wilful child that she was, not unless Paula and I had taken it in turns to stay up all night and watch her.

It really was the most dreadful luck that Paula was the teacher to accompany me on camp. Up until this year, Henrietta, who was head of history, and I have been in charge of the year eleven camp. I have been the year eleven patron for five years and teaching at the school for over two decades. I am fully aware of the level of discipline that is needed to run such a camp. Sixteen-year-old girls can be a trial but they can be handled.

Last year, the girls behaved beautifully. On Sunday night only half of them chose to go into town because the other half were happy to sit with me and Henrietta around the campfire.

I must admit I was devastated when Henrietta decided to retire to the Gold Coast to be closer to her daughter and grandchildren.

Detective Gold bumbles back into the room with a paper cup filled with water, dropping his file as he resumes his seat. He places the drink on the laminate coffee table in front of me, spilling some as he does so.

'Thank you,' I say and I pick up the cup and drain it. The water tastes of soap for some reason.

'Okay, so the difficulties?' I can hear a shade of frustration in his voice.

'Yes, as I said, I got Paula to search the bags. It's a simple process. Each girl brings her bag to the table set up in the main hall that also functions as a dining room, unzips or unclips it and moves the things around so the teacher in charge can see inside. We don't touch anything, and as I said before, we allow them their treats. We were about halfway through when it was Zoe's turn. I was standing with the girls waiting to take their bags up. Zoe took hers to the table and opened it and then I heard Paula say, "Oh, Zoe, love, you know we can't allow that."'

'And what was she talking about?'

'Well, obviously I had to find out, so I moved over to Zoe's case and I saw that she had an enormous bottle of vodka in there. She hadn't even bothered to conceal it, and what's more, she didn't even seem surprised or upset to have been caught.' I don't mention the other things I saw as I glanced into Zoe's bag. I don't say anything about that which is not my business. She caught me peeking, and for a moment we looked at each other, her pretty green eyes shining with mischief. I almost smiled at her. She thought she was so grown up but she was still just a child, pushing boundaries and waiting, wanting to get caught.

'Right, so obviously you took the alcohol away?'

'Well, I tried to. I reached into her case and then Paula said, "It's okay, Bernadette, Zoe can take it out," and she smiled at the girl. I don't like to speak ill of other teachers but Paula is far too liberal. She has teenagers of her own and she is forever telling me how they have to be loved through a difficult time rather than confronted. These are my *students*, not my children – I have no intention of loving them. I am there to guide them to achieve their best. I had been dealing with Zoe all year and I had had just about enough of her cavalier attitude towards the rules, so I reached into the case, grabbed the bottle and then I dropped it into the bin.'

'And what happened then?' asks Detective Gold. I can see he's getting bored and I can just picture him in his final years of school, staring out of the window imagining some future for himself where he got to be the hero, like in a movie. Students like that irritate me no end. I do have a soft spot for the slightly awkward ones like Leeanne, the ones whose minds are crowded with thoughts on everything and anything and who are open to every new idea. I have been very fortunate to have had a lot of these pupils pass through my classes over the years. They are the girls that I occasionally hear about doing wonderful things with their lives and I am always so proud to have been able to play some small part in their growing up.

The detective clears his throat, letting me know he is waiting for my answer.

'She said, "What did you have to do that for? I could have taken it home." I was, of course, incensed, and I assumed that Paula would leap in to my defence, but instead she replied, "Now, Zoe, you know very well that you're too young to have alcohol and you shouldn't have brought it with you. I know that you feel frustrated right now but maybe have a little time to cool off and we can pretend this whole thing never happened." Now, that to me was unacceptable.'

'Right, and what do you think the appropriate response would have been?'

'She should have separated Zoe from everyone, immediately called her parents and had her removed from camp. Instead she got all… I don't even know what to call it but it was a ridiculously lukewarm response, and right then and there I told her so. I also told Zoe I would be calling her parents to come and get her and that she should go and wait in the office.'

'But that's not what happened because she was still there on Friday night.'

'No, obviously.' I am proud that I manage, at the last moment, to moderate my tone. It is sometimes difficult to remember that I am not speaking with a student when I talk to someone of the younger generation, and this boy looks like he's only just left high school.

'She started crying and she apologised, saying that she would behave if I just gave her another chance. I told her that there were no second chances and she became completely hysterical. Eventually she was sobbing in Paula's arms and then we handed her over to her friends and Paula and I had a discussion in the office about what to do.'

'So you decided to let her stay.'

'I wanted to send her home but Paula has a ludicrously soft heart.' I run my hands down my pants again. If Paula had agreed with me and Zoe had been sent home, none of this would have happened. Instead of the whole of year eleven being told to stay home until Wednesday, they would all be back in school right now, reminiscing about camp.

Now everything will be overshadowed by this incident. And what is worse is that my ability to supervise children is being called into question, all because Paula wanted to be the good guy.

I can see her now. She was so angry with me, filled with righteous indignation. She stood in the office with her hands on her ample hips, her face flushed and her brown eyes shining with anger. 'Bernadette, there are better ways to handle this. She knew we would find it and it would get taken away. It was probably just a prank or a dare of some sort. She's apologised and she's very upset. I say we let her stay and I know we will have a very well- behaved young lady for the rest of the camp.'

But I don't explain this to the young detective. I just say, 'Eventually I accepted Paula's argument that it would be better for morale to let her stay. I insisted that she miss out on the first activity, which was a hike up to the waterfall, and that she write a three-page essay on the effects of alcohol on a developing brain, which was a topic they covered in personal development classes.'

'And she did that, correct? Mrs Fitzsimmons said that Zoe gave her the essay when you returned from the hike and that Zoe was cooperative for the rest of the day and that night.'

It is rather maddening to know that this detective has already spoken to Paula, whom I am sure shed tears through her entire interview. I was the senior teacher in charge. Surely, he should have been more interested in my version of events?

'Let me tell you something, Detective Gold,' I say, because I have had enough of trying to remain polite. I lean forward in my seat and clasp my hands together, hating the sticky feeling. 'I knew that Zoe wasn't sorry. She didn't want to go home because she had plans to meet a boy from St John's. At least that's what I assume because a girl like Zoe always has plans to meet a boy. This is not my first merry-go-round, you know. I've been teaching for decades and I have seen all sorts of students come and go. I knew what kind of a girl Zoe was from the moment she entered year seven wearing more make-up than any twelve-year-old girl should have access to. If you ask me, she sneaked out once Paula and I had retired for the night and got lost trying to get to him. That's why she was so desperate to stay, because she was up to something, and I can tell you this for nothing: Zoe Bloom was always up to something.'

'So, it's fair to say you didn't like her?'

You're being stupid, I want to say to him but I try for a more measured approach. I fold my arms and give him a stern look. 'That's an absurd question. She wasn't my child. She was a student. I felt for her the same as I do for all the others.'

The detective looks suitably chastened. I am not here to indulge any theories he may have.

I realise that I have actually lied about this. In all my years I have rarely come across a student I disliked as much as I disliked Zoe Bloom. I am a very good teacher and I pride myself on always managing to find something, even the smallest thing, about a student to like. I am able to greet every pupil I pass by name and I could also tell this detective at least one thing about every girl, one thing that makes her special or different. Young girls need to be seen and acknowledged so that they grow up to become brilliant, independent women able to take on the challenges of the world. I have helped hundreds of girls achieve this and, in turn, teaching has given me a life filled with passion and purpose.

If I find myself disliking a student, I work even harder to find something positive about them. I remember one girl last year named Leslie who styled herself as a Goth with black painted nails and dark eye shadow in total contravention of the uniform code. She was rude and arrogant and she spent many afternoons in detention. But the thing about Leslie was that she was a poet, and once I discovered this, I found a way to not only like her but mentor her as well. I am very proud to say that she is currently studying creative writing at university. I didn't give up on her. I rarely give up on a student but, despite my best efforts, I have never been able to find one thing to like about Zoe Bloom. I feel this as a failure in myself.

The girl was everything I have hated all my life. She was beautiful, popular, intelligent and from a loving family, wanting for nothing. Instead of appreciating what she had, she seemed determined to push every boundary until she got herself into a situation she couldn't smile or flirt or talk her way out of. And that's exactly what happened.

I, of course, do not say this to Detective Gold.

'I really have no idea what else could have happened to her. As soon as we were told by her friends that she was missing, we began searching. And although I usually would have waited an hour or so before calling the police, I called them immediately.'

'Yes, I understand that you did that. Is there any reason why you would have waited? I mean, it's a student missing from a school camp.'

I cannot help the sigh that escapes me. It's nearly five o'clock and Oliver likes to have his dinner at five o'clock. He will be most upset at having to wait. I should have asked Henry to feed him.

'The camp is set out over a fairly large area,' I explain in the hopes that this will be the end of it. 'There are twenty cabins for students, although we were only using ten, and then a separate area of cabins and a bathroom that the teachers use. It is open to the bush and students have been known to get lost making their way to the dining hall or looking for the bathroom. A couple of years ago a pupil left the path to look at a bird as she was making her way to the dining room and got lost for over an hour. But we found her and everything was fine. The trouble with being in the bush is that once you leave a familiar spot, you can find yourself going around in circles. The girls are instructed, should they get lost, to stop where they are and wait to be found, but sometimes panic sets in. I have never lost a student for more than an hour. And they are always extremely grateful to be found and able to laugh about the incident afterwards, so that's why I usually wait an hour. It's only happened four times in the more than twenty years I have been supervising the camp. The first time I called the police immediately, and when the student was found I got the impression that they felt I had wasted their time.'

'And yet you didn't feel you should wait to call the police in Zoe's case?'

'As I said, Detective Gold,' I reply and I can feel that I am almost baring my teeth at him, 'I knew what Zoe was like. She would not have gotten lost looking at a bird and she would not have simply gone for a walk. She hated everything to do with camp except for the opportunity to go into town on Sunday night. I knew that if she was missing, she had probably been gone the whole night.' I bite down on my lip as I say this, realising that I have just thrown up a whole host of questions for him to ask me. He will, of course, want to know why I thought she had been gone the whole night, and I have no desire to elaborate on that. I think about what was in her bag. Who brings such provocative underwear on a school camp?

'I still don't understand why you think that…' the detective continues but I have had enough.

'I am really feeling very tired and I need to go home and feed Oliver,' I say. 'I believe I have given you all the answers that I can.' I stand up and make for the door, feeling my shoulders hunch. I worry he will stop me, but he doesn't.

'We may need to speak to you again,' he says as I open the door.

'Fine,' I reply without turning back.

He can ask me questions all day. He's not going to get anything from me. I am more worried about Principal Bennet – or George as he likes to be called by the senior teachers – and what Paula will have said to him about me. I am worried about parents demanding a sacrifice for a lost child. I am worried about losing my job because, without it, I have nothing.

Exhaustion settles over me and I feel as though I have been interviewed for days instead of just an hour or so. I am not one for guarding my tongue. I am known for my absolute honesty in all matters, so the idea that I have to watch everything I say about camp and the Friday night she disappeared is tiring. But when the chips are down, self-preservation is all important. I cannot let what happened change my world.

As I leave the station and climb into my small blue car, I cannot help the thought that I am not one iota sorry that I will never have to see Zoe Bloom again.

CHAPTER FOUR

Jessie – The Sister

Jessie stares down at her notes. She is supposed to be studying for exams but she's been staring at the list of options for paediatric heart repair for hours. She knows that it will be easy enough to receive extra time or to be allowed to miss the exams completely. They are just over a week away. The death of her sister gives her a gold-plated excuse but she cannot summon the energy to begin the necessary form-filling to explain to the medical faculty that her sister has died and she cannot seem to study.

Her mother has said that she will help but Jessie would rather just take the exams and hope for the best.

She looks around her room, where she has covered the walls in posters of the human body so that even if she is just getting dressed in the morning, she is still working. 'This room is completely depressing,' Zoe told her last week when she came in to ask if her sister knew where the shampoo from the bathroom had gone.

'Yeah, well, I have plans for my life,' Jessie said.

'Everyone has plans, Jess. Don't you ever just want to, you know, have some fun?'

Jessie looked at her little sister, whose face was perfectly made up and who was dressed in tight jeans and a black T-shirt accessorised with a cute pink vest with tassels, and didn't know what to say to her. Zoe was about to go and have a shower and yet she looked like she was off for a night out.

Jessie wears black pants with a collared shirt of some kind every day. It's a uniform for her and means that she looks smart enough for practical work at the hospital and she doesn't have to think about what to wear in the morning. 'I need to work, Zoe,' she muttered.

'You've always needed to work,' Zoe replied, and Jessie thought she heard a touch of anger in her voice as though her career choice had somehow let her little sister down.

At the time she didn't care. Zoe had enough attention from everyone else. She didn't need Jessie's attention as well. But now she wishes she had said, 'Want to have coffee and some cake in the kitchen?' It would only have taken a few minutes, a few precious minutes, and then she could have gone back to work. And now she would be able to recall her sister's face as she chatted about her life; she would be able to picture her smile and the way her eyes lit up when she laughed. She would have a final three-dimensional memory of her little sister to hold onto, but instead her memory feels flat, artificial, as though she cannot summon the real Zoe to think about.

As it was, she just shook her head and returned to studying.

They share… They shared the same genetic material and yet they could have been strangers. Standing next to each other in photographs, they look alike, but they ran out of things to say to each other a long time ago. She should have tried harder with her. It wouldn't have hurt to express an interest in her Instagram feed or the squabble she was having with a friend.

Jessie sighs. You can't choose your family but she has always worried about how little she likes her sister. 'Liked, liked, liked,' she mutters, reminding herself. She had always assumed that at some point they would both be adults and would somehow find themselves on common ground, and now that can never happen. It can never happen. It's such a strange thing and so final, and she feels like she should be able to call someone and say, 'I wasn't done being a big sister, I need more time with her.' And the fact that she can't do that, that there is no way to undo what has happened, makes her so angry she can feel her body shaking whenever she thinks about it.

She has also found herself irrationally jealous of her friend Valerie, who is studying medicine with her and who has an older sister who she can call on for help with everything.

'I'm so sorry, Jessie,' Valerie said when she told her, 'tell me what I can do to help.'

Turn back time, Jessie had thought but hadn't said because Val was only being kind.

She should have been better at her job of big sister but she has always felt like it was one of the things she wasn't very good at. Maybe it was because when Zoe was born, she was already six years old and quite happy with being an only child. The seeds of resentment against her younger sibling began as she looked down at the small doll-like creature in the bassinette next to her mother's hospital bed and was exhorted by her grandmother, Ellis, not to touch until she had washed her hands because they were covered in germs that could be dangerous for the baby. Jessie had felt herself to be too large, too clumsy and too dirty. As she grew, Jessie couldn't help but be aware of how much Zoe was allowed to get away with. 'She's just a baby, she doesn't understand,' their mother said when Zoe was eight months and crawling and knocking over Jessie's precious Lego projects.

'She's just little,' their mother said when Zoe was two and took herself into her big sister's room while Jessie was at school and broke three of her beautiful porcelain dolls.

'She didn't mean to,' their mother said when Zoe was five and destroyed the pyramid Jessie had painstakingly built for a school project.

Jessie always felt the rules were different for her and her sister. When their father died, Zoe was four and Jessie was ten. Jessie remembers the funeral, remembers standing next to her devastated mother. Clutching her hand and being aware that even though her mother seemed to be comforting her, she was actually squeezing her hand tightly enough to hurt. Jessie allowed the pain, knowing that she needed her strength. Lydia had pulled her blonde hair back into a ponytail that was so tight Jessie could see that her skin was being stretched. She wasn't wearing any make-up and was ghost-pale. She didn't cry at the funeral, not at first. She chewed her bottom lip until Jessie's grandmother handed her a tissue and whispered, 'Just look what you're doing to yourself for heaven's sake.' Her mother had dabbed at her lip while the rabbi talked about what a wonderful man her husband had been, and Jessie had felt her stomach turn as the tissue was stained with her mother's blood.

'Eli Bloom was a loving and devoted husband and father who understood that time with his family was the most precious time of all. Despite his work commitments he never missed a dancing concert, a soccer game or a prize giving.' The stain of red on the tissue had grown and spread as it mingled with her mother's tears that finally arrived, and as she looked around her, Jessie could see people nodding with approval at her mother's correct reaction. She had scowled at the floor, hating everyone, hating where she was and what it meant.

And now she will have to stand at another funeral – the funeral of her little sister, her only sister – and be gawked at and watched for appropriate behaviour.

Zoe was not at their father's funeral. According to everyone, she was too young. She stayed home with a babysitter, helping to lay out food for when the mourners returned to the house.

Zoe had laughed and chatted with people when they came over all through the week of shiva, the official week of mourning. She was delighted by the attention and the surfeit of cakes and food that came through the door all day every day. She thought she was at a week-long party. Both Jessie and her mother had grown paler and thinner and more distant as the week progressed. Unable to taste the food, unable to swallow the food, unable to stand the sight of the endless dishes. 'It makes me sick to look at all this,' Lydia told her as they cleaned up one afternoon. 'I wish people would just leave me alone.'

'But everything tastes so good, Mum,' Zoe said with a giggle.

Jessie wanted to shake her. 'She doesn't care,' she told her mother bitterly.

'Oh, Jess, she's just too little to understand,' was her reply and then she smiled as Zoe offered her a bite of her muffin, seeming to be comforted by her younger daughter's lack of understanding. Jessie hated her little sister, even more than she hated the cancer that stole her wonderful father away.

Now, she lies back on her bed and stares at the ceiling, remembering her father's last day. He died at home. A hospital bed had been set up in the living room and nurses came and went at all hours of the day and night. On the day he passed away, Jessie woke early, before dawn, by what she now feels was certain knowledge that this was his last day. It was summer and she was dressed in purple pyjamas with butterflies across her chest. She climbed out of bed and crept downstairs to the living room where her father lay.

Her mother was asleep on the sofa next to his bed, as she always was. Jessie stared at her shrunken father in the dim light of the living room, where a small lamp burned all night. He had been a big man with broad shoulders, a thick head of sandy-brown hair and vivid green eyes. He had loved being out in the garden every chance he got and his face was always browned by the sun, despite his wife's constant lectures about sunscreen. Jessie breathlessly took in his appearance, not able even then to believe the change. The bones on his face pushed against the skin and he looked light enough for Jessie to lift.

She turned to her mother, seeing that her sleep was deep and dreamless, and then she climbed onto her father's bed, positioning herself next to him. She didn't like the way he smelled, hated the sourness that her mother tried to cover with the scented lotion she massaged into his skin, but she reminded herself that he was still her dad – her lovely dad who, until he got sick, had been reading her *Oliver Twist*, even though she was too old to be read to. Her lovely dad who had taken her to school every morning and said, 'Knock 'em dead,' as she climbed out of the car. Her dad who didn't feel like he needed to give endless advice like her mum did. He just listened and let her figure things out for herself. He was her lovely dad and her throat was tight and her heart heavy because she knew that he was fading, that she was losing him and no amount of love could keep him here.

She draped her arm carefully across his chest, not wanting the weight of it to hurt him.

She felt him move and, for a moment, regretted getting onto his bed because she had disturbed him but then she felt his hand touch her long blonde hair, stroking it as he had always done. 'You…' he said, his voice soft and breathless, 'you… you are my bright, shining star.' And then his hand dropped onto her back and Jessie's tears fell on the hospital sheets that her mother changed every day. She cried softly until she fell asleep, and she only woke when her mother shook her gently. 'Come, baby, time to have something to eat.'

He died just as the sun set that day, finally out of pain and at peace.

Jessie thought it would be easier to die with him. She couldn't understand how it was possible for her to be in so much pain and yet function, but her body kept needing to be fed – however little – needing to go to the bathroom, needing to breathe. And she had to take care of Zoe so her mother could have some time. 'Please just play with her for a bit,' her mum would beg in the weeks after her father's death, and she would take Zoe to her room and listen as her little sister chatted and laughed and used her dolls to tell funny stories.

Jessie could not help hating her, grabbing her by the shoulders one afternoon and shaking her until her teeth clicked together. 'Daddy is dead and you don't even care,' she shouted and was rewarded with Zoe's tears. When her mother came to see what was going on, she took Zoe away to comfort her, leaving Jessie with her pain and her shame at having lost control with her little sister, who had no idea of what had happened to her life.

Jessie doesn't think their relationship ever recovered and they have – had – grown even more distant as the years passed. Zoe was a periphery figure in her life, someone who lived in the same house, who shared the same bathroom, who sat across from her at dinner if she was home instead of studying at the library, but Jessie had no idea of who Zoe was. It is this thought that makes her saddest of all because she wonders what it says about her as a person. Is she incapable of feeling for others, of thinking about others? 'No,' she says aloud, shaking her head. She loves, she feels. She knows she does. But talking to Zoe had felt like hard work and she had enough hard work as she tried to stay on top of her studies for medical school and find a way to live an authentic life. But maybe if she had worked on her relationship with her sister the same way she works on everything else in her life, things would have eventually become easy and natural. 'Give me another chance to be a better big sister,' she would like to shout but she has no idea who to direct her entreaty to. There will not be another chance.

She hears the doorbell ring again. It's been going all day with people dropping off food or flowers. She has no idea why people imagine that the first thing you want to do after a death is eat, but she supposes that she would do the same thing for someone else. It's a societal convention, isn't it? She can imagine each person climbing back into their car after dropping off whatever they have brought and saying, 'First the father and now the daughter – what terrible luck they have.' The thing is that Eli's death was bad luck or faulty genes or something else cruel and unfair but Jessie has a sinking feeling that Zoe was actually responsible for her own death. She knows that her sister would have thought nothing of putting herself in harm's way. Who goes for a walk in the dark in the mountains? Who would be stupid enough to imagine that the Blue Mountains, where paths disappear into bush and drop away into green valleys, would be a safe place to wander? Only someone with no concept of their own mortality. She assumes that Zoe was smarter than that so maybe she did it for the thrill of it. Maybe she was meeting Callum, her ridiculous boyfriend who always smiled at Jessie like he believed he was gracing her with his attention. No, she probably wasn't meeting Callum. Not after what had happened. Not after what Callum had said and Zoe had told her. The knowledge of that sits in her stomach like a stone. She should, she knows, mention it to her mother, to the police, but what does it matter? Her sister is gone, and nothing will bring her back.

She gives up attempting to study and gets off the bed. Looking out of her window, she watches their dog Walter ambling around the manicured green lawn, sniffing out the scents of other garden dwellers. He doesn't know Zoe is gone. He cannot understand that the girl who surreptitiously fed him bits of toast as she ate breakfast while he sat at her feet will never return. Jessie sighs and feels the heaviness of tears push against her eyes but she bites down on her lip, letting the pain of that focus her.

There is something else she needs to talk to her mother about before the funeral, before the police tell her, because they are definitely going to find out. She needs to explain why she was in the Blue Mountains on Friday night when she told her mother she was going to be at the library all evening. Since the beginning of exam period, the university library has been open twenty-four hours a day and Jessie regularly stays there until three or four in the morning, along with the rest of the medical students. But Friday night was not one of those nights. She shouldn't have gone, of course, not at all, but she couldn't help herself. It was only an hour and a half drive, and even though she should have been studying, she hadn't been able to resist going. Feelings, strong feelings, were overwhelming for Jessie. She was already finding what was going on in her life difficult to deal with. She has no idea what to even think or feel right now.

Zoe once called Jessie frigid. 'Don't you ever think about having a boyfriend?'

'No,' Jessie replied. 'I don't want one.'

'You are just, like, frigid.'

'Anything else you want to call me before I leave the kitchen, Zoe?' she asked. She had only come in to refill her water bottle. She hadn't even greeted her sister as she stood in front of the open fridge, staring at everything on offer. The only reason Zoe had started speaking to her was because she was desperate to tell someone, anyone, about her latest crush. That's what she called them – 'crushes' – like she was some 1950s teeny-bopper.

'You have to hear about him,' she said to Jessie, 'he is just the most, like, oh my God, gorgeous man.' Zoe was dating Callum and Jessie thought that she shouldn't be looking at anyone else, but when she suggested this to her sister, her sister replied with, 'Okay, boomer.' Her latest insult for anyone who questioned her.

'He's a boy, Zoe, not a man,' Jessie replied, 'and I have no desire to hear about another one of your interests.'

Things went downhill from there. Jessie thought that her sister pushed her because she was looking for an argument, looking for someone to disagree with her because not many people did. Her mother and Gabriel just smiled and tittered and indulged every little whim of hers, and Jessie had seen the way her friends behaved around her, like she could do and say no wrong. Jessie didn't think

Zoe even got into much trouble at school, except with Bernadette Fischer, because she batted her eyelashes at everyone and teachers both male and female were charmed by her. It wasn't just because she was pretty; it was something more – a kind of entitled charm, Jessie supposes. Zoe assumed that everyone would love her and they did. She assumed that she would get whatever she wanted, and if she didn't, she became such a nightmare that eventually her mother gave in, and Jessie is sure that the teachers at school also found themselves giving in where other students would have been punished. It felt good to make Zoe smile, to make her happy. People couldn't resist it.

Zoe came to her sister for an argument, even though Jessie would never give her the satisfaction. But now she will never come to her again and Jessie would like to sit and cry and mourn the loss of her own flesh and blood, but what she mostly feels is tired and numb.

She opens her bedroom door and hears her mother talking to someone downstairs. Listening for a moment, she realises that it's a detective. She sits back down on her bed. 'Shit,' she mutters. She hopes the woman isn't saying anything about her. But why would she? What happened to Zoe was an accident. She went for a walk in the dark and fell, that's all. It has nothing to do with Jessie being in the mountains on Friday night.

Nothing at all.

CHAPTER FIVE

I think people use the word 'guilty' too much. I've heard people say they feel guilty after eating a piece of chocolate cake, after spending the afternoon watching television instead of working or when they neglect to take their dog out for a walk.

But guilt is not about that. Guilt, or the act of feeling guilty, happens when someone realises they have compromised their own moral code or society's moral code. When they have done something so terrible that they wonder at themselves, that they question who they are and how they got to a place where they could do such a thing.

If you ask me, guilt should be saved for bigger things than a piece of chocolate cake. It should be saved for when you do something so awful that you know, without a shadow of a doubt, that if anyone found out about it, they would never look at you the same way again. When you know that your action was contrary to everything you feel and think. When you have behaved in such a way that you have shocked yourself with how dreadful you can be.

That's what the word 'guilt' should be applied to.

I could wear the word as a badge instead of my name. I could introduce myself as 'Guilt' and when people found out what I'd done, they would say, 'Oh yes, that seems right.'

There are other words I could use to describe myself. Words that might explain why I did it in the first place. Angry, betrayed, hurt. Those all work as well but right now, right now there is only one emotion that is eating away at me. Churning inside me, twisting my brain, keeping me awake.

It began innocently enough… well, not innocently, that's not true. It began with an intention to hurt but it was never meant to go as far as it did, and no one could have expected the repercussions that have rippled through the lives of everyone involved. It got out of control.

The guilt I feel makes my hands shake. I'm always hot and unable to think about anything else. It is consuming me, and I know that I'm not going to be able to hide it for much longer. I know that, and what I'm afraid of is what's going to happen when I can't conceal it anymore, at what's going to happen and how many more people are going to get hurt.

CHAPTER SIX

Lydia

Lydia hands Detective Ellie Holland a cup of coffee and then she sits down opposite her in the living room. 'Thanks,' says the detective. Her smooth cap of black hair doesn't move an inch and her dark eyes have a penetrating gaze that Lydia is finding unnerving. The detective sits slightly to the side, making Lydia aware that she has a gun at her hip, disturbing the way her jacket falls. She is at once feminine and masculine, threatening and non-threatening, and Lydia wonders if all female detectives evoke this feeling or if Detective Holland is unique in this way.

'So, have you found out anything more?' she asks. It is late afternoon and she knows that the detective and her partner, a man named Lucas, have been speaking to people all day, just like they were speaking to people the day before. Zoe was found at six yesterday morning. She has been the mother of one living child and one dead child for thirty-five hours now and she wishes she could put up her hand and say, 'I'm done with this now. Can I go back to my real life?' She swallows quickly. This is her life, her real life, forever and ever. On the wall behind the detective is a picture of Zoe and Jessie aged three and nine. They are dressed in identical pale blue sundresses with little capped sleeves, the blonde hair of each girl falling over her shoulders, a waterfall of gold. Their smiles are wide but slightly fake because the photograph was done by a professional and they had been told to smile. They are beautiful and perfect, and looking at the picture always makes Lydia remember that what they were thinking about was the ice cream treat down at the beach they would be rewarded with afterwards for behaving for the photographs. She looks away from the image quickly, sadness slicing through her at their innocence and everything that has been lost since the picture was taken.

The detective takes the smallest sip of coffee. Then she leans forward and lets the cup hover for a moment above the polished wood coffee table until Lydia moves quickly to place a glass coaster in position.

'Well, we know she was in her room at nine. She must have left after that. We assume that she left on purpose since she was dressed for the weather and Shayna says that she remembers her being in pyjamas at around midnight or a bit earlier than that when they all agreed to turn off the lights. The girls were very good about figuring out what she would be wearing, so that at least helped us locate her relatively quickly.'

'That parka won't be warm enough, Zoe. The mountains are very cold at night,' she'd said the night before camp as she went over the list of things Zoe was supposed to bring with her.

'OMG, Mum, I'm not some little kid. I know how to stay warm,' Zoe muttered in response as she searched through her cupboard for the silver sneakers she wanted to take.

'Don't you think you should have proper shoes in case you go on a hike?' Lydia asked as her daughter put the sneakers next to the jeans and top she would wear on the bus the next day.

'I have the boots I bought with Gabriel. They're for hiking. These shoes are for the bus.'

'Your backpack is going to be very heavy,' she said, thinking that her petite daughter didn't look capable of toting the large bag around.

'I'll be fine,' she said.

Lydia thinks about the bright pink parka with the silver buttons. *They found her quickly.* 'But not quickly enough,' says Lydia and then she bites down on her lip, unsure why she felt the need to point this out. *If they had found her just after she fell, would they have been able to save her? Did she lie there, in pain, afraid and alone, unable to call for help?* The questions about her daughter's death will not take a break. They are on an endless loop in her head. This morning, after a restless night of little sleep, she woke up to find herself holding her pillow tightly and she knew that she had been cradling her child, that at some point in the early hours of the morning, she had found herself locked in a dream where she was holding Zoe's hand as she dangled off the side of a steep, grey cliff, jagged rocks waiting below. In the dream she had finally pulled her to safety, even as pain tore at her arm, and then she had held her tightly, vowing to never let her go. When she woke later and reality swamped her with the truth, she wanted, for a moment, to die. To simply close her eyes once more and never wake up. There is an ache in her arm that has been there all day as though she had held onto something heavy, as though she had lifted and saved her child.

'No,' agrees the detective, 'but then no one knew she was missing until the next morning.'

Lydia nods and Detective Holland clears her throat, continuing.

'Shayna says that she and Becca and Leeanne were tired because they had hiked to the waterfall but that Zoe wanted to stay up talking. The three girls convinced her to let them get some sleep. They'd all had a fair amount of junk food but nothing else – no alcohol because that had been confiscated. So sometime between midnight and seven thirty the next morning, when the girls realised that Zoe was not using a different bathroom but was in fact missing, is when she left the campsite. We are operating under the theory that she got up and went for a walk and unfortunately slipped and fell. It was very dark, and although she had her phone, which would have been able to act as a torch, it may not have helped her to see every obstacle.'

Lydia nods as Detective Holland speaks. Her voice is even and deep, sympathy in her tone. Lydia knows that this is not the first time the detective has spoken to someone about a dead relative. She looks like she's about Lydia's age so she must have been doing this job a while, but she wonders if it's the first time the detective has spoken to a mother about a dead child. She wonders if there is training for that.

The detective is not telling her anything new. Except there is a flaw in her theory. Zoe was not a fan of nature. She was terrified of spiders and creepy-crawlies, as she called them, and was unlikely to simply decide to take a walk in the middle of the night for no apparent reason. It was unfathomable.

'I don't see why she would have gone for a walk,' Lydia says. 'I know that it's spring but it's still really cold in the mountains at night, and she hated being outside. It wasn't her thing.'

'I understand. The other theory we have is that this may have been a deliberate act on her part.'

'She went for a walk deliberately?' Lydia questions, unsure if she should point out the stupidity of this statement.

'No,' the detective clears her throat again, clearly uncomfortable, 'I mean that it's possible Zoe meant to take her life.'

Lydia understands that she is the only stupid one in the room. She bites down hard on her lip. 'You… you think she killed herself?' Her tone is flat, wooden. This is not something she hasn't considered. Zoe is sixteen, was sixteen, and the last few months of her life were fraught with arguments and drama. She was either laughing hysterically or crying in her room, happily chatting or sullen and silent. Lydia had expected a level of unpredictability from her daughter because Jessie had been a little difficult herself at sixteen but nothing like what she experienced with her younger child. *It's my fault,* she realises. She had been too lax and then she'd tried to turn that around in the last few months. It was too late – Zoe was obviously not going to stand for it. But her daughter wasn't depressed; at least Lydia doesn't think she was. She knows that only a week ago she and Robyn, Shayna's mother, were discussing the unpredictability of teenage girls.

'She told me this morning that she wants to drop out of school and this afternoon that she's thinking about studying to be a vet,' Robyn said. 'I never quite know what to say and I'm always a little afraid of getting it wrong.'

'I know I'm getting it wrong,' Lydia told her. 'I'm too strict, I'm too nosy, I'm too old to understand.'

'You're just too much of a mother,' laughed Robyn.

'I worry so much all the time that she's unhappy, that all of this is just concealing some real issues.'

'She's fine,' said Robyn, 'they're fine. We pay such close attention to them, not like our parents. I don't think my mum and dad knew half the stuff I was getting up to at sixteen.'

'My mother just wanted to be left alone,' said Lydia. 'She was always busy with her friends or her books. I don't think I talked to her as much as my girls talk to me.'

'It's better this way though, isn't it?'

'I guess,' Lydia said but she felt like she was never not worrying about one of her children. Yet maybe she hadn't been worrying about Zoe enough.

She clasps her hands together and squeezes. Maybe she has been too focused on work and on getting Jessie through medical school and on making sure that Zoe didn't do anything she would one day regret. Maybe in the ticking off of lists and the getting through of days she missed really connecting with her daughter. Had she stopped really looking at and listening to her child?

'Do you think it's possible?' asks Detective Holland gently.

Lydia wishes she was one of those mothers who could reply with an unequivocal no, who was completely sure that they knew their child, but she isn't. 'I…' she begins and then she looks down at her hands, where she is twisting the gold band she wears on her right hand. It's the ring Eli gave her when they got married, a simple plait of white and yellow gold.

Gabriel would prefer that she not wear it at all but the only concession, because she can see how uncomfortable it makes him, has been for Lydia to wear it on her right hand. On her left hand, the diamond and white gold wedding band from Gabriel finds the sunlight coming in from the window and shines its expensive beauty. It's too big and Lydia would be happy to leave it in a drawer most of the time, having never been one for ostentation, but Gabriel would be horrified. She remembers his face, flushed with pleasure at her affirmative answer as he showed her the ring. She slipped it on her finger and he kissed her hand. 'I will do everything in my power to make you happy,' he said. It had been two years since Eli died and she had felt them rush past at the same time as she felt she was living through more hours than a day should possibly have. Gabriel made things easier, better. It felt like he brought some light into the house with him when he came home. Perhaps it was just a lightness of spirit.

'Oh, Gabriel, you already do, you do make me happy.' She smiled at him, at his desire to please, at his generosity in whole-heartedly taking on two children who weren't his own, at his embracing her broken little family.

'Do you have children?' she asks the detective abruptly, leaving her thoughts behind.

'I do. I have a fifteen-year-old girl and a twelve-year-old boy.'

Lydia nods. 'So then you understand that I can't answer that question. I think I know but what if I'm wrong? What if I missed something?'

'I understand,' replies the detective. 'Would it be possible for us to take a look at her phone?'

'Why?'

'It might give us some insight into her thinking.'

Lydia is carrying the phone in her pocket, has been carrying it since they handed it to her after they had strapped her child's body onto a stretcher and hauled her into the rescue helicopter that had taken its time to arrive. There was no urgency after all.

'I need to come with,' she said as she watched the paramedic manoeuvre the stretcher into place.

'We'll drive there,' Gabriel replied and Lydia was not able to answer him, her mind so focused on her daughter. 'I need to come with,' she repeated and the paramedic extended his hand and then showed her where to sit. He had, kindly, not zipped up the body bag all the way and Lydia stroked her daughter's cold cheek, admiring the perfect paleness of her skin and the contrast of her dark lashes, tinted regularly, Lydia knew. She was just sleeping. She looked like she was just sleeping. When Zoe was a baby, Lydia had stood and watched her sleep, laughing at how expressions flitted across her perfect little face as she dreamed. In the helicopter everything was still. The roar of the motor faded away and Lydia stroked Zoe's cold cheek. *Wake up*, she prayed silently, *wake up. Please wake up.*

It didn't take long to arrive at the hospital. Lydia knows that when they landed and the roaring blades of the helicopter ceased, she realised that she had not heard or felt anything on the trip. She usually got airsick, even on large aeroplanes. On her honeymoon with Eli they had taken a small plane to an island off the mainland of Fiji and she had thrown up the whole way. But for the trip in the helicopter, for her daughter's final trip, she had felt suspended in a bubble of space where all she could feel was Zoe's cold cheek and all she could see was her unmoving face. It was a few minutes of peace. And then the blades had stopped and the noise had faded away and people from the hospital had slid open the doors. She had been instructed to move here and go there and sit down and her peace was shattered and her soul was crushed.

All she has been left with is her child's phone. Her child's phone in its holographic pink and purple case. The colours on the case change depending on how you hold it and Lydia always thought it the perfect case for her changeable daughter. She doesn't want to let it go now. She is comforted by being able to touch something Zoe has touched, something she loved. An image of her daughter staring down at the phone comes to her, her thumbs moving over the keyboard with lightning speed as she lifted her eyes to meet her mother's gaze, a smile appearing as her thumbs kept moving. The phone was an extension of her child. She doesn't want it to leave her side.

'Sure,' she says to the detective now as though handing it over is not tearing at her insides. She charged it overnight because it had run flat, and as she gives the phone to the detective the screen lights up. The screensaver is a picture of Zoe, Becca and Shayna. The three of them are lying on the grass in the sunshine, smiling at the camera. On the green grass the fanned-out blonde hair of each girl blends into the hair of the girl lying next to her. A trio of youth and beauty.

Lydia had a moment of rage last night, just a moment, as she looked at the three beautiful girls, that Robyn, Shayna's mother, and Linda, Becca's mother, could both call for their daughters and have them answer, could hear their voices. She has no idea why she has been singled out for this pain, especially after Eli. Wasn't his death enough for one lifetime? Why is her daughter the one who didn't come home?

She wonders now, as she looks at the photo, when Zoe changed it from a picture of her and Callum. It had been a picture of the two of them dressed up for a school dance. Lydia remembers Callum in his dark suit with his hair perfectly styled and Zoe in a black cocktail dress. Her waist had looked impossibly small. The two of them were beyond beautiful.

'Do you know the passcode?' asks the detective.

'I don't. I've tried all sorts of things, like her birthday and her sister's birthday and the dog's birthday. I've even tried my birthday and her late father's birthday but nothing has worked.'

'Is there somewhere she may have written it down?' asks the detective.

'I don't know, I haven't been through everything. I did look for a diary but I have a feeling that if she had one it would have been online. Her computer is locked as well but I think it was mostly for schoolwork. She's always glued to her phone… She was always glued to her phone.'

'Do you think her older sister would know?'

Lydia sighs. 'Jessie and Zoe haven't exactly been close in the last few years. Jessie is a very serious student. She's studying medicine. All her life her only ambition has been to be a paediatric surgeon, and that's what she worked towards her whole high school career. She's in her fourth year now and we don't get to see her much, but when we do, I think that she finds Zoe to be a bit… that she found Zoe to be frivolous. They didn't talk much.'

'Do you think I could speak to her anyway?'

'She's lying down. She's taken things really… hard. I mean, how else could she have taken it, but it's been this terrible shock. I keep expecting Zoe to walk back into the room, and my husband… well… he's Zoe's stepfather. I told you that, didn't I?'

Detective Holland nods.

'Of course, I told you – sorry…' Lydia runs her hands through her hair. Two weeks ago, she had it cut into a neat blonde bob, hoping that would make it feel thicker. She's always had long hair but in a moment of clarity she realised, as she sat in the chair at the salon, that she was too old to have long blonde hair. She is fifty-two and she was tired of trying to look forty. She wanted to simply be fifty-two. Gabriel doesn't love her new hairstyle. 'It makes you look… different,' he said carefully, 'but nothing could make you less beautiful.' He meant that it made her look older but he would never say the words. The thought of looking older stung because she is six months older than he is, just six months, and yet she has felt, ever since they got married ten years ago, that she needed to look ten years younger than he was. It wasn't hard. He's bald and has a paunch and he's never taken particularly good care of himself so the lines on his face make him look older than his years, but Lydia has always had a thing about being older than him. She has no idea why. Maybe it's because Eli was ten years older than she was. She always felt like a kid around him and his friends. She pushes her hand to her chest now as she thinks about her first husband, about how he would have felt to know that his youngest child was gone. She's almost glad he's not here to see this, to feel this. Zoe was four when Eli died. Pancreatic cancer took him away in just six weeks, so fast it made Lydia's head spin. She barely feels like she mourned him properly as she had no choice but to get on with caring for her four-year-old and ten-year-old daughters.

She and Eli had run a property styling business together: he chose furniture for their warehouse and she did the styling. She went back to work just two weeks after he died. They had bills to pay and a staff of five. There was no other option. It was only a year after he died that she realised she had never really had time to mourn him, to truly mourn him, with the result that she still, twelve years later, mourns him every day. Gabriel understands but she knows it bothers him. 'I get it, of course I do, but I can't ever live up to him because for you it still feels like it just happened.'

'But I married you,' she always says when he talks like this. But he's right. Some days it does feel like she has only just lost Eli, and now… now she has lost their precious daughter.

'Her father died when she was only four,' she says to the detective.

'I'm sorry. Did Zoe get on with her stepfather?'

'I don't know how much she remembers Eli. She never called Gabriel "Dad" but I think that's because Jessie doesn't. I think he is… sorry, was, a father figure to her. They got along.'

Lydia and Gabriel had been friends since they were children. He had been in the year below her at school and their families had spent Sunday afternoons together, swimming and barbecuing in the hot summer sun. She had always thought of him as good-looking with his hazel eyes and cheeky smile but they didn't speak much at school. He would seek her out and chat easily about school and other students, always managing to make her laugh. He had a dry, observational sense of humour, quick and clever.

He contacted her a year after Eli died, having returned from working in America. He was divorced and horrified to discover she had lost her husband. They had connected on Facebook and progressed to speaking on the phone and then eventually seeing each other.

On their first proper date he took her to a Greek restaurant and they ate taramasalata and a salad rich with salty feta and juicy black olives. They shared a bottle of sweet red wine and savoured lamb so soft it melted in their mouths. 'Oh, this is just divine,' she said.

'It's all over your chin,' he replied and he started laughing and then she joined him and soon they were both hysterical, except her laughter had turned to tears because she hadn't been able to imagine laughing with another man ever again. Gabriel leaned forward and grabbed her hand. 'It's okay,' he said as she wept into her serviette, 'it's okay.' She hadn't realised how much she missed laughing with a man, how much she missed sharing her day with all its frustrations and triumphs. Gabriel had brought that back to her.

She was comfortable with him. It was nothing like what she had felt with Eli but she was comfortable and content and he got on with the girls. It was just easy. It was effortless and that was everything to her. It felt as though he had moved into the large space left by Eli. He didn't quite fill it but she and the girls knew they could count on him. He helped with school projects and fetched them from parties, accepting that Jessie was still standoffish after all these years. When Lydia felt her nerves fraying from the pressures of running a business and raising children, he would take them off for the day, treating them to minigolf or an amusement park, giving her some space and time on her own. He liked going out to different restaurants with her as Eli had done, trying new foods and enjoying each other's company. She knew she was lucky to have found someone who worked with her family because she could never have been with someone who didn't get on with the girls.

'Do you think it's possible that Zoe was planning on meeting someone that night?' the detective asks, drawing Lydia back to the conversation she would rather not be having. 'I know that the year eleven boys from St John's were in the mountains as well and that both groups usually met up on Sunday evening. And we know she was dating, um… Callum Winters, but he's from year twelve, we've been told.'

'She and Callum were together for about six months. But I'm not sure if they planned to meet up or not.'

'But it's possible, right? We're going to speak to Callum but I wanted to check with you if she said anything about it.'

Lydia starts to shake her head. 'No, nothing. The truth is that I don't know much about what she had planned. We had kind of been going through a bad patch. She was… difficult, you know in the way that sixteen-year-old girls can be difficult. She didn't really talk to me about him, about anything really.' Lydia allows herself a rueful laugh. 'She really challenged my idea of myself as a mother,' she admits. 'Jessie was so easy. She just got on with things and I thought I had somehow found the key to mothering a teenage girl, but I was sorely mistaken.'

'In what ways was she difficult? I'm sorry to ask the question because I know it's hard to answer, but I am just trying to get a picture of who she was. It may help to figure out why she decided to leave the cabin alone.'

Lydia drops her head into her hands. It's easier if she doesn't think about it, doesn't talk about it. She has found, over the last two days, that she is managing to function by simply pretending that Zoe is still at camp. She knows this is ridiculous but she can't help it. She cannot lose another member of her family, she simply can't, and yet that is what has happened. It still didn't stop her from going into Zoe's room this morning and changing the sheets on her bed, so she would have fresh sheets to come back to. And all the time while she was doing it, she had been thinking, *Zoe is sixteen and should really be able to do this herself.* She knows that if she lets her guard down even a little bit and allows herself to acknowledge the truth, then she will be undone. Completely undone.

'I know she was drinking and I know that she had tried marijuana. I think she may have… may have tried other things too. She came back from a party about a month ago and I heard her in the kitchen. She was way past her curfew so I went to tell her that it was unacceptable but she couldn't really have a conversation with me. She was almost incoherent. I was worried enough to wake Gabriel and then to wake Jessie because of her medical training. We were going to take her to the hospital but then she fell asleep and Jessie said she would sit with her. She was fine the next day and denied taking anything.'

'So, would you say Zoe was engaging in risky behaviour? I understand from my colleague that she brought a bottle of vodka to the camp.'

'Yes, I heard about that. St Anne's has been around for over fifty years. I attended school there and I can tell you that at the same age and on the same camp, there was more than one bottle of alcohol brought along. It wasn't just the drinking that bothered me – of course it bothered me and of course I lectured her time after time about the dangers of alcohol, but I assumed that she would go through the phase and then… I don't know… grow up. But what mostly bothered me about her was her defiance and her secretiveness, although none of that has anything to do with what happened to her, or maybe it does – I don't know, I really just don't know.'

Detective Holland looks at Lydia without saying anything for a moment and she knows she's being judged. Of course she's being judged. She should have confronted Zoe about her drinking, about the possibility that she was partaking in illicit drugs and about the fact that she was having sex with Callum. That was something Lydia only found out when she went looking for some headache tablets in Zoe's bedside drawer and discovered condoms.

'What do I do?' she asked Gabriel at the time.

'She's sixteen,' he replied. 'At least they're using protection. What are you going to do? Tell her to stop?'

Gabriel sometimes seemed blasé about these things. His children were eighteen and twenty and so he had been through it all already. He understood, but at the same time did not understand, her panic. He maintained a relationship with his kids and he still sent them money and he was interested in their lives, but his ex-wife, Sandra, dealt with the day-to-day hiccups.

'It's not a fight worth having,' Gabriel said. 'It's her choice. She's not the kind of girl who would make that decision unless she wanted to.'

So, she didn't confront Zoe about the condoms but she did lecture her about alcohol and drugs even as she watched her daughter roll her eyes and zone out as soon as she began speaking.

She tried – she believes she tried. But maybe she didn't try hard enough. Somehow, she missed something. She obviously missed many things. What if something had been bothering her child, really bothering her? And what if Lydia had persevered, had tried harder, had asked her daughter, 'What's going on, sweetheart?' Would Zoe still be here?

If she does allow the idea of Zoe being gone to emerge for even a moment, she realises that what she feels is not just guilt because she should have done better as a mother but anger as well. A raging anger at the school. All they had to do was to take care of Zoe for three nights. It was not an impossible task and yet they had lost her, allowed her to become lost. It is easier, Lydia has found over the last two days, to concentrate on how angry she is at the school if she thinks about what has happened at all.

Her anger exists in juxtaposition to her denial that her daughter will never walk through the front door of their home again. She is a mess of contradictions as she tries to get a handle on what has happened to her life.

She knows the detective in front of her wants her to say that Zoe was unhappy, that she might have taken her own life, meaning that nothing but Lydia's poor parenting is responsible for her child's death. She feels her skin grow hot as she has this thought. She will not conveniently say that her child was depressed. Zoe was not depressed.

'Listen to me, Detective. I understand that it would be easy for the police and the school to write Zoe off as a depressed teenager or as a teenager who did something that brought about her own death, but I am not going to allow that to happen. She was on a school camp, in the care of teachers. She should have been properly supervised and looked after. The teachers on the camp had a duty of care to her and they failed. I hope that once you've finished asking all these questions, you're going to charge them and the school with that failure. I would hate for anyone else to have to experience this, and now you'll forgive me, Detective Holland, but I think I'm tired of answering these questions.'

Lydia reads the look of surprise on the detective's face. She has gone from cooperative to belligerent in a few seconds. She can see that the detective was looking to find a way to blame Zoe for her own death, but Lydia isn't about to let that happen. She isn't going to let her blame her mothering either. Detective Holland has children and therefore she should be aware that you can get to a point where you're simply tired of being a mother, tired of always being the one that everyone turns to. Tired of being the one who has to make sure there's a different meal on the table every night and the clothes are clean and the house is tidy and the bills are paid and everyone has done their homework and studied for their exams and is getting on with their friends and not feeling sick. And she reached that point but she was still doing everything she could to reach her young daughter. Her young daughter who is now gone.

Quite suddenly she realises that she will not have control of herself for much longer.

'I need to lie down,' she says, hearing the tremble of her voice, biting down on her lip. She will not cry in front of the detective.

She shows Detective Holland to the door and then she stops in Zoe's room. She lies down on her bed, smoothing the sheets, regretting that she has washed away her daughter's scent of the musky rose bodywash she liked from the bed. She has no idea why she did that. How could she have been so stupid?

She lays her arm across her face, blocking out the light. She would like to curl up and sleep for days and days but there is a funeral to organise. There are three houses that have to be filled with furniture by Wednesday. Ordinarily she would have been there to supervise the loading up of the trucks and to accompany Betty, the interior designer, to each house to make sure everything looked right.

'I will take care of everything,' Nathan, her second in command, told her on the phone this morning, his slight Russian accent making 'everything' sound like 'everythink'. He believes he's managed to rid himself of his accent almost completely but he hasn't, and clients find him charming. She knows she can trust him to make sure everything runs smoothly. She has a good staff and they will do what needs to be done.

Next to her in Zoe's bedside drawer, something beeps. She opens it to discover Zoe's old Tamagotchi. She must have replaced the battery and started it again. The little electronic pet demands that she feed it but she has no idea of the right buttons to push. 'What do I do, Zoe?' she whispers, and when there is no answer, she feels an ache in her chest, a terrible ache that spreads throughout her whole body and rises into her throat, bringing tears so forceful that she feels like she cannot breathe. Her daughter is not here to tell her what to do. She never will be again.

CHAPTER SEVEN

Tuesday – Three Days Since the Accident

Shayna

I'm not really sure what to do with myself. I can't stay in my room for another minute but Mum says I don't have to go to school. I kind of want to go back, and I feel bad for that. It's only Tuesday and Zoe was found on Sunday morning. I know they have brought a whole lot of counsellors into school so anyone who wants to talk about what happened can. But my mum and Becca's mum have agreed that we shouldn't have to go back until next term. Becca texted me this morning:

I might go back tomorrow with everyone else.

I replied:

It doesn't feel like she's gone.

Yeah. It feels like we just haven't spoken to her in a couple of days.

I can't stop thinking about the way she looked at you when you told her the truth.

I know I shouldn't have texted her that. I was being what my mother calls 'deliberately provocative'. I wanted to see what she would say. I wanted to talk about what happened without all the bullshit and lies but Becca isn't interested in that.

You were part of that too but I don't want to talk about it. We agreed not to discuss it. I should have just kept my mouth shut. I was going to take that particular incident to my grave.

Maybe. Maybe we all should have kept our mouths shut.

Becca doesn't text back. I know she's thinking the same thing. Too much stuff was said. Too many secrets leaked out and stained the air. I don't know why Becca confessed —anger, I suppose. She felt a little bit guilty when it happened, but mostly she felt triumphant, I think.

This morning a detective came to speak to me at home. Mum sat with me in the lounge, looking uncomfortable. The room is usually only for when she has her friends over to dinner. Jason and I are not allowed in because it has these striped fabric couches and some glass ornaments she inherited from our great-grandmother. I don't like going in there anyway because even though I should be old enough to be there, I still feel like if I turn around too fast, I'll break something.

But she asked the detective to come into the lounge and then she left me with him while she went to make him a cup of tea.

He looks like he should be in movies. He's much older but so cute. He has curly brown hair and big chocolate-brown eyes and long eyelashes and a dimple when he smiles and I could see that he is really ripped. When he lifted his arm to take the tea from Mum, the sleeve of his pale blue shirt slid back a little and I could see he has a tattoo. I couldn't see what it is but it looked like the tail of a snake.

Him being so good-looking made it kind of hard to concentrate, but I told him everything I had told the constables on Saturday. I had been rehearsing the story in my mind so I would say exactly the same thing to anyone who asked. I felt bad about thinking the detective was cute when he was only there because Zoe was not. But then there is so much to feel bad about. I have never lied to an adult before. I never imagined I would have to. I'm not sure how this all got so complicated, and I had to keep pushing down the urge to just tell him everything so it could all just be out there.

But I only gave him the prepared story. I told him that we turned off the light in the cabin around midnight, even though Zoe wanted to keep talking and eating, and that I didn't see or hear her leave. I said that she seemed normal, fine.

He nodded a lot while I talked, and at the end he said, 'Okay, now I'm going to leave my card with your mum. Will you call me if you think of anything else? Anything at all.'

I nodded back but I felt like he could tell that I was hiding stuff. It didn't matter though – Becca and I agreed before the police arrived. We agreed that it wasn't worth discussing. It's not worth it.

I scroll through my Instagram again. People are putting up pictures of themselves with Zoe as if to prove that they were friends with the girl who died on camp, writing long messages about how much they'll miss her and what a great person she was. Then they get all these supportive comments from everyone else, like, 'I hope you're okay. Sending you hugs. Thinking of you,' followed by a sad-face emoji. I haven't put anything on Instagram, but maybe I should. People know she was my best friend and they will wonder why I haven't. I wonder what would happen if I put up a picture of her and follow it with #sorry #guilty #myfault. I can just imagine the thousands of comments and replies.

I choose a picture of her and me and Becca dressed up before we went to a sixteenth birthday party. I can't remember whose – there have been a lot of them this year. It was a black and white theme, and Becca and I are dressed in tight black trousers with white crop tops but Zoe is all in white. She's wearing a dress with shoestring straps. She looks amazing.

I will never forget you. You will always be my best friend. There are no words, I type.

The instant I post the picture, the comments flood in, and I should take comfort from them but it's all bullshit. I know it's all bullshit.

I put my phone down and stare at the ceiling, wishing I could sleep but it's impossible.

We're not really sure when the funeral is going to be because they have to do an autopsy, just like they do on television. It sounds horrendous. When I close my eyes, I can see Zoe on a cold metal table with great big cuts all over her body and it makes me feel completely sick.

Zoe used to like talking to my mum. 'She's funny and so relaxed,' she always said. Some of the best times of our friendship were just her and me and my mum, drinking hot chocolate and talking late into the night when she came for a sleepover. In my phone we have one booked for next weekend. I want to delete the entry from my calendar but at the same time I don't want to delete it, as though I can still keep a little bit of her here if her name is in my diary.

I wonder if Zoe's mum is sad about her. I mean, I know she must be sad because of course she loved her daughter, but according to Zoe all they did was fight. I get up off my bed and stare out of the window at the garden. It's warm outside today. I love spring. I love the smell of jasmine and the pink blossoms that appear on the tree outside my window. I know I could go and sit in the garden but it seems a little disrespectful to Zoe to be enjoying myself. The only problem is that I can't stay sad all the time. It doesn't feel real that she's gone. I keep expecting to get a text from her saying, 'Got you, you bitches.'

I pick up my phone again when I hear it ping with another text from Becca. I thought she was angry with me about the last message. I know she's lying in bed feeling all guilty. She can tell me she doesn't want to discuss it all she likes but I know she's feeling as bad as I am, maybe even worse. She has texted:

> *You're right. We should have just kept quiet. You aren't going to tell anyone, are you? I know you talk to your mum more than any of us but you have to promise me that you're not going to say anything. We'll both get into trouble, real trouble.*

> *I told you already. I'm not going to say anything. I told the detective exactly what we rehearsed.*

> *Okay good. I did the same thing. Delete this text and the others as well. Just in case they ask to look at our phones.*

I agree and then I go through the texts I have sent her, making sure there's nothing that anyone would be suspicious about.

I feel horrible about what happened, like really horrible. I look around my room for something to eat. I think I finally understand what it means when people say they eat their feelings. I find half a chocolate bar that Jason gave me last night. He didn't say anything because he's not sure what to say but he did give me this Flake that I know he had hidden in the cupboard. Mum buys lots of chocolate and Jason hides it from me because I ask him to.

'Here you go, squiggle,' he said after he knocked on my door last night. He threw the chocolate onto the bed and then he just stood there trying to find something to do with his arms that look too long for his body right now.

'Thanks, fudge,' I said and I almost wanted to cry at how cute he was. We don't talk much anymore but I really love him even though he's smelly and his voice is all weird. I knew what he was doing by giving me the chocolate. I shove the half I have left into my mouth, feeling the sweet flakes break up on my tongue. I swallow and then I'm instantly hungry again.

I don't think I could ever eat enough to fill this hole inside me. It's a Zoe-shaped hole, a best-friend-shaped hole.

When I was twelve, I got my period for the first time when I was at school. I went to the bathroom and pulled down my underwear and it was stained with rusty-brown blood. I remember how my heart raced and I felt like I couldn't breathe. Fortunately, it hadn't gone through to my skirt but I had no idea what to do and so I just sat there, trying to figure it out. I think I was in shock, even though I knew what it was.

After about five minutes I heard the bathroom door open and Zoe called, 'Shay, Shay… are you still here?'

I remember the relief at hearing her voice was like warm liquid seeping through my body. 'I'm in here. I got my period for the first time and… and now…' I started to cry.

'Okay… just sit tight,' Zoe said. 'I've got an emergency pack from my mum in my school bag. I've got clean underwear and pads and everything. I'll get it for you.'

And she did. By the time lunch was over, I was fine. She even gave me a small chocolate bar that her mum had packed in the kit. It turned what could have been something traumatic and horrible into something kind of fun and something that we shared and could laugh about for years afterwards.

I smile now as I think about that and I pick up my phone, meaning to text her and remind her of that, and then I realise how stupid I've just been. She will never respond to another text from me.

I curl up on my bed, trying not to remember what happened on Friday night, trying not to think about all the things I didn't tell the detective.

Because there was a lot I didn't tell him.

The truth. That's mostly what I left out. I left out the truth.

CHAPTER EIGHT

Bernadette

I cannot seem to calm my racing heart. I have been instructed to take the whole week off school. It was bad enough that I could only go back tomorrow but this is ridiculous.

I had no desire to take the final week of term off. My year ten English class have an exam this week and it was my intention to watch over them as they did a practice essay on *The Tempest* in class. I have devised, I believe, a wonderful question about Shakespeare's use of magic in the text, and as they are my advanced English class and quite the brightest group of girls I have ever taught, I was looking forward to seeing what they came up with. There is something so special about a group of clever girls, about watching them untangle a Shakespeare play and bring their own ideas of the world to themes in a work that has been around for hundreds of years. And now I can only hope that any substitute brought in to replace me is worthy of my students.

Instead of being with them, I have been asked to not contact anyone at school. 'We are taking this week very slowly,' Principal Bennet told me. 'We want the girls to be able to express themselves and to be allowed to mourn this terrible incident.'

'Most of them will not be in mourning, George,' I told him. 'You know what teenage girls are like. They will, instead, be revelling in all the drama.'

I had been speaking to him on the phone at the time and he grew very quiet when I said that. And then he said, 'Sometimes, Bernadette, I wonder why you became a teacher.'

'Don't be ridiculous,' I responded.

It's only Tuesday and I have been going slightly stir-crazy without work, but I have managed to tidy the flat and clean out all the cupboards. I have also planned nearly half a term of lessons for my year seven classes. I am most resentful at not being there now. I like to leave things in a neat and orderly manner before school holidays. George has assured me that I will be able to come in during the break and sort things out. 'If the police investigation is concluded,' he said. 'And if…'

'And if what, George? Spit it out.'

'If the police have decided against charging you and Paula.'

I didn't even know what to say to him. It's such a preposterous idea. What happened has nothing to do with me and Paula.

'I also feel I should let you know that the board will be meeting in the holidays and we will be taking legal advice.'

'What for?'

'I'm worried that this could get difficult. You had a duty of care to the students, and what has happened could be seen as negligence on your part.'

'So is it going to be your assertion that either Paula or I should have stayed up all night to watch these girls and make sure that no one decided to leave their cabin? We have never had something like this happen before. These girls are sixteen and fully aware of how to behave. I cannot be held responsible for the one recalcitrant student who comes my way after twenty-five years of teaching for this school.'

'That's not what I'm saying but I have spoken to Paula about the incident with Zoe and perhaps it would have been better for her to have been sent home or for you and Paula to have watched her more closely.'

'I said she should be sent home, George. I told Paula exactly that!'

'Yes, but when you agreed to allow her to stay at the camp, more care should have been taken. She had been very upset during the day and… look, we probably shouldn't be discussing this now. I just wanted to let you know what will be happening over the break. You may want to get in touch with the union and see what help they can give you if things get difficult.'

I didn't manage to summon a reply. I was incandescent with rage and I didn't trust myself to say anything else to him. I just hung up the phone. I have an impeccable reputation as a teacher and I will not allow what happened at this camp to destroy me and my career.

I open up the linen cupboard, where towels and bedding are neatly stacked, and take everything out. I have to keep busy or I will go mad. It amazes me how much time there is in a day without work. The school holidays are different, of course. Then I use the time to get ready for the next year or the next term and I always go into school anyway. I do allow myself the afternoon off in the summer holidays. Oliver likes the beach.

I am sure that the police will want to interview me again. I am sure that this is about to get very ugly but I have no idea what to do about it all. I should call the union and ask about legal representation but I seem to be paralysed in that regard. I can clean and I can tidy but I don't want to talk about this to anyone. Paula has left me two messages.

'Hi Bernadette, I would like to be able to have a chat. I know you're devastated about this, as am I. I would like to talk about a way we can help the students and perhaps about attending the funeral, which I believe will be soon. Give me a call.'

'Hi Bernadette, I really think we should talk. Give me a call.'

She wants to speak to me so we can get our stories straight, I'm sure. She has already spoken to one of the detectives and there is nothing to get straight anyway. I have explained what happened and she will say the same thing.

She was asleep when I got up to go outside and have a cigarette in the cold mountain air at midnight. I hated sharing a room with her. She snores and I had been tossing and turning for an hour when the need for a cigarette overtook me. I allow myself one a day, just one, but I made an exception on Friday night, what with one thing and another. The incident with Zoe had rattled me more than I felt it should have. I've dealt with difficult students before but I was worried that I seemed to be losing the knack for remaining calm in such a situation.

It was a beautiful moment at first. The air was frigid despite it being spring, and all was silent as though the cold had driven all the creatures of the bush into shelter. I did see an owl glide across the sky, its wings creating a whooshing sound, but that was all. The sky was completely cloudless and the stars stood out, abundant and bright. There were no lights to detract from the beauty of that midnight sky and I felt myself breathe calmly for the first time that day. Just as I finished my cigarette, I felt my eyes grow heavy and I knew I would be able to sleep. As I turned to go back into the cabin I was sharing with Paula, I saw her. Even in the dark I knew it was her from the ridiculous silver sneakers she was wearing that flashed as she angled her phone onto the ground so she wouldn't fall.

I didn't expect the other girl. It was difficult to see who it was. She obviously had not expected to be followed. She jumped a little when the other girl tapped her on her shoulder. They began speaking in hushed tones, obviously mindful of the silent camp. I watched for a moment, my body weary, and then I resolved to leave them to it even though the exchange between the two of them seemed to be becoming heated. I turned and went back into my cabin.

I was very tired. I reasoned that they were probably just on their way to the bathroom and that whatever was happening between them would quickly be resolved. I had no desire to get involved in a spat between the girls. They usually end as quickly as they start, and I know that when parents and teachers get involved, it only prolongs things. Teenage girls are mercurial creatures governed by their emotions. Disputes flare instantly and are over just as quickly.

It was only when I was comfortable in my warm sleeping bag, on the edge of sleep, that I realised the bathroom was in the opposite direction to where they had been walking. I am not proud of the thought I had then. It was not my finest moment as a teacher but I could never have known that it would lead to this. *Not my problem. It's not my problem.* I will never tell anyone, but that's exactly what I thought.

It was only then that I noticed the silence in the cabin, and at first, I was relieved because I assumed that Paula had finally stopped snoring, but then I realised that it was because she wasn't in the cabin at all. I worried that I had woken her but then I grew angry about that since she had been the one to prevent me from sleeping.

The cabin door opened and closed quietly and I muttered, 'Not my fault,' just in case she was about to accuse me of waking her. And then I slept. Deep, dreamless and quite restful for the location.

In the morning, I was going to speak to Zoe and whoever she had been talking to about where they had been going. I really was, but once she was found to be missing, I couldn't speak to her and I wasn't certain who the other girl was so I couldn't speak to her either.

I know the other girl was angry with her – I had been able to discern that much at least – but from what I know about Zoe Bloom, that could have been anyone in the camp.

She had a rather nasty streak. I'm sure she had no idea but her nickname amongst the girls other than her best friends was 'the witch'. Apparently, her beauty was a little marred by a slightly pointy nose.

'Well, it's not necessary to think about any of that, is it?' I say to Oliver now, who has been sitting patiently, watching me as I fold and stack towels. I have the balcony doors open and the spring breeze has filled my flat with the salty scent of the ocean. I am so grateful to have bought this apartment before the area became popular. I would never have been able to afford it otherwise but I have lived here for nearly thirty years as buildings were slowly gentrified and trendy restaurants opened up. While I value my privacy, I do enjoy the bustle of the beach during summer. Oliver enjoys it as well, and on our walks, he is much admired by all who see him.

'Would you like a walk?' I ask him, and he lifts his paws, motioning that he would.

I am going to try and be calm about my week off. I shall use it to prepare for next term and next year. I may even take in a movie or two. I am unsure about attending the funeral but it may be that I have to go. I will keep checking the school Facebook page for updates on when that might be.

As I leave the building with Oliver, I spot Henry coming up the road. He looks at me and opens his hands as if to ask what I'm doing home, but I simply shake my head and walk the other way. For some reason I don't feel able to explain all this to him. I have no idea why.

CHAPTER NINE

Jessie

She finds her mother in the kitchen, surrounded by food as though they are about to give a party. There are casserole dishes and cake plates and Tupperware full of home-baked biscuits everywhere. The same queasiness that took over her body after her father died floods her. She swallows a few times. In the dining room, the table is covered with vases of flowers, their smells mingling to create a sickly sweet perfume that makes Jessie sneeze any time she walks past. She cannot wait for the flowers to wilt and fade so that they can be thrown out.

'I don't know what to do with all this. I just don't know what to do,' her mother says, looking close to a breakdown. Her mum always knows what to do. When Jessie couldn't manage to get herself up off the bathroom floor three days after her father died, her mother had known what to do then. She had dropped down next to her and stayed there, just breathing in and out with her, holding her hand, until Jessie thought that she might finally be able to get up. She had known what to do two weeks later when she had gone back to work. At first Jessie was profoundly angry about this, as though even her mum thought it was better to just forget about her father like Zoe had, but deep down, she knows her mother has not forgotten about him. She knows that she thinks about him every day – even now after she's been married to Gabriel for ten years. Going back to work was a necessity so they could stay in their house surrounded by memories of Eli.

When Jessie was waiting for her final exam results – certain that she would not be granted admittance to medicine – her mother had known what to do then as well. 'Girls' day,' she had said, and she handed everything over to Nathan, and they spent the day sampling pastry at five different bakeries, which is Jessie's version of the ideal girls' day. She has never had much interest in shopping or facials or manicures. Her mother had known what to do when the text message flashed up on the screen of Jessie's phone, letting her know that she had received the mark she needed: dance around the living room, singing, 'You did it, you did it,' and then taking her to visit her father at the cemetery so she could tell him that she had achieved her dream. Her mother has always known what to do, and it occurs to Jessie as she looks at her, at how red her eyes are and how pale her skin is, that her mother may finally have no idea what to do at all. Perhaps there is only so much grief a person can take.

Jessie wants to reach out for her, to enclose her in a hug like Gabriel would do, but she can't seem to do anything other than look at all the food, trying to resist the urge to cram it into the garbage bin so she won't have to see it anymore, won't have to acknowledge what it represents. She remembers all the food after her dad died. So much food. Lasagne seems to be a favourite for the grieving. Jessie cannot eat lasagne. The smell of the bubbling meat and cheese dish turns her stomach, which she finds sad because it was her father's favourite meal.

How can Zoe simply be gone? What a strange, weird thing. When her father passed away, it happened quickly, but it happened as they watched. First, he was just more tired than usual, falling asleep after dinner when usually he was filled with energy at story time. And then he didn't seem to have an appetite anymore, which meant that he lost weight. But it was the slightly olive tinge to his skin that made her mother force him to visit the doctor. 'It's a tan,' he said. 'Everyone says I look wonderful.'

But her mother insisted and so he went, reluctantly, to begin the tests that led to the diagnoses and the immediate start of chemotherapy, despite the doctor telling them that, by that point, it was too late. Jessie did not know this at the time. Her mother tried to shield her and her sister from the awful truth of it but she wishes she had known. At the time she thought that the doctors just weren't trying to help him and she had vowed to do better when she grew up.

She remembers the very moment she decided she would train to be a doctor. It was the child at the hospital. She was no more than six or seven, trailing a drip. Her little head was bald and she was holding a fluffy stuffed dog. Jessie had seen her when she went to visit her father for the week he was in the hospital after the operation that did little to help anything at all.

She had been terrified about losing him but had looked at the mother following the small child – hope, fear and love written nakedly across her face – and even though she had been too young to understand it, she had wanted to tell the mother that her child would get better.

That moment had crystallised her desire to become a doctor. She didn't just want to save her father; she wanted to save everyone.

Once he came home to his bed in the living room, they knew with each passing day that he was getting closer and closer and then, one day, he died.

But Zoe went to camp. She just went to camp and didn't come back. How is such a thing possible?

She closes her eyes as she tries to think of something, anything to say that would help, and she remembers the last time she and her mother and Zoe were together. It happened less and less over the years as their lives became busier. But in January, in the summer school holidays, Jessie had returned home from a shift at the hospital at 8 p.m. to find her mother and sister sitting together on the wooden front porch swing that her father had built when her parents moved into the house. They were both dressed in shorts, their legs dangling as the swing moved back and forth in the dying rays of the summer sun. Jessie, exhausted, sat down next to Zoe without saying anything and felt her eyes immediately begin to close. Her head fell sideways to rest on her sister's shoulder. Zoe didn't move. Jessie felt her mother get up as she dozed but Zoe stayed where she was. She sat there for half an hour while Jessie drifted, gently pushing the swing and gazing at her phone in the warm evening.

She opens her eyes again. She cannot think how to describe this moment to her mother or what it meant to her. She discovers that she can't find the right words and not just because Zoe is gone but because of everything she has been hiding from her.

'Where's Gabriel?' she asks her mother.

'He's at work.'

Jessie nods. Zoe was not Gabriel's child. She is sure that he loved her but it's not the same.

Jessie found it difficult to accept Gabriel when he and her mother first started dating. She struggled with the idea that anyone could replace her father, even though her mother assured her, and Gabriel assured her, that this would never be the case.

He tried, in the beginning, to become a kind of fatherly friend to her and Zoe but Jessie wasn't having any of it, and to her mother's credit, she never pushed the relationship. But slowly as the years have gone on, Jessie has settled into a cautious friendship with him. He's not her father and he could never be but he is kind and supportive.

When Jessie first started medical school, Gabriel was full of information and advice and she had to bite her tongue and nod every time he said something. Gabriel is a dentist, and while he studied anatomy to a certain degree, he is not a doctor. But she knows that he only meant well. And he was able to help with some questions she had on the mouth and throat.

Most importantly, he is someone her mum can depend on, which means that Jessie was able, when they started seeing each other, to stop worrying about her broken mother so much. It was a relief, at twelve years old, to be able to just concentrate on her own concerns.

'I'll put it all away for you,' she says now to her mother, who looks at her with tear-filled blue eyes. She looks older and also like she hasn't slept since Saturday. 'Maybe you should just go and lie down.'

'Do you think Zoe will like any of this?' asks her mother.

'Mum,' says Jessie, alarmed.

'I mean… I'm sorry, Jess, I know she's… I know. How are you doing, love? Have you started the process to defer the exams?'

'I think I may just take them. Even if I do badly, it will be better to have them over.'

Her mother nods as though she's listening but she's still staring at the countertops as though she cannot comprehend what to do.

'What did the policewoman want yesterday?' Jessie asks, hoping to focus her mother.

'Just to ask if we knew any reason why Zoe would have left the cabin.'

'Have they spoken to Callum?' she asks because maybe Zoe had agreed to a meeting. Maybe. She thinks about telling her mother what she knows but decides against it. What difference could it make now?

'I'm sure if they haven't, they will soon. Oh, I can't bear it, I just can't bear it.' Her mother sinks into a chair, dropping her head into her hands, and Jessie finds herself wishing that Gabriel were here. He's been really good over the last few days. He sits next to her mum as she cries and then he always finds something to say about Zoe that allows her to remember something nice about her: 'Do you remember when she was dancing in the end of year ballet concert when she was twelve and the girl next to her fell and she leaned down and lifted her up but made it look like it was part of the dance? Remember when Shayna and Becca slept over and they made cookies in the middle of the night and you and I both dreamed about eating cake because of the smell drifting through the house?'

Jessie has listened from doorways as they speak. She wants to join them when they are together, to sit with them and remember her little sister, but she feels like all the stuff she's hiding from her mother will come tumbling out. Now is not the time.

She had planned to tell them this weekend. She had planned it for months. It was going to be a weekend of revelations, that's what she called it in her mind. She had woken up filled with purpose on Saturday morning, and only when she returned from her morning run, which she always liked to do as the sun rose, did she find her mother and Gabriel in the kitchen, each on their phones. 'What's happened?' she asked, seeing the shock on their faces.

'Zoe's missing. We're driving up there now.'

'Missing? But she's at camp.'

'She's missing from camp,' her mother snapped.

'How long has she been missing for?' Jessie asked, understanding her mother's anger was simply fear.

'They don't know. She wasn't in the cabin when the girls woke up this morning. They don't know. Gabriel, we have to go now.'

Jessie looked at her stepfather, who was sitting at the kitchen table, a cup of coffee steaming in front of him. His skin was pale.

'Sorry, yes. I was just trying to think of everything we might need. I have two torches and warm jackets – should we take some food?'

'I'll get my coat. I'll come and help look for her,' said Jessie.

'No, you just stay here. Take care of Walter and don't leave the house. If she's lost, she may call home. I don't know if her phone is still working because it's going straight to voicemail but I don't know. Just stay here, okay?' Her mother's voice kept rising, hysteria creeping in.

'Okay, okay. I'll stay here. I won't leave, I promise.'

After they left, Jessie tipped Gabriel's still full cup of coffee down the sink and gave Walter his breakfast. The old dog licked her hand as she put the food in front of him and she was moved to wrap her arms around his neck. She remembered him as a puppy – bought, she knows, by her mother to give her something else to focus on aside from her grief over her father. It had helped. Jessie never tired of taking care of Walter, named because he looked just like a Walter, even as a puppy.

She made herself some breakfast and took it up to her room to eat in front of her computer. Zoe missing was already all over the internet. 'Why do you have to be such a pain?' she muttered at her missing sister. She was absolutely certain that Zoe would soon be found and she was also certain that she would not get into trouble for driving everyone crazy. She is ashamed of that certainty now even though she understands that she couldn't have thought any other way. Students don't disappear from camp, and if they do, they are quickly found. She spent some time reading articles on the internet to confirm this theory.

When she couldn't wait any longer, she typed into her phone:

What's going on?

I don't know, it's all crazy here. She's missing and now the police have been called. You need to keep quiet about meeting me. Delete this text. I love you and I loved seeing you but we may have to stay apart for a while. Hopefully we'll find her soon and then we can talk. Until then please don't speak to your parents.

Okay. Please text me when they find her. I love you xx

She stared down at the phone, waiting for Paula to text her back. But she hasn't heard from her since. She has tried to get in touch with her but there's been no answer. She understands, logically, Paula cannot jeopardise her job any further. The police may want to see her phone. Paula has made the right decision in telling her not to contact her but she cannot help but be hurt. She would like to be able to sit with her, to discuss what has happened. She would like to be able to reassure her that she will not be blamed, that she doesn't blame her, because she knows what Zoe was like. If Zoe was meeting Callum or if she was sneaking out to have a cigarette… anything – no one could have stopped her. Jessie knows that her sister spent a lot of time sneaking out over the last year.

She thought that no one knew but Jessie was often awake to hear the scratching sound of her metal window opening and then the scuffling sounds of Zoe climbing out the window, down the trellis. The trellis is old and Jessie worried that it would break at some point but she never said anything to her sister.

Now, she drags her phone out of her pocket and looks at it, willing Paula to send her something, anything. Even just an emoji would do so she would know that Paula is thinking about her as much as Jessie is thinking about Paula.

Jessie was the one who pushed for a meeting on Friday night. She wishes she could approach this as she has approached most other aspects of her life – with logic and control – but she seems to have lost all control when it comes to Paula. She knows that she has held herself back from finding someone because she has always understood that being in love means exposing yourself to emotional devastation. She has watched her mother grieve for twelve years already, and she never wanted to open herself up to that kind of pain. But loving Paula feels so easy, so natural, and yet it has to be kept a secret. Being in a relationship with someone older is complicated. Add in children and a husband and a former student–teacher relationship and complicated becomes tangled and messy. Time together was snatched, rushed and nearly impossible. Jessie had been on shift at the hospital followed by hours in the library for two weeks straight before Zoe went on camp. Two weeks of text conversations and nothing else. Friday night had been the first night when she felt she could take a little time off and they had planned a meeting until Paula remembered camp. Jessie had typed impulsively:

I'll drive up there.

Don't be ridiculous. I won't be able to spend time with you.

Just for an hour, just so I can see you.

Jessie felt herself colour even though the conversation was over text and there was no one to see her at the time. She felt like she was begging.

Paula texted:

But you have to work or study.

I deserve a night off. I'll drive up and spend an hour and then I'll leave.

I'll have to sneak out of my cabin.

I'll tell my mother I'm at the library.

Okay, but if we get caught...

We won't get caught.

'Text me, please,' she mutters at her phone. But her screen remains blank and so she gets on with putting away all the food, surreptitiously throwing out two lasagnes so she won't have to look at them or smell them.

Students don't disappear from camp, but Jessie knows now that she should have understood that her family was cursed with impossible statistics. Statistically, pancreatic cancer is one of the lesser-diagnosed cancers in the world. Statistically, it is mostly diagnosed in older patients over the age of seventy. Statistically, fit young men of forty with no genetic predispositions or underlying health issues don't get pancreatic cancer. Statistically, Eli was just really, really unlucky. Statistically, no student from St Anne's had ever been lost for longer than an hour or two or died on a camp until the statistics met the Bloom family.

Jessie opens up a Tupperware filled with what look like brownies. *Who sends brownies to a house in mourning?* She takes one out and crams it in her mouth. It is thick and a little dry but she keeps chewing and takes the container up to her room.

She decides she will leave one on Zoe's bedside table for her and then she realises how ridiculous her thought has just been.

It was the same after her father died. When she went back to school, a month after he passed away, she was told she had placed third in a national maths competition.

When her mother picked her up that afternoon, she climbed into the car and gushed, 'I came third in the whole country, Mum. Dad told me I was the best at maths. I can't wait to show him.'

'Oh, Jess,' her mother said. And there were tears from both of them.

In her room she throws the whole Tupperware into the bin next to her bed.

'Oh, Jess,' she says out loud. 'Oh, Jess.'

CHAPTER TEN

It began innocently enough.

I started it with a like on one of her Instagram photos. It was of her in gym clothes —bright pink leggings and a matching crop top. She was holding a giant chocolate chip cookie and she had captioned it: My reward #workout #sweat #treat. Her face was glowing, her cheeks just a little pink, her smile wide and her teeth perfect. You could see the curve of her pert breasts and admire the way her blonde hair shimmered down her back, as though it had just been released from her ponytail. It wasn't real. When I saw it, I knew it wasn't real because very little on Instagram is, and I knew it was unlikely that she had just finished a workout – more likely that she just got dressed up, applied her make-up and took the photo – but she was beautiful, just so beautiful, and it was a great photo and that's all that mattered.

A new like on a photo from someone you don't know is always interesting and so she stalked across the internet, trying to find out more about her new fan.

And she liked what she found. She was meant to. Curly brown hair, sun-streaked with gold, and ocean-blue eyes. Ripped muscles from lifting weights and there was even a dog named Baxter, a German shepherd with the most intelligent look in his eyes. A beautiful boy for a beautiful girl. I was perfect. I made sure I was.

She liked a whole lot of the photos, including the one of me tucking into a burger. It isn't the best photo of me because I had just taken a bite of the burger and my cheeks are bulging with food but you can see the thick piece of meat in the centre, and the bright yellow of the cheese contrasts with the crispy brown onion rings. We all know how to take a good Instagram photo. My mouth waters when I look at that picture.

She commented on that one: 'Someone likes his food.'

I liked her comment, and just like that we were chatting.

Like I said, it began innocently enough.

I wonder if even the people who were really close to her, like her family, understand exactly what it's like to have the full force of her love and admiration directed at them.

I never understood it until it was directed at me. It's like standing in sunshine.

Once we'd been exchanging memes and one-liners for a week, she suggested we play ten questions.

I agreed. I thought I was ready for all her questions.

Name?

You know that already.

It's part of the game. Name?

Xavier. Name?

Zoe. Age?

17. Age?

16. School?

Home-schooled. School?

Really? Why?

I had to think fast then. Home-schooled meant she wouldn't ask me where I went to school and that I wouldn't have to lie but I hadn't thought about a reason.

I live in Glenbrook – you know, right next to the Blue Mountains – and my mother is an artist so she can home-school me.

Why do you want to be at home with your mother all day long?

I didn't exactly enjoy the high school experience.

Why?

I think we've stopped playing the game now.

I guess.

I thought about it for a bit…

I got into a bit of trouble for bullying. Some little kid complained.

I hate the way you're not allowed to say anything to anyone anymore. The whole world is so PC now. What did you do to him?

Um, can we not talk about that? I have moments where I feel bad about it.

Sure. Favourite food?

Burgers.

And we went on like that.

I didn't want to talk about the incident. I think that there are pivotal moments in everyone's life, when they do something that makes them take a good hard look at themselves. The incident with the kid, that kid, happened when I was twelve and he was ten. I've never really been able to let it go. A friend – a good friend who is still my friend today – and I had watched him on the playground as he picked his nose and ate it, in full view of the whole school.

'It's like he doesn't even care,' I said.

'I'll tell you how we could make him care…' my friend replied.

That Friday afternoon we grabbed him, stripped him down to his underwear and shoved him out on stage during a school assembly. We were supposed to be at the back of the stage to carry out chairs for the teachers to sit on. We told him to come and help us, and because he was only ten, he just did what we said. He was a scrawny kid with some kind of weird skin thing on his chest. He just stood there while the students laughed. He dropped his head and I saw a tear splash onto the stage. He only stood there for a few seconds before a teacher leapt up and stood in front of him, shielding him from everyone.

We got suspended but he left the school. I lay in bed that night and thought about what I'd done, about the way his face had turned beetroot-red and also about the way his parents had looked at me later that day when all our parents were called in. I felt like I was a monster and my mother and father were completely horrified. They looked at me like they didn't know who I was.

I decided that I didn't want to be that kind of person anymore. I would never tell anyone this but I wrote a letter to him a few days later. He didn't write back but I wrote him another and another. And eventually he replied. We eventually moved to email and we still talk now. I'm not a bad person. I've done bad things but I've always believed I'm not a bad person – until now. Maybe even I don't know who I am.

I keep saying to myself that I started talking to her for a joke. But it wasn't just for a joke. Here's the truth, the really unpalatable truth. Here is the truth that I can taste in the back of my throat, bitter and mean: I wanted to hurt her. But I didn't intend for anything like what happened. That decision wasn't my decision.

I tried to end it when I had had my laughs, when I had enjoyed the fact that I had fooled her and when I'd achieved exactly what I'd set out to achieve.

But every time I tried to end it, she would lure me back. It was amazing to have her attention. It goes some way to explaining why she was so popular. She was charming and lovely when she wanted to be.

And she was vicious and nasty when she wanted to be, and I could be just as terrible when I wanted to be. But never as terrible as I have been. Never as terrible as that.

CHAPTER ELEVEN

Wednesday – Four Days Since the Accident

Lydia

'Can I please bring you something to eat?' begs Gabriel but Lydia shakes her head. She hears him sigh as he leaves the room. He is finding his inability to help her frustrating. He is usually able to jolly her out of a bad mood or help her calm down after a frenzied day at work. Even though he understands it, he still hates that he can't make her feel better.

She has spent the morning in Zoe's room, going through everything again, looking for… She doesn't even know what she's looking for. She wishes she could stumble across a journal or some notes – anything. But everything private and secret about her daughter is on her phone, and the police have that. Her whole life is contained in that metal rectangle and it is password-protected. Her entry to her daughter's life has been barred for years, and even though that's the case with most mothers these days, she should have realised that she needed to know more.

The word 'bitch', the terrible word she called her daughter just before camp keeps coming back to her, and she has to shake her whole body to rid herself of the memory of that terrible few minutes. *How can that be the last thing I said to her? How could I have done that?*

Trying to erase the word, longing for absolution, she climbs right into Zoe's closet, moving aside clothing and searching in pockets, still looking for something she can't name. At the back of the cupboard are all of Zoe's old dance costumes, and she rubs her hands along the slippery satin and Lycra, catching her nails on loose sequins. The sweet chemical smell of stage make-up still clings to the costumes, and she pulls one out and takes it back to her bedroom with her.

She lies on her side on her bed, a photo album from Zoe's first year open in front of her. She wishes that she had taken more pictures of her or that Facebook had been a thing when Zoe was born so she would have a record of virtually every day with her daughter. She has a cousin who had a little girl last year and she's pretty sure Miriam posts a picture of Leah on Facebook every single day. Lydia scrolls past after giving each photo a quick like but she's never considered that Miriam has a record of every day of Leah's life forever and ever. The pictures in the album she is looking through don't even cover every month, and the loss almost winds her.

Zoe was born in the middle of a February heatwave that was so bad, Lydia thought she wouldn't survive it. Eli started taking Jessie to school a few days before Lydia was due, so she could just lie on the couch with the air conditioner blasting on her. She remembers he came home every day with a treat for her. 'I can't even look at myself anymore,' she told him.

'You are and always will be the most beautiful woman in the world,' Eli said.

Her contractions began as she walked around the house at 2 a.m., unable to sleep. Labour was quick and sharp and then there was little Zoe, blonde-haired and blue-eyed, angelic-looking Zoe.

For the first few weeks after she was born Eli took lots of pictures. Pictures of a red-faced, squalling newborn Zoe, as she was being weighed just after birth. Pictures of Lydia holding Zoe and then Jessie holding Zoe and their grandparents holding her. She runs her fingers over a photo taken when her daughter was around three weeks old. They'd had a tea party to welcome her and let everyone meet her. In the image she and Eli are standing in the centre, baby Zoe cocooned in a light pink blanket in her father's arms. His parents are on one side of him and her parents are on the other, standing next to her. A tear splashes onto the picture and she wipes it away. Only three people in the image are still alive. In the sixteen years since Zoe was born, she has lost both her parents: her mother to a heart attack and her father to a car accident – they will never know for sure but she believes he fell asleep at the wheel. He had used alcohol to cope after her mother died. Fortunately, he didn't kill anyone else. Eli is gone, the cancer taking him so quickly Lydia feels like she didn't even get time to understand what was happening. His parents moved to Queensland and she knows she should have been better at maintaining contact but she has always been so busy with work and the girls. She also knows that Graham and Michelle took her marriage to Gabriel badly. They didn't understand how she could have moved on after only two years. But the marriage wasn't something she planned. It was just something that happened. And now Zoe is gone. Before her paternal grandparents and after her father but before her mother. How can she be gone?

She closes the album and lies on her back, staring at the ceiling, her head pounding. She's sure she is dehydrated. She cannot seem to stop crying for more than a few minutes. The visit from the detective broke through the numbness and she has been sobbing for hours, for days. She thinks she cried as she slept last night because this morning her pillow was damp. At least the sleeping pill helped her get some rest. She didn't think she could go another night without sleep. She was starting to see things, hallucinations of her daughter walking past the room she was in. The first time it happened she shrieked and ran to the door of Zoe's room only to find the corridor empty. The next time it happened, when she was in the kitchen, she stood very still, hoping that the ghost of her child would walk across the doorway again. It was then that she realised she needed to sleep, real deep sleep.

How can you be gone, Zoe? How can you be gone? She lifts the costume she has brought from Zoe's room to her face, touching the beaded fabric against her cheek. Zoe wore it when she was thirteen for a jazz dance concert. It is a bright green with silver beads all over the torso and a black fringed skirt. She knows Zoe wore it all day before the concert that night. 'I have to get used to the way it feels, Mum,' she said. But Lydia knew that she loved the feeling of the fringing around her legs as she twisted and turned and practised for her moment in the limelight. Her daughter had started dance classes at three years old, loving the medium from the very beginning. On stage she looked as light as a feather as she leapt and twirled and stood on her toes. Until last year, Lydia had assumed she was interested in dance as a profession. She had taken ballet and tap and jazz and hip-hop classes over the years. The whole back half of her closet is filled with sparkly costumes from all the recitals Lydia has attended over the years. She wants to watch the videos she took but it feels like it's too soon. She doesn't know if she will be able to stand seeing her vibrant daughter smiling her way through a performance onstage.

Last year Zoe seemed to lose interest in dance. She quit her classes one after the other.

'But you love to dance,' Lydia had protested. 'Why don't you just do it until the end of your schooling? It's great exercise and great for stress release.'

'I'm bored with dancing now. I don't have the time anymore either.'

Lydia put that down to her increasing interest in boys and that becoming the most important thing in her life. More important than dance, than school, than her friends and certainly more important than anything her mother had to say. And then this year she started dating Callum seriously and she couldn't even be persuaded to think about dancing for the end-of-year concert at school.

Was Callum the problem? Did he drive up to the Blue Mountains and have a fight with Zoe? Did it all just get too much or was it an accident?

The questions have been circling in her head and she's not getting anywhere with the answers. She hears the bell ring downstairs and sighs. She cannot imagine who is left to drop off food or flowers. The whole neighbourhood seems to have been by already, and Zoe has only been gone for five days. It's not even a week. The fridge is full to bursting and Gabriel has resorted to taking food to work to give away to his staff. And still it keeps coming.

Do people have casseroles and cakes in the fridge just waiting for a tragedy? It feels like they do.

She needs something to drink but she will wait until she hears the front door close so she knows that whoever has dropped off a dish has gone. She will have to start thinking about sending thank you emails or texts at some point, she realises, although the thought almost makes her retch with its finality.

This morning Detective Gold called and spoke to Gabriel, telling him that they could go ahead with the funeral.

'There were no drugs or alcohol in her system,' Gabriel reported.

'I wish there had been,' she said and her husband nodded, understanding. It would be easier if there was some outside influence, something they could point to, some tangible reason.

The funeral will be tomorrow afternoon.

She and Gabriel had already chosen a casket online. At the thought of the mahogany box lined in pink silk, encasing her precious daughter, Lydia places her hand on her chest. How is she going to survive this pain?

Ordinarily Zoe would have been buried immediately after death as is their tradition but the autopsy delayed things. Lydia believes that this must have been requested by the school who are looking to mitigate blame and she also knows that she could have refused to allow it. But she wanted to know as well. If she did have alcohol or drugs in her system, then surely that was the school's fault as well? But there was nothing and so Lydia is back to her endless questions.

Gabriel comes into the room.

'Have they gone?' she asks as she wipes her constantly watering eyes.

'Um, no, and you need… It's the woman detective, the one in charge of Zoe's case.'

'But I just saw her on Monday and you spoke to the other detective this morning. Why is she back here?'

Gabriel shrugs and looks down at his shoes. He is a little red in the face. 'Why did you give her Zoe's phone?' he asks.

'She wanted to look at it. She thought maybe it would give us a clue as to what happened. Anyway, what difference does it make…?' Her voice catches. 'It's not as if she's going to be angry.'

'No, no, I suppose not. She says she wants to speak to both of us. I can tell her to come back tomorrow or I can talk to her alone.'

'No, it's fine.' She sighs.

She levers her body off the bed, feeling old and tired. She is only wearing socks and contemplates putting on shoes and giving her hair a brush but decides against it. The detective saw her like this two days ago. Not much has changed since then.

In the living room, Detective Holland is sitting straight-backed on the grey sofa. She looks uncomfortable and stands up when she sees Lydia. For no reason she can understand Lydia feels her skin tingle. *She knows something. She's found out something.*

'What is it?' she asks, too overwrought, too grief-stricken, too everything for pleasantries.

The detective nods her head, just a small nod, an acknowledgement of how Lydia feels, of who she is and what she's dealing with, and just that small gesture calms Lydia a little. She returns the detective's nod. It's the best she can do.

'Can we get you anything to drink?' asks Gabriel.

'No, thanks, look, Mr—'

'Gabriel, please.'

'Gabriel, Lydia, I've been going through Zoe's phone. Our tech guy, Zack, managed to override the need for a password. I'm a little concerned because I've found something, someone she was speaking to and sending pictures to.'

'Pictures,' repeats Lydia. Of course the detective found pictures. From the time she was fourteen and got her first smartphone, Zoe lived her whole life in front of her phone camera lens. Lydia is glad to have her Instagram account to look at now even though she knows that she said, 'If you are only ever taking photos of your life, Zoe, you are not really living it,' many times.

'You are such a boomer,' Zoe would reply, rolling her eyes. She will have to deactivate the account or close it down or something. She will have to do this for all Zoe's social media, she thinks. Or she supposes she could leave it all there and her daughter will live on, suspended on the internet at age sixteen forever.

'Of course you found pictures,' says Lydia.

'Shall we sit down?' The detective gestures to the grey linen sofas as though they are in her house. Lydia's unease grows.

'We've been going through everything, just to see if she posted something that would help explain what happened. Zack found some private messages on Instagram between her and a boy—'

Lydia holds up her hand to stop the detective. 'I'm not sure this has anything to do with what happened. You know she was dating Callum. I'm sure that whatever was said between the two of them was private, Detective. I don't really want to see any photos she might have sent him. You know what this generation is like. They seem to have no boundaries.'

'Absolutely. I understand. But this is not Callum she was talking to. We have discovered she was speaking to someone who is identified only as an Instagrammer with a number.'

'What does that mean?' asks Gabriel.

'First,' says the detective, 'I feel I should let you know that Zoe and Callum broke up weeks ago.'

'What?' says Lydia.

'Yes,' says Gabriel at the same time, and his wife turns to look at him.

'What do you mean yes? Did you know about this?'

'I ah… yes, she told me… I thought you knew. She told me.'

'No.' Lydia shakes her head. 'I didn't know. I don't understand. She adored Callum. Are you sure?'

'We are,' says the detective firmly. 'She broke up with Callum around three weeks ago.'

'Was it her choice? Did she want to break up with him? Maybe that's why she was so upset?' Even as she says this, Lydia realises that in the last few weeks Zoe hadn't seemed particularly upset. Her daughter did, in fact, have moments of even seeming relatively happy when she wasn't arguing with her.

'Callum says he was very unhappy about breaking up,' says the detective. 'I had a quick chat with his mother as well and she says that he was quite devastated. She doesn't know what happened but he did tell her that he felt she had betrayed him.'

'Betrayed him how?'

'I am going to get Detective Gold to speak to him privately so we can find that out but she does seem to have been talking to this other boy for a while.'

'Oh my God. Do you think Callum did something to her? Did he drive up there and, I don't know, ask to meet her or something and then…' She stops speaking, the horror of what she's imagining too much to bear.

'We don't feel that's what happened,' says the detective.

'But you don't know,' says Gabriel.

'No, but I did want to discuss the other person, the boy she was speaking to.'

'You don't know who it is?' asks Gabriel.

'Here's the thing,' says the detective patiently, and Lydia knows she wants them to just listen for a moment.

'The reason the person is called Instagrammer instead of having a handle is because they've deleted their account. However, in the messages between the two of them we've managed to ascertain that it's a boy – or a man – named Xavier.'

'Why a man? Why would it be a man?' asks Gabriel, his voice tight.

'We're not sure. We're never really sure but we have to explore all possibilities. They seem to have been speaking for the last six weeks or so and she also sent him pictures. It's not unusual for teenagers these days to send each other photos. We are assuming that it is a boy, but because we can't trace whoever this is, we have to operate under the assumption that it could be anyone.'

'You mean it could be an older man?' says Lydia, aghast. 'I'm sure Zoe was smarter than that. She wouldn't be interested in an older man.'

'Everyone on the internet is vulnerable. She could have believed that it was a boy.'

The detective turns the phone around to show Lydia some of the images, and Lydia immediately recoils at seeing her child posed in such a manner, dressed in such a way.

'Oh God,' says Gabriel and he turns pale.

Zoe sent Xavier – whoever he is – pictures of herself in her underwear, white lacy panties or a black thong, with her hands barely covering her breasts. There are also pictures of her in her school uniform with her top tied up under her breasts, obviously wearing no bra. Lydia shudders at the way her child, who will always be her little girl, pouts at the camera in some kind of strange imitation of a porn star.

'There are a lot of them like that. She started sending them to him a couple of weeks ago.'

'So surely you should be talking to him,' says Lydia.

'Yes, we would, but we have looked into him, and his Instagram account has disappeared. In fact, everything to do with him has disappeared. We can't even trace an IP address right now. It's like he never existed at all.'

'I just don't…'

'We're wondering if she ever mentioned him? If she said something about him that could help us trace who he is? Because there may be a reason why he's gone to ground now. He does say in one of the messages that he lives in Glenbrook, which is near the Blue Mountains.'

'No, she never mentioned him,' says Lydia, and she rubs at her face with her hands. The pictures make her feel dirty. 'Gabriel, did she ever say anything to you?'

'No, but… a couple of weeks ago when I took her to get some hiking boots – remember on the day that you were styling that house for a photo shoot? She needed them for camp. She did spend a lot of time giggling at her phone, and when I asked her what was so funny, she wouldn't answer me, and I know that usually she would just say it was Callum. But she was a little secretive. I didn't think anything of it because, well, she'd been like that for a while. Then I asked her how her boyfriend was and she told me they'd broken up, so I did wonder why she seemed so happy and if she was talking to another boy.'

Lydia runs her hands through her hair. 'Why didn't you tell me?'

'I thought… thought you knew, Lydia,' stutters Gabriel.

'Are you going to be able to find him? What if she left the cabin to meet him? He lives near there. They could have arranged to meet up and then she got lost and fell… or he could be… he could be… he could be someone who wanted to hurt her.'

'Look, anything is possible. I just wanted to check if you'd ever heard of him.'

'But just because he says he lives near the Blue Mountains doesn't mean he arranged to meet her,' says Gabriel.

'Well,' says the detective, 'in the last messages she does ask him to do just that.'

'What?' says Lydia.

'She asks him to meet her and then she tells him exactly where to go.'

'And where was that?'

'It was at a spot near the camp. I'm not sure how she would have found it unless she'd been there before.'

'She had,' says Gabriel.

Lydia feels her mouth drop open. She has no idea how to even pose the question to her husband. She leaves it to the detective to speak for her.

'How do you know that?'

'A month or so ago. You remember, don't you? Please tell me you remember that I took her and Becca and Shayna up there?'

'I don't…' begins Lydia.

'Liddy, please,' says Gabriel. He sounds desperate but Lydia just shakes her head. She has no idea what he's talking about.

'Why don't you explain it to me?' says the detective.

Gabriel stands up from the sofa and starts pacing around the room, his feet marking the newly vacuumed carpet. Lydia wonders who has vacuumed since she knows it's not her.

'I took the three of them up to the mountains for the day because I went to visit Geoff. Geoff is an old friend from dental school. He's recently moved from Sydney to the Blue Mountains for a, you know, what do they call it? A tree change. I told Lydia I was going up to visit him on a Saturday – I think it was three or four weeks ago – and Zoe overheard me and asked if she and Shayna and Becca could come. They wanted to ride the scenic railway –you know, the one that goes up the side of the mountain?'

'Oh God, oh yes… of course,' says Lydia. 'Of course, I remember. I'm sorry, I have no idea why I would have forgotten that.'

Gabriel takes a deep, relieved breath. 'Right, and so I treated them to lunch and then they started talking about camp and Shayna wanted to see where it was, and so we went up there to have a look. It was empty so we walked around a bit and I took them down a path. I don't know where this… this person suggested they meet but she had seen the camp before she went away.'

The detective nods her head. 'That fits with what we've read. Zoe was the one who suggested they meet and she was the one who told him where. She described it pretty well so we could tell that it was a spot near where we found her.'

'How did she describe it?' asks Lydia.

The detective takes out her own phone on which she has obviously made notes about the conversations between Zoe and the boy or man who calls himself Xavier.

'She wrote, "Meet me at midnight. Everyone will be fast asleep by then, including the ogre Fischer. Down the side of the camp is a path that leads to a clearing where they have bonfires and stuff. It's easy to see because there is a ring of stones in the middle. I'll be there."'

'And does he agree?'

'That's the thing – he doesn't. He tells her it's too soon and that he wants to make sure they really love each other.'

'That's ridiculous,' says Lydia. 'They'd only been speaking for a few weeks.'

'That's right, but you know what teenagers can be like… Or it may just be that he got scared and didn't want to meet her and was trying to get out of it. But if that's the case, we are wondering why, and why he then deleted everything.'

The detective hands the phone to Lydia so she can read it for herself.

I don't understand why you won't meet me. You said you live right near where camp will be. You can get here if you want to.

I know but I don't want it to be at night. I don't want us to have to sneak around. I want to really see your beautiful face.

But every time I try to arrange that, you say that you can't. What's going on? Don't you like me?

Yeah, I do. How could I not? I'm just shy.

You'll meet me if you want to keep talking to me. Meet me on Friday night, exactly where I said.

Lydia tries to scroll down but sees that this is the last message.

'And how close to where she wanted to meet him was she found? How close? Neither of us was there. We were with other volunteers. If it was that close to the camp, how come they didn't find her right away? I don't understand.'

'It's about forty or fifty metres,' says Detective Holland. 'If he did meet her, they may have walked away from the clearing. But it's off the path and down the side a little. The searchers walk in specific grids so they know they've covered everything. This area was tucked away. If he didn't turn up, she may have been upset and lost her way trying to get back to camp, or she may have just wanted to get away. There are a lot of possibilities.'

'But no answers,' says Gabriel. 'This should have been something simple to figure out. How has it all gotten so complicated?'

'That's exactly what we want to know and why we have to keep asking questions.'

Lydia thinks about Zoe running through the bush. Was she chased by a man, a man who was supposed to be a boy? Or was she running, crushed with disappointment at the fact that he didn't turn up? If she would have just spoken to her more, pressed her more, taken more time to get her child to tell her what she was thinking, maybe none of this would have happened.

The school is trying to find a way to shift the blame onto Zoe, but right now Lydia can see that the only person to blame is herself.

'I just…' she says.

'I know,' replied the detective. 'I will let you know the moment we find out what happened on Friday night.'

'I lost my child,' says Lydia. 'That's what happened. I lost my child.'

CHAPTER TWELVE

Shayna

I close down my computer and pick up my phone. It's been buzzing next to me for the past hour and a half as I tried and failed to concentrate on the movie of the novel *Frankenstein*, which we are supposed to read but which is so incredibly boring that I now really regret taking advanced English. I know, without even asking, that my mum will not let me drop down to the easier course. She's big on not giving up. She nearly failed her first year of nursing because she was too busy partying but then she decided that there was no way she would give up and she ended up coming in the top five of her year at the end of her degree.

'There is very little in life that cannot be achieved with perseverance,' she tells me and Jason every second day.

My dad agrees 100 per cent with everything she says. Zoe used to say that if she wanted something, she went to her stepfather. 'His kids are older so nothing fazes him, and I can usually get him to talk Mum round on just about anything,' she would laugh. 'All I have to do is pout and cry and he always tells Mum to go easy on me.'

'My father also tells my mother to go easy on me,' said Becca when we were having this discussion, 'but she just goes, "Roland, you don't know the first thing about raising children," and he nods his head and leaves the room. I hate it when she does that. It makes him look like an idiot.'

'My parents are big on "presenting the children with a united front",' I told them. And they both looked at me like they couldn't imagine anything worse.

Becca has been messaging me from school:

I couldn't stay in that house for one more minute with my mum looking at me like I'm about to blow.

Mum said I could go back today if I wanted or I could just leave it until after the holidays. But it really sounds like the shit has hit the fan. I don't think I want to be there for all of it.

Apparently, Ms Fischer has been arrested by the police. Principal Bennet fired her and now she's going to jail.

I find that hard to believe. It's not as if Ms Fischer had anything to do with what happened to Zoe. I know that for sure.

Just heard she hasn't been arrested but Lulu said she would definitely be fired, something to do with duty of care. Those are the words everyone keeps using.

There are five counsellors here and they've set up tables in the staffroom and the hall and they're just sitting there because no one wants to go and talk to them.

I ate lunch with Leeanne. She's kind of okay to hang out with. I feel like we're the only ones who really get how awful this is.

Why don't you come back to school?

The whole atmosphere here is so weird. The teachers all look at me like I'm the one who died.

Do you think I should tell Mr Roberts that I can't do my chemistry exam next period? It's been super hard to concentrate.

Leeanne said they cancelled tests and exams for the rest of term. I didn't even need to try and study.

I should have gone back. Maybe if I was there for the day everyone would have looked at me strangely but then at least it would be over. I hope that by the time we come back from holidays, everyone will have forgotten about it. I don't want them to forget about Zoe but I just want to go back to my normal life.

My mum says that most people are only interested in themselves anyway.

If I'm honest with myself, I'm worried about not looking sad enough. People will want me to look like I've been crying. They'll want me to be unable to concentrate in class. They'll want evidence that my best friend died, but the truth is that I'm not really sure she was my best friend anymore.

Things had changed between us and our friendship seemed less… I don't know how to describe it – maybe less friendly. When we were younger, I knew I could trust Zoe with everything and I could count on her to always be there for me, but as we got older, we sometimes seemed to be in competition with each other.

Zoe preferred it if Becca and I were a little insecure. If we went out together on a Saturday night, she would get dressed first, sure of the compliments she would get from both of us, and then she would lie on the bed and take selfies and comment on everything Becca and I wore and everything we did with our make-up. By the time all three of us would be ready to go out, we'd have all agreed that Zoe looked amazing but that Becca and I looked okay, but it was too late to do anything about that.

She also liked to pick on the girls who were a little vulnerable. For someone so tiny she could be a really big bully. But we never really minded it. For one thing, if she was picking on some other girl, she wasn't starting with me and Becca, and for another thing she was usually very funny. You couldn't help laughing.

She liked to make up nicknames for everyone. She once dated a boy with small hands and she called him 'sparrow boy', and every time I saw him, I felt like I could see that he had wings and I imagined him hopping along a branch. She called the tallest girl in our year 'the giraffe', and while that wasn't exactly an inspired nickname, Julie does kind of have a face like a giraffe, and so whenever I see her, I imagine her tearing leaves off the top of a tree with her teeth and I get the giggles, but it isn't nice. I know it isn't nice, and I was always aware, even as I laughed with Zoe, that my mum would be kind of ashamed of me. I was ashamed of myself.

And there was other stuff that was happening, more serious stuff.

The night before I left for camp, I had a conversation with my mum about Zoe. I told her all the stuff that had been bothering me for nearly the whole year.

She was sitting on my bedroom floor, trying to roll up the sleeping bag tightly enough so that it would fit back into its bag.

'I did ask your brother to roll this up when he came home from his sleepover but he just threw it at the bottom of the linen cupboard.'

'He can be such a dick,' I said. I was busy trying to pack everything into the case that I was taking.

My mum laughed. 'Teenage boys can be a little bit selfish. You could just take a bigger case, you know.'

'Yeah, but I'll have to lug it on and off the bus. Besides, I know it's going to fit, I just have to get it right – like Tetris.'

'You always did like puzzles.'

I pushed a pair of sneakers to one side and moved my toiletry bag into the slot I had created.

'Well done, sweetheart. I knew you could do it. I think you have everything. I'll go down and start on dinner.' She stood up and stretched because her back always gets stiff when she sits in one place for a long time. 'I wish I liked going to the gym. I'm sure my back would feel better if I did.'

'Maybe if you persevered, you would like it.'

'Ha ha… well done on throwing that back at me. I would persevere if it meant enough.'

'Maybe we could join a gym together.'

'Maybe,' she said and then she looked at me and sat down on my bed, smoothing the white duvet and running her hands over the embroidered roses. Her fingertips were still stained with the blue paint for the picture she'd been working on in the afternoon. She's a really gifted artist, and when she's not running the house and taking care of us, she paints landscapes that she sometimes sells on Facebook. I watched her hand move over my duvet, liking the way the blue on her fingers contrasted with the snow-white of the cover. Everything felt so simple and so safe then.

'Is anything wrong?' she asked. She was looking down as she said it. I know she didn't want me to feel like she was watching me too closely. I was going to say 'nothing'. I planned on saying 'nothing' but instead the words came out of my mouth without my permission.

'I wish I didn't have to share a cabin with Zoe.'

She nodded her head and I climbed onto my bed and lay down so that I was staring at the ceiling. Sometimes it's easier to say important stuff when you're not looking directly at a person. There is a crack on my bedroom ceiling that runs all the way across. It's only a hairline crack, and Mum says that when we next paint the house, we'll get it fixed. I don't mind; I kind of like the way it makes jagged little turns all the way across the ceiling. It calms me down to look at it. It looks like it was drawn there by someone and I imagine standing up on a chair and tracing over it with a pencil. I stared at the crack as I waited for Mum to reply.

She was quiet for a few minutes. I knew that she wanted to jump in with, 'But Zoe's your best friend,' or, 'If you've had a fight, you'll make up – you always do.' But she didn't say any of that. Finally, she just said, 'Why?'

I didn't really know how to put it into words… I just knew that eventually I wouldn't be able to say no to Zoe anymore. Then I would be the one who ended up in trouble – or worse.

'Okay, so you can't say anything to her mum,' I began, because our parents speak all the time.

'I won't.'

I twisted my hands together, not even sure that I wanted to keep the conversation going. 'Okay… okay, so Zoe has been having sex with Callum for a few months now.'

'Oh,' said my mum, 'well I guess she is sixteen… but I hope—'

'This is not about me, Mum. I've told you I'll talk to you before I do anything like that, and anyway, I don't have a boyfriend and I wouldn't want to… do it with someone who was… just there.' As I spoke, I could feel my face getting red and hot. Mum's easy enough to talk to but some stuff is just too embarrassing.

'I know, love. Does it bother you that she's having sex?'

'No, it's just that she keeps telling me and Becca we're losers because we aren't. She keeps inviting us to come out with her and Callum and his friends, and each time she tells us that this is the night we get to have sex, and I don't want to do it just because she says it should happen. She stopped asking a few weeks ago but I just know she's going to start up again after camp.'

I stopped speaking, and even though I wasn't looking directly at Mum, I could hear her take a deep breath, which I knew meant that a lecture was coming on not giving in to peer pressure. I carried on before she could start.

'And it's not just that. She's nasty about a lot of other girls in the school. And I know that she and Callum are drinking and I think there's drugs stuff.'

'What kind of drugs?'

'I don't know, and you have to promise me you won't say anything, but it feels like I'm waiting for an accident to happen, like Zoe is about to crash her car into a tree and I don't want to be in there when she does.'

Mum lay down next to me on the bed, looking up at the ceiling as well. 'That crack looks bigger,' she said before carrying on. 'That's a lot. I understand why it's bothering you. Does Becca feel the same way?'

'Yeah.'

'Then you have two choices. You can both talk to her and explain how you're feeling – she might listen if it's the two of you. Or you can simply begin to distance yourselves from her. It may get difficult, especially if she tries to turn other girls against you, but it may be the only thing you can do.'

'But what about camp? We've already put down that we all want to be in the same cabin. I mean, she hasn't actually even talked about Callum in a bit, and I think they may have had a fight or something. I kind of hope they have and that they break up, but then I feel bad about thinking like that.'

'It's self-defence, you thinking like that – don't feel bad about it. It would be easier for you and Becca if Callum wasn't in the picture. I know that boyfriends can change the way friendships are. It's just something you have to adjust to.'

'Yeah, it would be easier if we all had boyfriends or none of us did. I still don't like how mean she is about other people though. Becca and I almost didn't put her name down on the form for who we wanted to share with but then I got scared that she would find out.'

'She's been your best friend for years, Shayna. I don't think she wants to hurt you. But,' said Mum, standing up, 'I'm afraid that you might just have to grin and bear camp. When you get back, we can talk about some strategies. I know you don't want me to talk to Lydia, but if something strange is going on with Zoe and drugs…' She shuddered as though a whole lot of disturbing thoughts had just run through her mind, and then I felt bad for saying anything.

'You promised!'

'I know,' said Mum, holding up her hands, 'I know and I will try to leave things for now, but Lydia and I have known each other for a decade. If there is something going on with Zoe, it would be irresponsible and cruel of me to say nothing.'

'Oh my God!' I yelled. 'You promised and now you're just being a typical mum. Look, forget everything I just said. It's fine, we're fine. Can you just go now?'

'Shayna—'

'No, Mum, just go. I don't want to talk about it anymore.'

I turned on my side so I was facing away from her. She stood there for a bit and then she left, closing the door quietly behind her. I felt terrible then because I knew I shouldn't have said anything. I knew she was going to tell Lydia and then Zoe was going to turn on me and she was going to make my final year of school a living hell.

So, what I'm worried about is that if I do go back to school, everyone will see that I'm not sad that Zoe is gone. I'm not sad at all. What I mostly feel is relief. Absolute relief that I will never have to deal with her again, and that makes me a bad friend and a bad person. But I'm not a bad person. I'm not.

CHAPTER THIRTEEN

Bernadette

I am not surprised to find Paula standing at my door when, I assume, she should be getting dinner ready for her children. Not surprised but irritated and frustrated. I have no desire to speak to her.

She looks dishevelled, with her mousy brown hair sticking up all over the place and what appears to be a red-wine stain on her yellow blouse. She also looks as though she's been crying.

'I suppose you'd better come in,' I tell her. 'Can I get you something to drink – red wine perhaps?' I say as I look her up and down, taking, I must admit, no small pleasure from the way she flushes.

It is only two more days until the end of term. I have emailed all my classes homework to do over the holidays. There is no sense in them starting the term without having kept their brains occupied over the next two weeks.

I am missing my students, all my students. I am missing the early-morning coffee I have in the staffroom as I watch out the window that looks down onto the front gate. I love seeing them arrive at school, greeting each other with hugs as though they haven't seen each other for years. There is such a lovely energy around young girls whose whole lives lie before them.

Today I got up early even though I had nowhere to go. I took Oliver for his morning walk and was cheered by the sun rising earlier and the slight warmth that has begun to permeate the air. Oliver enjoyed it too, bounding in and out of the bushes in the park and wagging his little tail at every other dog we met.

I met Henry as I returned to the building. 'You're running a little late this morning,' he said.

'I don't have school.'

'Ah, so the holidays have begun. Perhaps we could share a morning walk next week.'

'We can,' I said, and then, because I hate keeping secrets, I confessed that I was not at work because of what had happened at camp.

'Ah,' he nodded after I finished speaking, 'such a terrible thing. I did hear about it, but I didn't know it was your school.'

'Yes. From what I gather they have managed to keep the name of the school out of the press. I don't think that will be the case for much longer what with the way teenagers speak. I'm sure it's trending all over the internet anyway. I have no doubt that the girls at school are spreading the names of the teachers in charge far and wide. Nothing can be kept secret anymore.'

'But surely this cannot be your fault?' said Henry.

'I…' I began and then I'm ashamed to say that I felt my face grow hot, a sure sign that tears were on the way. I turned quickly and fled into the lift, leaving Henry calling after me. That was a rude thing to do but I had no desire to lose control of my emotions in front of Henry, in front of anyone. I took a few deep breaths in the lift and I was fine by the time I returned to my flat. I will call Henry tomorrow and apologise. Of all the people I know, he is the least deserving of my occasional abruptness.

I hadn't expected to feel like this but last night I dreamed of her, saw her plummeting through the air, her hand reaching out, a look of utter horror on her face. I understood in the dream that if I just reached out, I could save her. But I didn't. In the dream I simply watched her fall.

I woke up with my heart racing, covered in sweat. I couldn't get back to sleep for at least an hour. I have to keep repeating to myself that this is not my fault. Whatever happened to her, she brought it on herself. This is not my fault. It simply cannot be my fault.

'Thanks, I'm good,' says Paula, drawing me back to exactly what is happening now. I am not one to find myself lost in rumination, but over the last few days, I seem unable to think straight for extended periods of time. 'I just thought we should speak. I don't know what you've told the police and George but I don't want this to mean the end of my career, Bernadette. I can't lose my job. You may not know this but six months ago Ryan and I separated and he's being difficult about child support. My job is all I have to keep me and my kids fed and with a roof over our heads.' She wrings her hands as she speaks. I notice that her nails, which were painted a light pink on camp, are chipped and peeling. I never paint my nails for this very reason. Only a woman who does very little with her life can maintain painted nails. I gesture to the sofa and Paula perches on the edge of a cushion as though she is getting ready to dart out of my flat at any moment.

'You really need to calm down about this. What happened was not our fault and I will tell everyone I speak to that this is the case. She left her cabin of her own free will. She went somewhere other than the bathroom, which she had been expressly forbidden to do, and she, unfortunately, tripped and fell. It is a terrible thing, Paula, but it is not our fault.'

Paula begins to worry at one of her fingernails and I'm horrified to see a few pink chips fall onto my carpet.

'I don't think the police and the parents and the board are going to see it like that. St Anne's has never lost a student on a school camp. It's not something they have ever had to deal with. It's a terrible thing and I keep thinking about Zoe's mother, about her having to deal with all this. We failed in our duty of care. We failed her mother and I'm sure that we're going to be punished for it. I…' She has worked herself up into a flustered state. Her cheeks are red and she looks like she's going to burst into tears. I cannot stand overly dramatic people.

I find myself weary but I will not sit down. I stand over Paula, hoping to encourage her to get control of her emotions. 'Oh, please, you have to get a hold of yourself. If they start making noises about taking away our jobs, we will go to the union. They cannot simply dismiss us because of that irresponsible child.'

'You say that but you don't know. We don't have any idea what the board will be like. Do you know what is being said about us on social media?'

'Don't be ridiculous, of course I don't know. I would never indulge the stupidity of others by reading their ridiculous thoughts.'

Paula shakes her head and snorts. 'God, you're so superior. You have no idea that the world has moved on and that your whole life can be blown up by a few tweets.' She hauls her phone out of her messy patchwork bag; a few tissues fall on the floor, along with a tampon. I bite down on my lip. She's disgustingly disorganised. Scrolling through her phone, she begins to read. 'They've coined a hashtag – a hashtag is—'

'I know what a hashtag is!' I roar, completely fed up with her desperate stupidity.

'Great!' she yells back. 'Now you listen to this. They've coined a hashtag "school camp of death".'

'I don't want to hear it.'

'Yes, but I'm going to read you a few, Bernadette, because I don't believe you understand the gravity of our situation.' Her voice is pitched high and she sounds near hysteria so I huff and cross my arms. I won't sit down next to her on the sofa. In fact, I won't sit down at all. I would like to grab her and shove her out of my apartment but she's a bigger woman than me and I don't want to get hurt.

She reads, her head down, her eyes narrowed on her phone:

Imagine losing your child on camp because of incompetent teachers #schoolcampofdeath

There is no way I would allow my daughter to ever go on camp at this school again #schoolcampofdeath

We put our children into the hands of these teachers but they have no idea how to take care of them #schoolcampofdeath

I hope that someone is charged over this. No way should your child go to camp and not come home #schoolcampofdeath

What is being done about this? I was going to send my daughter to this school next year. Now? No way #schoolcampofdeath

My heart goes out to the mother of the student who died. I would never be able to forgive #schoolcampofdeath

'Yes, fine, I understand.' I stop her. 'It doesn't matter. We both know the facts and the facts are that we did nothing wrong. She made the decision. It had nothing to do with us.'

'Yes, but…' she says, and she looks down into her bag as though she is searching for something. 'There's… there's something, oh God… I don't even know how to say this and I don't want to say anything, especially not to you.' She leans down and picks up the things that have fallen out of her bag, shoving them back inside.

'Oh, for goodness' sake, just spit it out.'

Paula places her hands on her lap and spreads her fingers wide, staring down at her ravaged nails and the peeling skin on the back of her hand.

'Do you remember Jessie, Zoe's sister?' She looks up at me, her eyes shining with unshed tears.

'Of course. She was one of the best students we've ever had. She was an absolutely delightful girl. I believe she's studying medicine. She is the finest example of a young woman who refused to let adversity get in the way of her achieving her dreams. She lost her father very young.'

'Yes, they both did.'

'I imagined that Zoe would be like her. I was sorely mistaken.' Perhaps that is why I found Zoe so difficult to like. I compared her to her sister from the moment she began school. I kept expecting her to dazzle me with her thoughts as her sister had done but that never happened. I can remember looking forward to classes with Jessie, looking forward to the way she would interpret a text or write a creative story. She could have been anything she wanted to be, but she will make a wonderful doctor. It was perhaps unfair of me to have held her younger sister against such high expectations. Maybe I would have enjoyed teaching Zoe more if I had simply accepted her for who she was. I mentally add this regret to my list of regrets about Zoe Bloom.

'Yes, well, I taught Jessie biology. She was obviously a very good student and we've stayed in touch over the years, just a quick call now and then, you know?'

'I don't believe that teachers should stay in touch with students beyond a Christmas card but I'm sure I'm alone in that.' I have no idea where this conversation is leading but I feel a tickle of worry for no reason I can discern.

'Maybe, but about eight months ago we bumped into each other at the shopping centre and we went for coffee and then we started speaking every day and…'

'And what?' For the first time since Paula appeared at my door, I feel something other than irritation at her. It sounds like she is about to make a confession.

'And we sort of developed a friendship that is more than just a friendship.'

'What does that mean?'

'It means we're closer than friends.'

'I'm still not understanding you, Paula,' I begin and then of course it clicks. 'Are you saying that you're… together?' I cannot use the word 'lovers'.

'Yes, it's why Ryan and I separated, although I've always known, I guess.'

'But she's a child!'

'She's twenty-two and I know I'm a lot older than her, and believe me I wasn't expecting anything. I knew who I was but I have children and had a husband and I didn't want to hurt anyone. I had accepted that I would never really be happy but then there she was and… Oh God, I don't know what I'm going to do.'

She drops her head into her hands and I hear her sniffing.

I didn't want this information. I leave Paula snivelling into her hands and go to the kitchen, where I pour myself a stiff whisky. I gulp it down then pour one for Paula.

'I have no idea why you're telling me this,' I say when I return to the living room and nudge her with the glass. She accepts it and takes a sip, coughing dramatically after she swallows.

'Believe me, you are the last person I wanted to share this with. It's already led to the end of my marriage, but I'm telling you because Jessie came up to the mountains on Friday night. She came up and we met on the other side of the camp near the bathroom you and I were supposed to use. We only met for an hour and we just talked.'

'Why on earth would you do something so stupid? We were only on camp for three nights. Surely you could have waited for three nights?'

Paula shakes her head and sniffs, dabbing at her eyes with her crumpled tissue. 'We hadn't seen each other for weeks and it's so hard with the kids since they don't know about her, and I hate lying to them. I don't know. I know it was stupid. Believe me, I know, but we hadn't seen each other and she really seemed to need to connect and I just… I just let her come. It was only to talk, just to see each other.'

'I certainly don't need details.' I sink down into the chair I use at night to watch television, taking comfort from the soft, caramel-coloured leather.

'I don't want to give you details, Bernadette. Let me explain why I'm here,' she says and then she downs the rest of her whisky in one gulp, which leads to a ridiculous amount of coughing and choking. I don't offer her water. I don't say anything. Her tone has become strident. I simply wait for her to be done.

Finally, she takes a deep, gasping breath and then she wipes at her eyes and nose with her tissue. 'I'm telling you this for two reasons. Firstly, I got up when Jessie texted me that she was there. It was just before midnight. When I got up, your bed was empty.'

'I went to use the bathroom,' I say quickly.

'You did? I was meeting Jessie right there and I didn't see you.'

'Paula,' I sigh, 'I have no idea what my bathroom habits have to do with your tawdry little affair. Why do you care where I was?'

'Because when I came back to the cabin at around one in the morning and opened the door, you were back in your bed and you muttered, "Not my fault." I thought that was a strange thing to say. Why did you say that?'

Paula's brown eyes seem to have developed a certain malicious shine as I watch her, as though she believes she has caught me doing something wrong. I didn't do anything wrong.

I stand up from my chair and grab her by her soft, fleshy arm. 'Get up and get out of my house, you ridiculous woman!' I yell as I haul her up and shove her towards the door.

'Bernadette,' she shrieks, shocked at my behaviour, 'what's gotten into you? I just wanted to talk. I just wanted to find out what happened. We need to know what to say to the board if we—'

I don't let her finish. I manhandle her out of the flat and into the passage. I am thankful that there is no one about. I couldn't face any more humiliation in front of Henry. I shut the door on her midsentence and then I go to the kitchen and pour myself another whisky.

I am not a two-whisky-a-day kind of person but needs must. Once I have allowed the amber liquid to burn down my throat, I take a deep breath and look at Oliver, who has not moved from his bed next to the sofa. He seems to be cowering away from me. He is not used to me raising my voice.

'I'm sorry, Oliver,' I say quietly. I go over and sit next to him, stroking his little head. 'The nerve of that woman,' I say to him, and he sits up and offers me his paw.

I pick him up to put him on my lap. As I stroke his soft, grey-brown fur, I allow myself a few tears of self-pity.

This is not going to simply blow over, I realise. I can foresee a difficult road ahead for myself.

I should have stepped in and stopped Zoe arguing with whoever she was talking to. I know that the girl was not much bigger than she was, but I really couldn't say who it was. I should have told them to go back to bed. I should have called her parents when we found the vodka. Should have, would have, could have. I close my eyes and let myself calm down as I stroke Oliver, who rolls onto his back and stretches his legs out in bliss.

And then it strikes me that I *do* know who the other girl was. I know because she was wearing a beanie hat with pom-poms hanging from it. In the dark I couldn't see the colour, but I couldn't mistake the pom-poms.

I sigh, lift Oliver up and place him on the floor. I should say something about this. I should tell one of the detectives but I'm unsure as to what that would accomplish.

For the first time in decades, I really have no idea what to do about a situation. No idea at all.

CHAPTER FOURTEEN

Jessie

Jessie heard the doorbell ring but she has no desire to speak to whoever has come. When there is a knock at her bedroom door, she contemplates, for a moment, climbing out the window and down the trellis just like Zoe, but she stands up from her desk and goes to open the door instead.

'The detective in charge of the case is here and she would like to speak to you,' says Gabriel, standing in the doorway.

'Why?'

'She's spoken to all of us and now she needs to speak to you.' To Jessie, Gabriel looks pale, uncomfortable, and she wonders what the detective has told him but she doesn't want to speak to her. Aren't detectives trained to root out your deepest, darkest secrets? She can't have that. Not now.

'Yes, but what am I going to add to the conversation?'

Gabriel sighs. 'Shall I tell your mother you don't want to come down?'

'No, no, it's fine.'

Gabriel looks tired. Her mother looks tired as well and she's sure she looks the same. Zoe's death has exhausted them all.

In the living room Detective Holland is pacing up and down, listening to someone on her phone. 'Uh-huh,' she says, again and again and again, and then she glances quickly at Jessie and nods at her. 'Right, fine.' Then she hangs up the phone.

'Sorry about that,' she says, but to Jessie she doesn't look sorry; she looks like someone who is trying to figure out what to do with the information she's just been given. The feeling makes Jessie uncomfortable.

Her mother is holding Zoe's phone, looking down at it, discomfort obvious in her pale face. The detective sits down on the other end of the sofa and rests her hands on her knees.

'What's wrong?' Jessie asks her mother.

'Did you know that Zoe had broken up with Callum?'

Jessie bites down on her lip. The detective looks at her, her dark eyes searching Jessie's face, and she knows that she has to say something.

'Yes.'

'But how? When? Why didn't you say anything?' The questions burst out of her mother.

Jessie crosses her arms over her chest. Even though she and Zoe weren't close, there is an unspoken rule between sisters, all sisters. They protect each other's privacy against nosy parents. Jessie swallows quickly as she realises that she could have told Zoe the truth about herself. Zoe would have kept Jessie's secret until she was ready to reveal it to the world, and it would have meant that at least one person in the house knew what Jessie was going through.

She doesn't say anything as she looks at her stricken mother. Lydia's hair hasn't been brushed and she's dressed in an old tracksuit. She looks nothing like she usually does. Her mother has been through too many deaths. First her husband and then her parents and then her daughter. It is too much for anyone to bear.

Jessie, too, has been through those deaths, and as she looks at her mother, she finds herself surprised that the two of them are still standing. Surely it cannot be possible to be surrounded by this much death and still be standing?

Jessie would like to tell her that everything is going to be okay but it's not okay. And it never will be again.

'She told me not to,' she finally says. 'I wasn't supposed to know either but he came to the house and she wouldn't speak to him so I did instead.'

Her mother opens her mouth to yell at her daughter but the detective puts up her hand to silence her. 'Perhaps you could explain exactly what happened when he came to the house, Jessie. It's just so we can get a sense of what was happening in her life. Very few people seem to know that they'd broken up.'

Jessie sinks down into a leather chair that her father used to sit in. It doesn't exactly match the grey linen sofas and the pale grey silk curtains of the living room but she knows her mother will never get rid of it. It is still referred to as Eli's chair. Whenever Jessie sits in it, it always feels warm, as though he has just stood up from sitting there, and she likes to believe that she can still smell him, a kind of earthy scent from all the work he did in the garden combined with the smoky whisky he liked to drink.

'It was a few weeks ago,' she begins and she feels a stab of guilt. The only thing she felt at the time was profound irritation that she had to get involved with the teenage drama.

'It was a Tuesday afternoon. I'm always home on a Tuesday afternoon unless I'm at the library because it's the one day that my last lecture finishes at two o'clock. Otherwise I am at university five days a week or else on rotation at the hospital,' she explains and then she has no idea why she's doing so. The detective is not interested in her schedule but the woman looks at her keenly and nods her head for Jessie to go on.

'Zoe was home because she had a headache or a stomach ache or something that meant she couldn't go to school. But I knew she wasn't sick and Mum knew she wasn't sick and it was just easier to let Zoe stay home when she wanted to. Otherwise she would go to the school office during the day anyway and claim to be ill, and then they would call my mother and she would have to leave work to go and get her.'

Her mother lets out a short bark of laughter because this is the truth. Then she wipes her eyes and takes a deep, shuddering breath.

'The bell rang at around three and I knew Zoe was home and I was working so I ignored it. But then it rang again and again and again and finally I got up from my desk and went to open the door. Zoe was standing in the passage. "It's Callum," she said to me – she whispered it and then she told me that they'd broken up and she wasn't ready to tell anyone yet. She told me he was being weird and she just wanted him to go away and asked me to make him go away. I thought it was a bit strange because she seemed a little scared, and I don't know Callum very well but he's never struck me as someone to be scared of.'

'Scared?' her mother asks, horrified.

'So you went to answer the door for her?' asks the detective, encouraging Jessie to go on.

'Yeah, she told me to tell him she wasn't home, but he knew she was because of course she'd been posting on her social media all day. He was standing at the door, looking more like a lost little boy than anything else.'

Jessie realises that she has spoken the last sentence aloud and then she shrugs because he did look like a lost little boy. Callum is objectively very good-looking, almost pretty, with brown hair and blue eyes and a perfect smile. Zoe thought he looked like an actor, but to Jessie he just looked like a boy, and on this particular day he looked really sad. His eyes were red as though he'd been crying and she had felt instantly sorry for him. It wasn't the first time one of Zoe's boyfriends had turned up to the house wearing his broken heart on his sleeve.

'I told him that Zoe wasn't home. But he kind of begged me to go and get her. He told me he just wanted to talk to her for a minute. He sounded desperate to speak to her.'

'And did she speak to him?'

'No, I kept telling him she wasn't home and eventually he went away.'

'He just went away,' says the detective as though she doesn't really believe that's all that happened.

Jessie thinks about leaving it at that but then she decides that they might as well know everything. It's not like it makes any difference anyway. Zoe will still be gone. She is surprised to find her eyes filling with tears. She wipes quickly at her cheeks and Gabriel silently reaches forward and takes a tissue out of the box on the coffee table, handing it to her.

She doesn't know when they started keeping tissues in the living room and then she realises she doesn't know if they will ever, any of them, be able to be more than a few feet away from a box of tissues ever again. She remembers it being like this after her father died. Tears came unexpectedly, surprising her by turning up when she was in the middle of watching television or having a shower. She had not thought she would cry over her little sister in the same way she cried over her father. She believed that nothing could be as great as his loss, but as the days roll on, the tears are getting worse.

'No,' she finally sighs. 'He said that he gave up his best friend for her, and that she was making him look like an arse because she kept liking some other guy's photos. I asked what guy, and he said he didn't know – no one knew who he was. He asked me to tell her to be careful. That people aren't always what they seem. That she thought she was so smart but she wasn't that smart. And then he kind of laughed to himself and left.'

'But I don't understand,' says her mother. 'Why didn't you say anything to me? Why didn't you tell me what he said so I could talk to her and find out who he was?'

'She told me not to. She told me…' Here Jessie hesitates, trying to remember what Zoe had said when she asked her who Callum was referring to. 'She said that Callum was just jealous because he wasn't as cute as his replacement. And then she asked me to keep quiet about it. She didn't want to tell anyone about the new boy until they'd been together for a while.

'I didn't think it was anything serious, Mum,' she says, appealing to her mother. 'Just because Callum didn't know who he was didn't mean there was something wrong. I figured he was just from a different school or different state or something. I never imagined it could possibly be a problem.'

'So Callum had already tried to find out who Xavier was?' says the detective. Her brow furrows as though she's trying to understand. 'He didn't tell us any of this. He only said that they broke up.'

'Is that his name?' asks Jessie. 'Was she talking to some guy named Xavier?'

'Yes, we think so, although his account has been deleted and he's the young man… or the man… she was sending these photos to,' says her mother in a whisper, handing Jessie Zoe's phone.

The pictures don't surprise Jessie at all. Her sister liked attention and it didn't really matter to her how she got it, but she doesn't say this out loud. She simply shrugs and hands the phone back to her mother.

'Can I go now?'

'Actually, Jessie, I have been wanting to speak to you,' says the detective.

'About what?'

'Friday night. Would you like to speak to me alone?'

Jessie would like to say yes because she knows what this is going to be about but she shakes her head instead. It might as well come out now. It might as well all come out. They might as well all know.

'We can't find Xavier and that's a problem. He's simply disappeared, which makes us believe that this was an episode of catfishing, but in the messages she asks him to meet her on Friday night in the Blue Mountains. So, tell me,' says the detective, and she looks straight at Jessie, making her whole body grow cold with the absolute knowledge contained in that look, 'did you see anything on Friday night when you went up there to meet Paula?'

'What?' says her mother.

'What?' says Gabriel, and Jessie curls up tight in her father's chair and puts her head in her hands.

Everyone in the room is silent, and when Jessie lifts her head, she sees her mother opening and closing her mouth, like a fish out of water, and she feels like this is exactly how her mother must feel. Everything she thought she knew about her life is slipping away and all she can do is gasp for air and hope she survives.

'How do you know about that?' she asks the detective.

'I just took a call from my colleague. Paula rang the station and spoke to him. She was very distressed but thought that it was best if she told the truth. And it is best, Jessie. Trust me.'

'I don't know… who's Paula?' asks her mother, and then before anyone can answer her, she realises, 'Oh, Paula Fitzsimmons. Why on earth would you have gone to meet Paula? You told me you were at the library. Why weren't you at the library?'

Jessie feels a deep well of sorrow for her mother open up inside her. She gets up off her father's chair and goes to sit down next to Lydia, putting her arm around her shoulder. 'It's okay, Mum. It's okay. I did go and visit Paula. I went to visit her because I'm kind of… We've been… I don't know how to explain it. We've been seeing each other.' She says the words quickly, rips off the plaster, hoping that the pain will be more bearable that way.

'I don't understand,' says her mother woodenly. Her body is stiff and she doesn't look at Jessie but rather down at Zoe's phone, where the screensaver image of her and her friends has taken the place of a lurid photo of her younger daughter in her underwear.

Jessie sighs. This was supposed to be something she broke gently to her mother. She had assumed that when she was ready, it would be easy because she knew her mother would support her even if she did not support her relationship with Paula.

'I was going to tell you last weekend, Mum, I really was. I went up there on Friday night to see her because it's difficult to get time with her kids and… everything. We've been seeing each other for a few months – I mean *seeing each other* seeing each other, although we've been speaking to each other for much longer than that.'

Her mother stands up and pushes Zoe's phone into the pocket of her tracksuit pants. 'I don't understand any of this, Jessie. I didn't even know that you were gay. And Paula is so much older than you and she used to be your teacher. Surely there's something immoral about that? I don't… I just don't understand any of this at all and I can't anymore… I just can't.'

Her mother walks out of the room and Jessie listens as she pounds up the stairs to her bedroom, the door slamming so hard the sound reverberates through the house. Jessie, the detective and Gabriel sit in silence for a minute until Gabriel says, 'I should go and see if she's all right. You don't need me anymore, do you?'

'No, thank you, it should be fine. I'll just finish up with Jessie.'

Gabriel nods and then he turns to go but stops. 'Do you want me to stay?' he asks and Jessie wants to cry because not for the first time since her stepfather entered her life, she's glad he's here. It feels like she needs someone else in the room with her and the sharp-eyed detective, but she realises that her mother needs him more.

'No thanks, I'll be fine,' she says and Gabriel runs his hand over his bald head, a gesture he uses when he's very stressed.

'Jessie,' says the detective once he leaves. 'Did you see anything? Anything at all that could be of help?'

'When I was leaving, I saw her heading away from her cabin.' Jessie takes a deep breath once she says this. She feels instantly lighter. The two secrets she's been holding onto for the last few days have been exposed, and the secret she's been holding onto for years now is finally out in the open. And while she has no idea what the consequences will be, at least she doesn't have to worry about anyone finding out anymore. Although, at the back of her mind, she wonders why Paula called the police and told them without texting her first. She wonders about this but she doesn't want to dwell on it too much for fear of what it might reveal.

'But you didn't stop her or say anything to her?'

'No one was supposed to know I was there.'

'What did you think she was doing? Where did you think she was going? Did she look distressed?'

'I didn't… I was mostly concentrating on getting to my car. I didn't know where she was going, but yes… yes,' she says slowly, admitting to herself her failure in her role as big sister, 'she looked like she was crying.'

'And did you see anyone else, anyone talking to her?'

'No, I mean, I may have seen someone heading back away from her, towards the cabins, but I didn't look properly. I thought… I don't know what I thought. I had no idea what was going on so I didn't want to… to get involved and I didn't want anyone to know I was there. I just wanted to get home.' Jessie wrings her hands together as she speaks. 'I should have… I'm a bad sister. I was a bad sister,' she whispers, more to herself than to the detective.

'I don't think that's true,' the woman says. 'You had no idea what was going on, and you shouldn't have been there. I know you're an adult but perhaps an involvement with a former teacher is not healthy for either her or you.'

'I *am* an adult,' says Jessie, standing up. 'And as an adult, I imagine that no one has the right to tell me what to do as long as I'm not breaking the law.' She leaves the room without seeing the detective out as she knows she should.

She is halfway up the stairs when she hears the front door close. She has stated that she's an adult but she feels like a child, a confused, sad child.

In her room she checks her phone again. Paula has still not replied to any of her texts.

She thinks back to that night, to the way her breath condensed in the air, a puff of white against black, as she spoke to Paula. The feel of her hand, the warm flush of happiness that meant she wasn't shivering in the cold.

'Leave quickly so no one sees you,' Paula whispered, and Jessie darted to the parking lot, using cabins as cover so she was concealed. She had stopped to get her bearings when she saw her sister, saw the flash of her silver sneakers and heard the muffled sounds of her crying.

She took a step, just one step forward, because it was her intention, it had been her intention, to go after Zoe. But then a rush of thoughts stopped her. She would be exposed. Paula would be exposed. Everything would be ruined.

She wasn't ready to stand in the light and so she stepped back into the darkness, walked softly to her car and drove away. She just drove away.

CHAPTER FIFTEEN

Online, she came across as kind of a ditz. She used a lot of emojis on Instagram, as though one tiny little sticker can somehow convey exactly what a person is thinking.

I've always hated emojis because, to me, they allow you to distance yourself from the world and from the people you're meant to be connecting with, but whatever. I've learned to use them with the best of them. Zoe was fond of the crying face, the laughing face and the kissing face, and then she liked the heart emoji. Zoe 'hearted' everything she liked. I got a lot of hearts.

But sometimes I would catch her at the right time, late at night usually when she was supposed to be asleep, and we would have a real conversation, and what I realised after a while was that Zoe was concealing a pretty good brain. Not good enough to see me for what I was, but she was intelligent and she could talk about most things. She didn't seem, from her online activity, as though she would have an opinion on what was going on in the world but she did. We discussed Brexit and the pandemic that had nearly destroyed the world economy and euthanasia and whether or not drugs should be legalised.

She had a lot to say about a lot of things and she was kind as well. Not about people. She was brutal when she talked about girls she knew. Everyone she knew was too fat or too thin or too up themselves or not as clever as they thought or a secret bitch. But she was kind about animals. She abhorred hunting for sport. She thought hunters should be forced to hunt each other. And she loved her dog, Walter: 'He has the kindest eyes and when he looks at me, I realise that he completely trusts me. I know that if I was cruel to him, he wouldn't understand but he would forgive me for it. And when I think about people who hurt animals, I get irrationally angry.'

'Me too,' I told her. I was surprised that we had so much in common, that there was so much about her that she didn't show the world. It made me feel bad for lying to her, for pretending. I had to keep reminding myself why I was doing what I was doing: what she had taken from me.

'I have never spoken to anyone the way I've spoken to you,' she told me the week before she wanted us to meet up.

'Me neither,' I replied.

'I feel like we may have known each other in another life, you know. I've talked to you about so much more than I have ever shared with my family or my friends or even Callum. I never said any of this stuff to him. I feel bad about that. Maybe I should have trusted him more.'

'Maybe… Do you miss him?' She didn't reply to that comment immediately but I waited. I wanted to know the truth.

'I kind of do but I don't feel like I connected with him the way I have with you. Don't you feel the same way?'

'I do,' I told her.

I could have confessed right there and then but that wasn't the plan. The plan was for her to feel heartbroken and hurt and humiliated just like she made a lot of people feel heartbroken and humiliated. I wanted to hurt her.

But not like I did.

I never planned that. I keep repeating that to myself because I have to believe it. I never planned to hurt her like I did. I never planned it.

CHAPTER SIXTEEN

Thursday – Five Days Since the Accident

Lydia

Summer feels very far away in the early-morning spring weather. Lydia should not be outside, should not be walking in the wind. She could have waited for it to warm up but she knows that people, the well-meaning neighbours and family and friends, would frown upon the idea of her leaving the house at all. Yet she cannot stay cooped up any longer. It feels like her thoughts are chasing her through all the rooms of the house, and no matter where she goes, she cannot simply just be. She has assumed that a walk will help, and Walter has deigned to accompany her, despite the cold. She needs a walk and some space today before this afternoon, before the terrible afternoon that is to come.

She cannot think of what to make of Jessie's revelations. Her daughter is gay and was seeing a much older woman, and she went, secretly, up to the camp on Friday night. She was secretly seeing a former teacher, the very teacher who was meant to be looking after Zoe on the school trip.

Gabriel had left the room after she stormed out, but before heading upstairs, he had stood outside the living room while Jessie spoke to the detective.

'She told the detective that she saw Zoe heading away from the camp and that she seemed distressed,' he reported to Lydia.

'What? Why on earth didn't she stop her?'

'I don't know. I guess she didn't want anyone to know she was up there…'

'But she could have… It wouldn't have mattered. She could have helped her.'

'I can't explain it,' said Gabriel.

Her daughter was seeing a much older woman and she had seen her sister out of her cabin and in a distressed state and done nothing. Not only that but she had failed to report this to anyone when they first found out Zoe was missing. This is what she cannot let go of. Jessie saw Zoe heading away from camp and she saw she was upset and then not only did she do nothing about that, when she found out she was missing she still said nothing. Nothing. Maybe she would have pointed the searchers in the right direction and they would have found Zoe earlier and maybe, just maybe, she would have been alive. But she got in her car and drove away. Jessie saw her sister and drove away and then she said nothing.

Lydia keeps listing these facts to herself, trying to make sense of them, trying to find a thread she can pull so she can understand why her child has betrayed her, betrayed her sister, in such a way.

Concealing that she is gay is understandable even though it's hurtful. As a mother you want to believe that your children trust you enough to open up to you. But she understands that Jessie may have needed time to work out exactly how she felt. Jessie being gay is simply who she is and Lydia is fine with that, but she lied about where she was. She lied about what she saw, and Lydia is not fine with that.

How is all this possible? This is not Jessie. Jessie is an honest, open-hearted young woman who wants to save the whole world if she possibly can. Before yesterday, if someone had asked Lydia if Jessie had ever lied to her, she would have said, 'No. There was never a reason for her to lie to me.' But there obviously was.

The fact that Jessie is gay is not really a surprise, more a confirmation of what Lydia already suspected, but she had been waiting patiently for Jessie to come to her with this news. And the fact that she didn't, that even at twenty-two she has never introduced Lydia to a girlfriend, feels like an indictment of their relationship because she knows, without doubt, that Jessie would have gone to Eli as soon as she became aware of herself. She would have gone to her father and said, 'I feel this way,' and he would have said, 'Then that's who you are and that's fine.' She would have said the same thing, of course she would have, so why did Jessie not come to her? What happened to her relationship with her daughters? How did it go so wrong?

She stops near a telephone pole and waits for Walter to finish his slow, sniffing inspection of other visitors to the spot. He lifts his leg and then looks at her. There is a slight glaze to his eyes these days. 'He is getting on,' the vet told her at his last check-up, 'but he seems in good spirits.'

In the sky a few grey clouds drift in the breeze. Lydia would like them to gather and grow, to bring a storm that batters the city. She wants it to be cold and rainy today. The weather needs to reflect her life, to reflect what's happening today of all days. She's not sure how she will feel if she has to stand in the sun to say goodbye to her child. At Eli's funeral it had been cold and windy with a light drizzle that hit everyone in the face as the wind blew the drops sideways, stinging cheeks and mingling with tears. That had felt appropriate.

'Are you in good spirits, Walter?' she asks him and he wags his tail at her. They continue their walk as Lydia wonders if the dog has registered that Zoe is gone forever. He has, as he has always done, gone to her room every day, looking for her. He goes to her room, and when he finds she's not there, he returns to his comfortable pillow in the kitchen to wait for her return. He does the same thing with Jessie. He likes to have the girls home with him. He is very protective and she smiles as she remembers that when Callum first started coming over, Walter wouldn't let him sit next to Zoe on the couch. He would deliberately squeeze in between them, his large, golden body preventing them from being too close.

'Can't you put him outside?' Lydia remembers hearing Callum ask.

'No,' Zoe replied. 'He's the boss of this house. He'll get used to you eventually if you're nice to me.'

He did get used to Callum because Callum is a nice boy – a little superficial but nice nonetheless. Harmless is how she's always thought of him. But is he actually harmless? Why would Zoe have been scared to speak to him? She knows their relationship was a little volatile.

Twice in the last few months, a selection of chocolates addressed to Zoe had been delivered to the house, and when Lydia had asked about them, her daughter laughed and said, 'It's the best way to say sorry.'

'What on earth could you two have to fight about?'

'Just because we're sixteen and seventeen doesn't mean we don't have issues like every other relationship. He's trying to control who I talk to online and I'm not going to let that happen.'

'You shouldn't,' Lydia had agreed.

'Yeah, and I told him to back off. And now he's sorry.'

She seemed to have more control in the relationship than he did. But perhaps he handled the break-up badly? Zoe had broken up with a lot of boyfriends and she'd never been scared to speak to any of them afterwards.

She stops walking and drags Zoe's phone out of her pocket. She's been carrying it everywhere with her since the detective gave it back. This morning she has left her own phone at home, not wanting to be disturbed, but she has brought Zoe's phone with her, brought Zoe with her. It is unlocked now and she's keeping it charged. She taps on Callum's name before she can think about it, and to the sound of her heartbeat in her ear, she holds the phone and waits for him to answer. It's very early and she knows that he probably won't even be up for school yet, but she wants to surprise him. She doesn't want him to have time to prepare his answers for her as he must have had before he spoke to the detectives.

He answers after only three rings.

'Zoe!' he gasps, his voice thick with sleep, and for a moment Lydia feels bad. He probably thinks he's dreaming. She should have, perhaps, called from her own phone, but it's too late now.

'No, Callum, I'm sorry but it's Lydia, Zoe's mother.'

'Oh… oh Mrs… oh.'

'Look, I know you've spoken to the police but I just wanted to ask you what happened between you and Zoe, why you broke up.'

'Um… we just… she just… I don't know what you want me to say. We just broke up. It wasn't… working.'

Lydia can hear his awkwardness, his shock at her call. She's sure that if she was Callum's mother, she would be furious about the mother of another child calling her son. But she needs to do this.

'Jessie told me that you told her Zoe was speaking to another boy and the police know that as well. Do you know anything about the boy? Is there something you may have forgotten to mention to the police?'

'No… I don't know… I didn't forget anything.'

'Something you didn't want to tell them then?' she responds quickly.

There is silence for a moment, and when Callum speaks again, his voice has changed. He sounds wide awake. 'Why would I know anything about him? I didn't know everyone she was speaking to on her Instagram. She talked to lots of people.'

'Yes, but you said to Jessie that she had no idea who she was speaking to. You only said that about this one particular boy or… or man.'

'It's not a man.'

'How do you know?' she snaps, anger beginning to rise inside her.

'I just… look, I'm sorry about what happened to Zoe, like really, really sorry. But I don't know anything. I told the police that. I don't know anything. I have to get ready for school now.'

'But Callum,' says Lydia and then she looks at the phone. He has hung up on her. He's hiding something. She's sure of that but what? Is he just embarrassed that Zoe broke up with him over a boy she hadn't met yet? Is it something else?

Who could this person have been? Anyone really. He could have been anyone from anywhere in the whole world. She has no idea what kind of a person Xavier is or if his name is even Xavier. She shivers but not from the cold, more from the idea that someone was talking to her daughter, was possibly pretending to be someone else, was allowed to enter her home and infiltrate her daughter's life through Zoe's phone. The only reason for him to delete his account would be because he was afraid of getting caught, and why would he be afraid of getting caught? Last night she and Gabriel had decided, with a sickening feeling, that he was probably older.

'He probably saw the comments on her Instagram after she… died and he got spooked,' Gabriel said last night.

'What kind of a man talks to a sixteen-year-old? Who does something like that?' she said. She knew the answer so she didn't expect him to reply. But she's sure that there are a lot of older men who disguise their true age when they first speak to someone a lot younger than they are. Zoe liked to think of herself as too smart to be scammed over the internet. Lydia has been talking to the girls about cyber safety for years and has always only received rolled eyes and 'we know' in response. But what if Zoe didn't know? It isn't very hard to disguise your identity on the internet.

She rubs at her eyes. Whoever she was or was not talking to, it's too late now.

Zoe is gone but Jessie has obviously been lost to her for a while, she realises with a crushed heart. Dating a former teacher, and a married former teacher at that, is not the choice of the daughter she thought she knew. And why would Paula Fitzsimmons have made such a choice? Eli was ten years older than she was, and she knows that when they met, her mother had been concerned, but for Lydia it was love at first sight and nothing would have stopped her being with him. But Paula is a former teacher – a former teacher who has children and a husband of her own. It feels like Jessie has lost the ability to reason properly. Maybe that's what love is? But it still doesn't feel like this is who Jessie is – or was. How is it possible that she has no idea who her children are?

Zoe's funeral will be held this afternoon. She is grateful that at least it's going ahead. Over the last few dark days she has found herself wishing that Zoe had been high or drunk or out of it. She hates to think of her daughter being fully aware, of her crippling fear as her body tumbled off the side of the small outcrop, struck with pain as she hit the ground. Did she know what was happening to her? Did she know she was dying? Lydia shakes her head, letting her tears flow freely. It's horrifying to contemplate. So awful to think that Zoe, in her last moments, may have cried out for her.

She is trying to not think about those last moments of her daughter's life even though they crowd in all the time. She is instead attempting to remember three wonderful moments in Zoe's life every single day. But, of course, Zoe's life was filled with wonderful moments so once she's thought of three, she can remember three more and then she feels her tears dry up and she can even manage a smile.

She breathes in the cold air as the sky begins to lighten. It's not even seven o'clock yet, but the peace she feels in the relative silence, despite her tears, was worth getting out of bed for. Only the warbling calls of the magpies disturb the peace, and she loves the sound of their chatter, feels as though they are waking up the suburb. She likes it when the area feels empty. She likes space. She and Gabriel were planning on renting a house near the beach on the south coast in the Christmas holidays.

'Let's make it a big one so Zoe can bring a friend and Jessie can bring someone too if she wants to come down for a few days. It will probably be the last time Zoe comes on holiday with us. I know she's planning a trip to Europe for after her final year of school,' she explained to Gabriel.

'I'll speak to Zeek – you remember he's in real estate down there. He'll be able to find us something.'

Lydia has no idea if Gabriel has spoken to Zeek or not. But the idea of it just being her and Gabriel in a big house by the beach is horrifying. The idea of ever attempting to do anything joyful again is impossible. She knows it seemed impossible after Eli's death as well but there was a little bit of light, a little bit of hope, from Zoe who didn't fully understand that her father was gone forever. It was hard not to smile when Zoe grinned or to laugh when Zoe giggled. Yet there were moments when her exuberance was too much for Lydia, who just wanted to lie on her bed and hold Eli's favourite sweater to her face, inhaling him and remembering their life before the cancer, and then she would ask Jessie to take her little sister away, to keep her entertained so she could have some time. Was that when she and Jessie first started to lose touch? Had Jessie resented taking care of her sister when her own heart was so completely broken?

'Come on, Walter,' says Lydia and she tugs at his lead so they can head back home. Others are appearing on the street now and while she would ordinarily greet the other regular dog walkers, she doesn't feel up to it today. How on earth would she answer the benign question of, 'How are you?'

'Come on,' she whispers, 'three things, three good things about Zoe.'

She stops for Walter to sniff at a tree and she lets go of her conversation with Callum although she knows she will mention it to the detective. She just breathes and lets go of everything but her daughter. She thinks about the first time Zoe saw the dog.

Lydia had not wanted a dog at all. She had enough to handle with trying to run the business on her own and keeping herself together emotionally. Every day she arrived home exhausted to two little girls who had no idea what had happened to their world. Zoe didn't understand why she never wanted to play with her anymore and Jessie was just… beyond sad. Lydia worried that she was depressed. She was a shell of the child she had been before Eli died, and every time Lydia tried to think about what to do in a concrete way, she felt herself shut down.

She tried grief counselling, just for her and Jessie at first, hoping that it would help, but her daughter hadn't wanted to share with the counsellor. At each session Lydia talked and talked, and the more she said the more distant she felt from her own feelings. Jessie would barely speak at all. 'How are you doing?' their counsellor would ask her each week. He was an older man with a neat grey beard and calm blue eyes.

'Okay,' Jessie would reply and then she would subside into silence.

'I don't want to go back,' she told her mother after three sessions.

'He's just trying to help. If you don't like him, we can find someone else.'

'No,' she replied, lifting her small chin, her blue eyes cloudy with emotion. 'I don't want to talk to anyone. Why do you think talking will help? Talking won't bring him back and I'm sick of people asking me how I feel. I feel horrible and awful and I will forever and ever.' She turned and left Lydia's room, slamming her own bedroom door behind her.

'Oh Eli,' Lydia whispered, 'what am I supposed to do now?'

She felt helpless, hopeless and like she had failed her child.

She had picked up her phone and opened Facebook, meaning to post a question about grief counsellors on a page that dealt with the loss of a loved one. The first thing she saw was an advert for golden retriever puppies and she felt, bizarrely, as though Eli was sending her a message. He had always wanted a dog and she had always responded, 'when the girls are big enough to handle the responsibility.' She regretted that after he died, hated herself for denying him the pleasure of a pet.

Instead of scrolling past, she clicked on the post, and three weeks later she was able to surprise the girls.

Walter had been for Jessie really. Lydia picked her up from school with the puppy asleep in a basket in the front passenger seat of her car. She had asked a friend to have Zoe for the afternoon, wanting to see how Jessie would react, unsure if she would love the idea or hate it. She didn't feel sure about anything anymore.

Her daughter climbed into the back seat and clicked her seatbelt.

'How was school?'

'Fine.'

Lydia waited.

'Why aren't we driving?'

And then Walter made a snuffling sound and Jessie took off her seatbelt and looked at what was in the front seat.

'Oh, oh, oh,' she cried. 'Is he for us? Is he?'

'He is.' Lydia smiled, and for the first time in many, many months, Jessie smiled back at her.

Later, when Zoe was home, Lydia took her to Jessie's room, where the puppy was curled up on her bed, fast asleep.

Zoe stared at him for a moment and then reached out to touch him gently, softly. 'I hope he makes you happy again, Jess,' she said, shocking Lydia with her perception.

'He will make both of us happy,' replied Jessie.

'What should we call him? He looks like his name is Walter,' Zoe said as the puppy opened his eyes to look at her.

'Why?' Lydia asked.

'Because his eyes are sweet and his face is kind of smushed like Mr Walter who works in the garden at my kindy.'

Lydia let out a bark of laughter and then she stopped abruptly. The sound was strange to her own ears. She had not laughed properly since Eli died. But then Zoe laughed and, miraculously, Jessie began to laugh as well. The younger girl grinned when her sister giggled and Lydia knew she was pleased to have been the one to make that happen. It felt like a victory.

And just like that an avalanche of memories – of Zoe laughing, Zoe telling jokes, Zoe pulling funny faces to make Jessie laugh – appears.

She realises that she's back at the house. The funeral is this afternoon and it cannot come quickly enough. She wants it to be over; she wants to be done with all the sympathetic glances and the kind words and the hugs. She wants to be left alone, just left alone. She knows that people will wish her 'long life' as is the tradition and that she will have to thank them but she won't feel thankful. How can she want to continue living? And just like that she is crying again.

She knows that for sure and suddenly, on the day of his daughter's funeral, she misses her late husband with a force so visceral it takes her breath away. She would be able to survive this if he were here, she thinks, but he's not. And she doesn't know how on earth she's going to get through the rest of the day.

At home Jessie is stretching on the front lawn, ready to go for her run.

'Mum…' says Jessie but Lydia just shakes her head. She can't. Not today. She simply cannot give anything more to anyone else today.

CHAPTER SEVENTEEN

Shayna

It looks like our whole school is here. You could fit 200 people in this chapel or whatever they call it, and there are people spilling out of the door into the foyer.

Outside it's pouring with rain. In the last hour the sky went from grey to black and then lightning streaked across the sky followed by huge claps of thunder. And then the rain came down. It's cold and miserable and I'm cold and miserable and I think that if Zoe is watching from wherever she is, she's happy that we're all going to get soaked. There have been moments, since it happened, when I think I can feel her anger at me, like it's in the air or something. I understand her fury.

My mum always says, 'The only thing necessary for the triumph of evil is for good men to do nothing.' Some American president said it in a speech once and it basically means that if you see something terrible happening and do nothing about it, then you're as guilty as if you'd done it yourself.

I know when my mum says it, it's to do with the world standing by and letting people starve to death in developing countries and stuff like that, but on Friday night I understood that saying completely, and I like to think of myself as a good person and so I couldn't just sit by and watch the evil that was occurring. Because something awful was happening in that cabin.

But I didn't just not stand by. I turned it around. Becca and I turned it around and then I did something dreadful and now I can't stop wondering if I was the evil that should have been prevented. That's what I can't stop thinking: that I'm the bad one and I deserve to be punished.

It went too far and there's no way to change what happened now.

Outside, thunder booms and I feel my body startle. I want to put my hands over my ears. I bite down on my lip instead.

'It's going to be ghastly to stand at the graveside out in the open,' my mum said as we parked our car and got ready to run inside.

When we walked in there was a spot where people left their umbrellas. They're all piled up there now, all different colours, dripping water onto the floor, and I have no idea how everyone is going to make sure they have the right umbrella for when we have to walk to the graveside.

This place has a tin roof and it's a good thing there's a microphone otherwise I don't think we would be able to hear anything.

I look up and around me.

All the teachers are here. Except for Ms Fischer. I don't know why she's not but maybe it's because she's been arrested. The rumours are swirling around – one minute she's in prison and one minute she's left the country.

Mrs Fitzsimmons is here so I'm sure Ms Fischer hasn't been arrested. She's standing at the back between Mr Jenkins and Mrs Gallagher and she looks like she wants to throw up. Her eyes are red from crying and her hair's a mess.

I feel really bad for her. I feel bad for Zoe's mother and sister as well. They're sitting at the front. The rabbi guy stands in front of the microphone and he starts talking about how nice Zoe was and what a special child she was and Zoe's mum looks like her face is made out of stone.

'Zoe was a beautiful dancer who lit up the stage. Her mother Lydia told me of her first ballet class at only three years old, when little Zoe excitedly donned her pink ballet shoes and then stood perfectly in first position waiting for the class to begin…'

Jessie is biting down on her lip as she listens to him talk but I can see that Zoe's mother is nodding occasionally as if to agree with the rabbi.

There is a second of silence as the rabbi takes a breath and the rain stops. Everyone automatically looks up at the roof. And in the silence, you can hear the electronic buzzing of everyone's phones vibrating at different times, like the phones are communicating with each other.

This is the second funeral I have been to in my whole life. The first one was for my grandfather but he was eighty-five when he died so even though everyone was upset, it wasn't like this. It wasn't like this at all. You can almost hear everyone's thoughts: *This is wrong, this is wrong, this is wrong.* I wonder how long the rain will stay away for.

All around the room people are sighing and sniffing. One woman a few rows behind me is crying loudly and I turn quickly to see who it is but I don't recognise her. A man next to her is squeezing her shoulders and whispering, 'Shh.'

It's weird to think about a life just stopping: one moment you're there and the next you're gone. We talked about that once at a sleepover, me and Zoe and Becca. I think we were about fourteen and it was really early in the morning, like 4 a.m., and we were tired but kind of hopped up on sugar.

'What do you think happens when you die?' Becca asked.

'You go to heaven,' I said. 'Like whatever heaven is supposed to be. I think you're still here but, you know, as, like, a spirit.'

'I don't believe that,' said Zoe. 'I think you're just gone.'

'Why do you think that?' Becca asked.

Zoe was quiet for a bit. 'I just do. If you were still here, then I would be able to feel my dad, and I don't. I don't feel him at all. It's like he never even existed.'

'But then—' I started to say.

'I'm tired,' said Zoe. 'It's time to go to sleep.' I would have liked to have asked her more but Zoe was always in charge when we were together. The next day when we woke up, we had other things to talk about. And now, it's awful to think that Zoe is just gone, just nowhere. I would rather think about her in a beautiful place, like a garden or something. I know our friendship had become strained but she was still my friend. I hope she's somewhere peaceful and nice, even if she is furious with me.

Mum is sitting next to me, crying, and Becca is on the other side, next to Leeanne. I look at the screen behind the rabbi, where they have put up some pictures of Zoe. There are pictures from her whole life there. There's even one of the three of us and I know that everyone keeps looking over to where we are sitting.

I met up with Becca this morning, just to have coffee and talk, and Leeanne was there. I know that Leeanne has been hanging out with Becca a lot. It seems like she's part of our group now, which is weird because she's so different to us. But it also feels right. We were the only ones in the cabin, the only ones who know what happened before we turned off the light and went to sleep. It puts us in this kind of bubble, I guess. We all know what happened but none of us will talk about it.

Everything would have been fine if Leeanne hadn't ended up in our cabin. Any other girl could have had that fourth bed and everyone would be back at school today, whispering about what did or did not happen with the boys from St John's.

Zoe sniggered when Ms Fisher told us that Leeanne would be sharing with us.

She called Leeanne 'stick insect' because of the way she looks, which is, like, completely different to the rest of her family who are all good looking. She is tall and flat-chested. Her eyes always look big and bulbous because of the glasses she wears and she's always a little hunched over. She is a bit weird-looking, as though she hasn't quite grown into her face and her long, straight nose. We've all gone through an awkward phase in our lives. Mine was when I was fourteen and my teeth looked too big for my mouth. Becca had bad skin at fifteen but that's sorted out now. But Leeanne is still battling her skin and her long skinny arms and a whole host of other things, all along with being the smartest in the year and telling everyone who will listen that she's going to be a Supreme Court judge.

Zoe never went through an awkward phase. She was just pretty when she was younger and then prettier as she got older, and she had a real thing about Leeanne. I know the real reason why she didn't like her, but I don't think Leeanne should have been blamed for something someone else did, and I could also never figure out exactly why she disliked her so much. Of all the people Zoe teased, Leeanne got the worst of it.

So, for Leeanne to end up in our cabin was not a good thing, and anyone who knew what had been going on and about how Leeanne and Zoe were connected – which was everyone – could have predicted how things would go.

This morning we met at Becca's house so we could be by ourselves without people constantly coming up to us with this weird look on their faces, like they're trying to show us how sad they are. To me they look like cartoon people and I know for a fact that not everyone is sad. They all just love the drama of the whole thing. Becca and Leeanne said they didn't want to go to school today, even though the funeral was only scheduled for this afternoon.

'I feel so guilty,' I told them when Becca handed me a cup of coffee.

Leeanne didn't say anything. She opened a Tupperware she had brought with her and showed us that she had three caramel slices. 'I thought we could use a treat,' she said, and even though Becca and I would never have had something like that on a weekday, we each took one anyway. It feels like the rules don't apply anymore.

'It wasn't our fault,' Becca said.

'It really wasn't – you guys were just defending me,' said Leeanne. 'I feel bad that she got upset but I'm also so grateful that you stood up for me.'

Then we all just ate our caramel slices, letting their gooey sweetness distract us, and talked about new Netflix shows as though that somehow erased everything that had happened, as though we weren't all going to a funeral in the afternoon.

I wanted to talk about it more. I wanted to try and pinpoint the exact moment when it all went wrong, but I keep going over it and I can't.

I know it was just after Ms Fischer did her check of our cabin, so it must have been just after nine.

'At least you didn't screw up Sunday night,' Becca said to Zoe and laughed.

'You dared me to bring it,' said Zoe.

'I didn't think you actually would.'

Zoe shrugged her shoulders. 'Time for a junk-food feast, I think.'

We all climbed out of our bunks and grabbed our junk food from our bags. It was cold in the cabin, with the wind whistling through tiny gaps in the metal where the tin walls met each other. We were all dressed in pyjamas with socks and jumpers, and I was wearing my beanie because I was freezing. We sat on Zoe's bunk and threw everything we had on her sleeping bag. 'What about you, Leeanne?' she said and she looked at Leeanne, who had the bunk underneath Becca's. She was just lying there really quietly. She hadn't said anything at all. She was like an animal that instinctively knew to be quiet or it would get hurt. I'd never really thought much about Leeanne, about what life must be like for her, until that night. I'd watched as Zoe said things to her but I'd always distanced myself from it. But in the cabin I'd been watching her, noticing how she waited for all of us to choose our bunks first before she put her sleeping bag down, and how when Zoe threw some tissues on the floor that she'd found in the bottom of her bag, Leeanne just got up, collected them and put them in the garbage. I don't think Zoe even noticed her do it. I felt bad for her, bad that she felt she had to be so careful with us.

'Well,' she said, 'I did bake some red velvet cupcakes. I thought I would share them with whoever was in my cabin.' She climbed out of her sleeping bag; her pyjamas were covered in flowers. When she bent over her bag to get the container of cupcakes, her glasses slipped off her face and clattered onto the floor.

I heard Zoe snigger.

'Don't, Zoe,' said Becca.

Zoe laughed. 'Hey, don't bite my head off – only a stick insect can do that.'

'Stick insects don't bite their mates heads off, Zoe, that's what a praying mantis does. If you're going to insult me, you should know your facts,' Leeanne snapped.

I held my breath because I had no idea why she would do something so stupid. And I had never ever heard her stand up for herself like that.

'Oh, really,' said Zoe. Her voice was high-pitched and I knew then… I knew exactly what was going to happen.

That's it, I realise now as the rabbi prays. That's the moment it all went wrong. The moment Leeanne fought back because I guess, in a funny way, she showed me and Becca that it was possible to fight back. Until then, we'd never said or done anything to upset Zoe even though she was never careful about upsetting us.

'Those cupcakes look amazing,' I said, really needing to distract Zoe. I could see by the way she was smiling that she was angry.

Zoe didn't say anything. She just sat quietly on her bunk, watching Leeanne, watching us.

I leaned forward and took a cupcake and they were delicious. Becca and Zoe took one as well, finishing them quickly and licking their fingers, and then we were all eyeing the other stuff on the bed – which included a bag of Doritos I had brought, some Skittles, some caramel candies and three blocks of chocolate that Becca had brought along with four packets of jelly snakes – wondering what to eat next.

Zoe had brought four packets of Tim Tam biscuits in the new flavours they have. One was salted caramel and one was strawberries and cream. I can't remember the others. Zoe smiled widely at Leeanne. She moved her hands in a circle over everything and said, 'So, Leeanne, maybe if you eat some more junk, you'll grow some boobs. Maybe then you could find yourself a boy stick insect – sorry, praying mantis – and bite his head off after he has sex with you.'

Leeanne laughed, just a small, sad laugh. 'I think I may just go to bed,' she said. 'That was a long walk we went on today. The waterfall was beautiful though.' She got off Zoe's bunk and climbed back into her sleeping bag. I knew she was trying to change the subject. I also knew that she wanted to have something else to eat but she wasn't going to.

'It was,' I agreed with her.

'You must have loved the waterfall and the bush, Leeanne. I mean, this is your natural habitat, isn't it? Bet you got to catch lots of lovely bugs to eat – snap, snap, snap.' Zoe moved her head and clicked her teeth together.

'That's enough, Zoe,' said Becca.

'Oh please, Saint Becca, stop defending her like you've never said anything nasty about anyone.'

'I've never been as nasty as you.'

'Except for when you told me that you thought Shayna was going to die a friendless virgin.'

'What?' I said.

Becca folded her arms and scowled at Zoe. 'I said that a long time ago when I was cranky with her. It was, like, two years ago,

Shayna, and I was mad at you because you wouldn't come over because you had homework. I was just being stupid and bitchy and I'm sorry. Zoe, you really don't know when to keep your mouth shut, do you? I have no idea why Shayna and I ever thought we could trust you as a friend.'

'Oh, and do you know when to keep quiet?'

'Yes,' smirked Becca, 'or I would have told you about hooking up with Callum.' Becca took a deep breath and clamped her hand over her mouth. It was like the words had launched themselves into the air without her knowing. She went pale. She was never ever going to tell Zoe about what had happened with Callum.

Someone else at the funeral sobs, dragging me away from the memory of that night. I move my shoulders a little because I can feel I'm getting a cramp in my neck from holding my body so straight. My mum sniffs and gets another tissue from her bag and then she hands me one, as though I should be crying. I dab at my eyes even though I'm not. I try to stop thinking about what happened by reminding myself of where I am, what is happening, but I find that I can't stop thinking about that night.

I turn to look at Becca but she's staring straight ahead. I have no idea why she told Zoe that night. It was supposed to be a secret, something she had only shared with me and something we had promised would never be shared with anyone else.

'Wh-when?' Zoe asked, her voice soft.

'I don't think we should talk about this,' I said.

'No, I want to know when. When, Becca?' Zoe's green eyes were bright with fury.

'At Emily's party,' said Becca, and I could hear the regret in her voice, but once you open Pandora's box, it stays open. Emily's party was four months ago, when Zoe was still gushing over Callum every minute of the day.

'How could you?' Zoe stood up, getting off the bed and moving towards the door. 'How could you? You're supposed to be my friend, my best friend.' She folded her arms, jutted out her chin and shot daggers at Becca.

'Okay, look,' said Becca and she started pushing her cuticles back on her nails like she always does when she doesn't want to look at someone. 'You drank too much and passed out and he was cranky because there was no one there from his year, so I said we should go for a walk. We didn't actually have sex, Zoe. Some stuff just happened and it meant nothing and I'm sorry. I'm sure he doesn't remember anyway. We were both drunk and I'm really, really sorry.' She looked up at Zoe and I could see that she was going to cry.

'She is really sorry,' I said. 'You can ask him and he'll probably say that he doesn't remember at all, not a thing – they were really drunk.'

'Oh, and you can just shut up as well, Shayna. You're the biggest bitch of all of us. You pretend you're always trying to be nice but it's all about show. You should be friends with stick insect Leeanne, and if you think that any of those boys from St John's are going to be interested in you, you're mistaken. You're a frigid nerd, Shayna, and no one will ever want to fuck you.'

The cabin didn't feel cold anymore. The heat of our anger at each other filled the air and I actually started to feel myself sweat underneath my layers. I wanted to scream and scream because it was all so scary and frustrating. We had never had a fight like that before. We'd had arguments but we weren't the kind of friends who yelled and screamed at each other. Everything was out of control.

'Don't say that to her!' shouted Becca.

'I can say whatever I like,' spat Zoe.

'You know what, Zoe? Just about everyone at school hates you,' said Becca. 'Talk to anyone, from year seven to year twelve – they all think you are a complete bitch. The only reason Callum is dating you is because you have sex with him, and everyone at St John's calls you EaZoe because you are. You're easy!'

I looked at Becca. That was a lie, unless she'd heard it and not told me, but I knew it was a lie. I thought then that she'd taken things a bit far but I still didn't want to stop. After all the months I had been worrying about what Zoe was doing and how she was treating people, I didn't want it to stop.

'Stop talking crap. Stop it!' shouted Zoe.

'You need to hear this, Zoe,' I said. 'Becca and I are tired of being treated like this, and you also need to know that after school, Becca and I are going travelling together, without you.' Then it was Becca's turn to look shocked. We hadn't planned on saying anything to Zoe about that until just before final exams.

'But we were…' said Zoe and then she went back to her bed, pushed all the food onto the floor and kicked it under Leeanne's bed, extra-hard so she kicked Leeanne as well, and she got into her bunk and burrowed down in her sleeping bag. I could hear her panting angrily from my bunk and I felt horrible and sick and I wanted to just wind back the clock.

But I also felt glad that we'd said what we'd said. I was glad we'd hurt her feelings.

No one said anything else, and after a few minutes of silence, Leeanne climbed out of her bunk and turned off the light.

And that was the last time I saw Zoe.

I bite down on my lip. That's a lie. It wasn't the last time.

In the chapel people begin to move, and I look around me and realise that it's time to walk to the graveside now. As we file out, I see a lot of the boys from years eleven and twelve at St John's. They are all walking together with their hands in their pockets and their heads down. I see Callum right in the middle of the group, as though he is being protected. I wonder what he's thinking.

I look up as we get outside, where the grey clouds are beginning to separate and some tiny patches of blue sky have become visible. The storm was over quickly, and maybe if I had just left it when

Leeanne turned the light off, the storm in our cabin would have been over quickly as well.

We stand at the graves and I watch Zoe's mum throw some dirt on top of the mahogany coffin as the rabbi prays.

The sound of the dirt hitting the wood is so final, so horrible, a thud of earth and my friend is gone. I think about Zoe inside the box, cold and still, and I feel sick. I can't hold back my tears. My mother hands me another tissue and I can see she's crying as well. Everyone is crying.

At the back, a little way off from everyone, are the two detectives who've been asking us all questions. I wipe my eyes and feel that my hands are shaking.

They are coming over this afternoon – well, this evening really. Just to talk, they told my mother. Just to make sure they have all the information they need. Without meaning to, I catch the detective's eye, and the look she gives me stops my tears. All I can feel is fear. Because I can see that she knows. I'm sure she knows.

CHAPTER EIGHTEEN

Bernadette

I did intend to go inside. I drove here early and parked my car at the other end of the lot so that I could make a quick getaway, and I fully intended to go inside.

The pouring rain obscures my vision and cocoons me inside my small car, safe from everything outside. The cemetery is a peaceful spot, surrounded by large trees with beautifully laid out garden beds, now a riot of spring colours in pinks and reds and oranges, although there is little to see today. This morning it seemed possible that the grey clouds would drift away, leaving a sunny afternoon, but instead a storm brewed and now there is rain and thunder. The sound of the rain on the roof of my car is soothing, and if I focus on it, I can listen only to that. I have cracked the window open just a tiny bit to allow a small amount of air into the car, where the windows are fogging up.

My parents are both buried here. It seems strange to be here for a child, for someone right at the beginning of their journey. Strange and ultimately very sad. I wish I could grieve this lost life properly but I cannot think much beyond self-preservation.

I really wanted to get out and go inside. But once people started arriving, once I heard snatches of conversation from people parking near me… I just couldn't bring myself to leave the car.

'I would be so angry,' I heard one mother mutter loudly over the rain to her daughter, whom I recognised as Nelly from year nine. I didn't realise that the whole school would be here. 'I heard Ms Fischer is going to jail forever,' the girl replied to her mother. Nelly is a proficient artist but struggles a little with English, and she regularly attends the extra lessons I hold at lunchtimes for those students who want a bit of extra help. I wonder if Nelly will return to these sessions next term, and I wonder how she will look at me, how they will all look at me.

They had parked right next to me but were oblivious to my small blue car and my slightly open window.

That's how they are speaking about me, as though I am a criminal, as though I have actually committed the crime of killing this girl. It is preposterous.

More cars arrived, and as I wiped away the condensation on my window, I even saw Paula turn up with Murray, who teaches science, and Grace, who teaches geography, for support I'm sure. I am certain that if they glanced this way, they would have seen me. Soon the whole parking lot was filled and I understood that it was time to get out, time to go and pay my respects, but I found myself unable to move. I still find myself unable to move. The rain stops and I become aware of the silence. It would be easy enough to go in now. But I don't seem to be able to find the strength to do so.

I don't think I can stand the stares, the whispers, the way that everyone will look at me. I understand that this is not what is happening to Paula, despite the fact that she has actually done something wrong. She left her room to meet her young lover. Her young lover who is a former student. The girl's sister, of all people. But none of that is common knowledge. What I saw isn't common knowledge either and yet I know that the majority of the blame is being placed on me. I was the senior teacher in charge. Will the students ever look at me the same way again? And if they don't, if they won't – why am I still keeping a secret about Friday night? Why am I protecting anyone at all if no one has even thought of protecting me and my reputation as a teacher after so many years of my loyalty and service?

I reflect on the two girls fighting outside the cabins, at the way they gesticulated at each other, at the sibilant whispers of anger that I couldn't really make out. The girl fighting with Zoe was wearing a beanie with pom-poms on the end. I watched them swirl around as she shook her head.

Shayna was wearing it when I went to do my check at 9 p.m.

'Ms Fischer, it's so cold in here that I have to wear a beanie to sleep,' she told me and I nodded my assent.

'I too will be wearing one, Shayna, and it will do us both good to be deprived of a little luxury for a night or two.'

I had forgotten about that part of the conversation because that was when Zoe asked about being allowed to go into town on Sunday night.

The memory is clear now but I am unsure what to do with the information.

If I tell the police that Zoe and Shayna were fighting at midnight, I will be asked why I didn't stop them and then why I didn't say anything in the days since then. Implicating Shayna will mean implicating myself and then the board will have a great deal to use against me. The police will also have a great deal to use against me, and I have no idea what will happen to Shayna. Of the three girls in that little group she is, perhaps, the sweetest. I have noticed her helping other students in class, and she has volunteered for homework club with the junior school students for a couple of years now. She strikes me as a girl who avoids confrontation. I have never heard her say an angry word to anyone. It was unusual to see her arguing with anyone, especially her best friend. I should have paid attention to that.

I am suddenly very tired. The parking lot has emptied of people and it's just me, sitting here in my car as the time passes. There are so many people here that I am sure I could sneak in at the back and no one would notice me. Unless, of course, they did.

I keep reassuring myself that I have done nothing wrong but I am starting to feel as though I am lying to myself.

I need to move now because the funeral will be over soon and I don't want to be caught sitting outside here in my car like a deranged voyeur.

Wearily, I start the engine and slowly back out of the space. I will return home to the safety of my apartment and to Oliver, who asks for nothing more from me than kindness and food.

There is no one I can call to discuss how I am feeling, no one that I would trust with the information I have, and I wonder as I get closer to home how I have managed to live such a very small life.

It was not my intention. It was never my intention, and yet here I am at sixty-two with literally no one to speak to at all.

CHAPTER NINETEEN

Jessie

That's my sister in there, Jessie repeats to herself as she stares at the hole slowly being filled. The words don't make sense. At least the rain has cleared but it has left the grass soggy and the air cold.

Dirt drops onto the wood of the coffin, the thud sound growing duller as the grave fills up and her sister is buried underneath mud and stones. The wind comes up as grey clouds move to block out the sun again. A few scattered drops of rain fall and Jessie shivers. It's the right weather for what's happening. A girl whose smile was bright and sunny is gone. Jessie knows that it was impossible not to smile back at Zoe when she offered one of her genuinely happy smiles.

Gabriel has his arm wrapped around her mother's shoulders. Jessie can see he is supporting her weight. This morning, after breakfast, she knows that her mother took a strong tranquilliser, unable to bear the thought of facing this feeling raw and uncocooned. Jessie came downstairs after her shower to find her weeping at the kitchen table but was unable to say anything, unable to find the right words. She had tried to speak to her this morning before she went for her run but her mother had no desire to talk to her. She had stood in the kitchen, watching her mother awkwardly, trying to find something to say, anything, and then Gabriel walked in and all she felt was relief that she didn't have to deal with her mother, who doesn't seem to want her now only daughter anywhere near her.

Jessie thought about taking something as well but in the end she didn't. She wishes she had now even though her mother's glazed and distant eyes make her seem removed from what's happening. Jessie supposes that it's better that she cannot feel the whole intensity of her daughter's death. She can imagine that her mum would simply collapse then, would lie on the floor and be unable to move at all. Her mother and Gabriel are standing together and yet Lydia seems completely alone. Only one person here at this funeral is watching the child they gave birth to being buried, and so she is alone in her grief. There is no grief like that of a mother who has lost her child. No one can break through it, no one can touch it, and so here, surrounded by hundreds of people, her mother is alone.

Jessie wraps her arms around herself, wishing she had brought a jacket so that she could hold it tightly around her body that is shivering. It occurs to her that one day her mother will die and then, because she has no father and no sister, she too will be completely alone. It is possible that if she lives for many years, there will be no one to watch her being buried. She shakes her head away from thoughts of herself. She would like to go and stand next to her mother but that feels impossible. She glances over at her father's gravestone, which is right next to where Zoe is being buried, in the plot intended, one day, for her mother. *Look what's happened to us, Daddy*, she thinks. *How are we going to survive this?*

She has only glimpsed Paula amongst the hoard of people who have arrived to say goodbye to her sister.

She has tried to catch her eye but Paula is refusing to look at her.

Jessie wants to be angry at her for telling the police but she is not. All she wants is for Paula to look at her, to speak to her, but she will not answer her texts or calls. All Jessie is getting is silence. In truth, Jessie had not expected to fall in love. She had simply been enjoying their chats over email and then, later, their meetings over coffee. She's not even sure how their discussion evolved beyond general stuff like what she was studying and the biology syllabus to more personal conversations about how Paula felt about her marriage and then about Jessie's late realisation – halfway through year twelve – that she was gay. Jessie understands that she always knew this about herself, always. It just seemed easier to deny it because she felt, after the death of her father, that it would be an unnecessary complication in her life. On the afternoon she was supposed to be studying for her final physics exam, she had instead stood in front of her mirror and said to herself, 'My name is Jessie Bloom and I'm gay.' And then she felt a hole open up inside her because her first thought had been, even after all the years he'd been gone, *I need to talk to Dad about this.* The realisation winded her.

She looks around now – as though it would be possible to see her father here, as though his ghost may have somehow appeared to say goodbye to his younger daughter. They are standing right next to his grave, after all, and she cannot help but keep looking at the black granite stone where his name is inscribed in gold lettering.

Eli Bloom
Beloved father to Jessie and Zoe
Wonderful husband to Lydia
Dearly missed son of Graham and Michelle

Her grandparents are on a cruise somewhere in the middle of the Mediterranean. They could not wait for them to return to hold the funeral. She knows that one of her cousins is holding a phone and filming the funeral so her grandparents can sit in their cabin on the ocean and watch their granddaughter being buried.

It feels like a horribly ghoulish thing to do and yet she knows that it's important for them. All her grandmother could say when they spoke last night was, 'I can't believe it, I just can't believe it.'

The rabbi is finished and he asks the mourners to form two lines so that she and her mother can walk through and be wished long life. It feels barbaric, as though they are on parade, their terrible tragedy on display, and yet she knows it is meant to comfort everyone.

She walks slowly, accepting hugs and kisses from everyone. Accepting sympathetic gazes and squeezed hands. Accepting it all.

She walks past a group of boys who all nod at her, and she has no idea who they are until she recognises Callum standing with them. They are from St John's. Callum is studiously avoiding catching her eye, looking at the horizon, almost pretending he isn't here. She doesn't blame him. No one wants to be here doing this.

Only the keenest observer would notice that her mother has not touched her or spoken to her, only someone who knows their family intricately – and it seems to Jessie that there is no one here who would fall into that category. People get caught up in their own lives and she realises that she has been so consumed with getting her degree, with achieving her goals, that she has barely seen her extended family over the last few years. She has missed family dinners and celebrations because she was working at the hospital or because she had to study, so there is no one to think, *Things between Jessie and her mother seem tense.* This is both a relief and overwhelmingly sad.

Paula might notice if she was looking at Jessie; if she even glanced her way, she might notice. But Paula refuses to look at her.

Only a few days ago she was in love, doing well at university and looking forward to her future. Today she is an only child, a woman alone, a scorned daughter, and she knows she will soon be a failed medical student.

The ripples of her sister's death will last forever.

CHAPTER TWENTY

I wonder if they know I'm here. I mean, obviously they know I'm here but have they considered the possibility that Xavier is here?

There are two police detectives standing at the back, far enough away that they almost look like they're here to visit someone else's grave, but they are watching everyone. Perhaps they are hoping for some graveyard confession. Or perhaps they are expecting to see some strange-looking older man with dark glasses and a trench coat. Xavier could be anyone.

By now I assume they've found our conversations. I thought she would refuse when I asked her for the photos or that she would insist on using Snapchat so the pictures would disappear, but she didn't seem to care so I assume that they are still on her phone.

Everyone around me is crying, and I wonder if it's because they really loved her and are going to miss her or if their tears are for the loss of a young life – any young life. Or if their tears are just for show.

I think when a young person dies, everyone is reminded of their own mortality, of the possibility that they too could be only a small misstep away from death.

I wish I hadn't come. I wish I didn't have to be here to see this grief, all this grief.

For about the millionth time I mentally go over all my accounts, making sure I've deleted everything that needs to be deleted.

I knew she was loved. Of course, she was loved, but you forget how much one person's life touches those around them.

I feel my stomach turn over. I haven't been able to sleep properly for days.

I took her from them, from all these people standing at her graveside. I took her away from them. I took her from everything she was going to be, from everything she could have been.

It wasn't the plan. The plan was only ever about humiliation and revenge and making sure that she was exposed for the truth of who she was. It was only ever to show her that she wasn't invincible, that she couldn't just go around hurting people on a whim.

But it all got very out of control. It got out of control because I couldn't keep what I was doing to myself, because I had to share it. I shouldn't have shared it and so I am to blame.

I did a terrible thing but I can't tell anyone because then my life would be over, and not just my life. The terror of the police being able to trace it back to me keeps me up at night.

The truth is I wasn't exactly sure what I was going to do. I had begun to feel that it had all gone too far and I wasn't quite sure how to extricate myself from it all.

I believe I've wiped away every trace of my existence on the internet, which was easy enough since I never really existed at all. Since Xavier never really existed at all. It's strange to think how real he became. I liked being him, living in his body and his world. I liked it but now I wish he could share this burden with me. It's all his fault really.

All his fault.

CHAPTER TWENTY-ONE

Monday – Nine Days Since the Accident

Lydia

Lydia lies on her bed, curled up, a pillow over her head so she doesn't have to hear the soft murmur of voices downstairs anymore. Her daughter was buried last Thursday and yet still the people come. Hundreds attended the funeral. Their faces all blended into one large mass eventually, and the touch of so many hands – warm or cold, soft or calloused – made her want to run from everyone.

She does remember seeing Callum. Their eyes met for a split second and he immediately dropped his head, hunched his shoulders and shoved his hands into the pockets of his jacket.

'He looked like he's hiding something, like he knows something,' she told Gabriel later that night.

'What could he be hiding, Lydia? He's a seventeen-year-old boy. What could he be hiding?'

She lifts the pillow from her head and hears the click of the front door closing, and she sighs with relief. Every day she thinks that maybe she will be left alone, maybe no one will come and she will have the hours and the space and privacy she needs to try and find a way to deal with this. But still, they come. They are still sitting shiva so visitors are to be expected but Lydia cannot deal with it anymore.

'When do you think you might… might return?' Nathan asked her carefully on the phone this morning. His voice was soft and she could hear that it pained him to ask the question, but she knew that her clients would be asking. Everyone's lives went on, after all. It's only been a week and Lydia cannot imagine ever opening her eyes again and not wanting to return to sleep, where she doesn't have to think about Zoe being gone and where she is sometimes gifted with blissful dreams of her daughter.

'I just don't know,' she replied. 'Can you manage without me for as long as possible?'

'For as long as you need,' he said but he didn't sound certain.

It would be impossible to get herself into the shower and make sure her hair and make-up were done so she could look presentable for a client whose only goal in life is to get the maximum amount of money for their home in the real-estate market. She cannot conceive of discussing throw pillows and paint colours as though those things were important ever again.

To some degree she doesn't mind people visiting. It helps to be able to speak about Zoe, to be able to collect the memories others have of her, to even see the collection of photos that other mothers may have on their phones that include her daughter. But the problem is that, inevitably, talk turns to something else.

Once the cake has been served and the tea made and Zoe discussed for a certain amount of time, people always begin to talk about something else. And that's, mostly, what Lydia can't stand. Because how on earth can the world simply be allowed to go on?

She lasted as long as she could today with the group of visitors who are downstairs, but when conversation began to turn to other things, she said to the woman she was speaking to… Was it Zoe's gym teacher? A teacher from her old primary school? She can't remember, but when the woman mentioned the weather and how lovely a day it was, Lydia said she needed the bathroom and stole away upstairs to Zoe's room, searching through drawers again, looking for… something but she has no idea what. In the bottom drawer of Zoe's desk, she found an old exercise book, half filled with notes for English. Lydia ran her hands over her daughter's large looped handwriting, over the words 'themes in *Macbeth*'. At the bottom of the page Zoe had written, 'Boring, boring, boring.' Lydia was unable to suppress a smile. Zoe was not a big fan of Shakespeare. She flipped through the rest of the book, listening for anyone coming up the stairs, not wanting to be disturbed. On the last page, in bright purple pen, Zoe had written, 'Bastard. It's him or me. Him or me. Him or me. I Love…' but the name was crossed out, covered in thick black lines so she could not even see one letter. Lydia stared at the words, unsure what to make of them. She assumed Callum's name was under the lines. Sighing, she gave up and took the book back to her room, closing the door behind her so that Gabriel would not try and bring her yet another cup of tea. People seem to think that endless cups of tea are the answer to grief.

Gabriel is doing everything he can to help and she's grateful. Downstairs she caught him watching her, making sure that whoever she was speaking to didn't upset her too much, but really there is not much else he can do. The Valium helps. She had only meant to take it for the day of the funeral but she has found herself taking it every day since. Not good, she knows. But it takes the edge off and allows her to thank people who come over, to appear as though she is able to function. She looks again at the words her daughter wrote. Was Callum the only one she loved? Who had she loved after they broke up? Xavier? Was that relationship already over when she went off to camp?

She slides the book into her own drawer, knowing it will stay there for years, possibly for the rest of her life. The empty pages will never be written on, another note will never be made.

I will never feel any differently to this, she thinks.

Jessie looks terrible whenever she sees her. She would like to put her arms around her now only daughter and tell her that she forgives her, that all is well, but she seems to have run out of the capacity for forgiveness.

And Jessie will not ask anyway. Instead she leaves the room as Lydia enters and they sit in silence over dinners that neither of them eats.

'It's not unusual for a child to keep a secret like this,' Gabriel said to her.

'It's not that,' she replied, 'it's got nothing to do with that. If she felt she needed to keep it a secret, I'm fine with that. She had a right to decide when she wanted to tell me, but I can't help feeling that she would have told Eli – she would have told him the minute she realised. That makes me feel like she doesn't trust me, and if she doesn't trust me, how can I trust her? But the worst thing is that she didn't tell us what she saw. She sneaked away without getting involved, and even after that she could have confessed immediately and maybe it would have meant we found her sooner. Do you understand, Gabriel? What if her keeping her secret about seeing Zoe was the difference between Zoe's life and death?'

'I don't think that's possible,' Gabriel said, but he didn't sound completely certain because no one could be completely certain. Zoe's death had been instant, the medical examiner thinks, which is a relief to Lydia. She had been dead for many hours by the time they found her. That's what the autopsy revealed but it is not completely accurate because everything could only be estimated. Maybe if they had known she was not in her cabin on Friday night and had immediately begun searching, they would have found her and taken her to hospital. Maybe, maybe, maybe.

'All Jessie saw was Zoe walking away from the camp,' Detective Holland has confirmed, which is exactly what Gabriel said. 'She saw she was upset but I guess she didn't want to interfere.'

In her mind, Lydia cannot help recreating the scene, cannot help changing the outcome. Instead of just leaving when she sees her sister, Jessie calls out to Zoe and asks her where she's going, if she's okay. She imagines Zoe confessing about Xavier and Jessie saying, 'But you've never met him before. You don't know who he is. I'll come with you.' Because it is necessary for her to make the scene as realistic as possible, Lydia adds in an argument between the two girls in which Zoe angrily tries to send Jessie away, irritated at her interfering sister, but in the end, she allows Jessie to go with her. In this fantasy Lydia has, either Xavier does turn up and Jessie is there to keep her sister safe, or he doesn't turn up and Jessie is there to comfort her sister. Either way, Zoe is safe. Zoe is alive. Zoe is loved. In the morning, she is able to sit next to her friends and grumble about cold toast and the freezing morning weather. When Lydia closes her eyes and allows this scenario to play out, she is immediately comforted. She hates opening her eyes and admitting that it is only a fantasy – and so she takes another Valium, numbing everything.

This morning the detective called her to discuss her interview with Shayna.

'Shayna did say that there was an argument between the girls just before they turned the lights out.'

'An argument? What were they arguing about?' Lydia asked, and she knows that at the time she asked to simply find something tangible to think about when she thought of her daughter's last hours.

Zoe, Shayna and Becca had been friends for a decade, and there were quite a few arguments over those years. When they were around thirteen there was a terrible fight over Shayna and Zoe scheduling birthday sleepovers on the same weekend. Their birthdays are only a week apart and it shouldn't have been a problem, but there were a whole lot of activities and other parties on at around the same time. Lydia remembers that Zoe and Shayna stopped speaking for at least three days until she and Robyn had a chat on the phone and sorted out a joint party. It shouldn't have been a big deal but the girls were thirteen, and hormones and egos and pride were involved. Lydia knows there have been lots of petty little arguments over the years and she had expected the detective to tell her that the girls had fought over who had eaten more of the junk food they had all brought to share.

'Shayna and Becca got quite angry with how Zoe was treating Leeanne – the other girl in the cabin. Apparently, she was saying some things that were… a bit unkind and Shayna and Becca called her out on it.'

'That's not like Zoe,' Lydia said and then she took a moment to think about it. She wants to believe that her daughter was incapable of being unkind but she knows that Zoe was, like most teenage girls, self-centred and difficult. She had heard her say things to Jessie that could be construed as unkind. She had heard Zoe call her older sister 'frigid' and 'boring', knows that she used to roll her eyes when Gabriel spoke sometimes, forcing him into silence. 'You're being rude, Zoe,' she knows she told her daughter more than a few times over the last six months. She had seemed to see herself in opposition to everyone else. But was Zoe unkind? Was this one more thing she didn't know about her daughter? She hadn't known about her breaking up with Callum or about the mysterious Xavier, who has now disappeared. But in her heart Lydia knows that Zoe's sometimes prickly demeanour was more self-defence than anything. Her daughter hated feeling attacked, just as anyone did.

'Look, I'm aware that girls exaggerate and that it may have just been a small disagreement,' Detective Holland said, dragging her away from her musings, 'but it could explain why Zoe decided to leave the cabin.'

'Really? How bad an argument could it have been?'

'I think that Becca and Shayna were quite angry.'

'But it's not as if they'd never had a fight before – it's never been that often, but when they did fight, everything was always fine in a few days.'

'Perhaps she felt she needed some air, just to clear her head. We do know that when Jessie saw her, she was alone.'

Lydia could feel, as the detective spoke, that the woman believed she was coming to the end of her investigation, and she understood that she didn't want that to happen. She cannot accept that Zoe simply went for a walk and tripped. It doesn't make sense no matter how many explanations she is given.

'But what about the meeting she was supposed to have with Xavier?'

'We are still trying to trace the owner of the account. It's very difficult to get any help from Instagram but there's nothing to indicate that a meeting occurred. It seems to us that she wanted it to happen but that's when Xavier backed off and deleted the account.'

'But why,' Lydia demanded, 'why aren't you asking people if they saw a boy or a man around the camp? Why aren't you asking everyone about him?'

'We are, we have.' The detective sighed. 'No one saw anything. No one knew he existed. We are now wondering if he actually lives overseas. You read those last few lines of messaging. He wasn't keen to meet up. It may be that he realised he had been caught out and deleted his account for that reason. We've been speaking with a psychologist and apparently that's not uncommon behaviour for a catfish from overseas.'

'But she still left the cabin to find him?'

'We're unsure. The end of the messaging leaves it pretty open, as you saw. As I said, she may have left the cabin just to get some air after the argument.'

'I spoke to Callum,' she said impulsively. 'I called him to ask why they'd broken up and he was… weird.'

'What do you mean by weird?'

'I don't… It felt like he was hiding something from me, like he didn't want to talk to me. Maybe you should question him again.'

'We have questioned him twice. He didn't know who she was speaking to over Instagram and he wasn't anywhere near the camp on Friday night. He was at home with three other year twelve students. We have confirmed this with all of them and their parents. He was here in Sydney all of Friday night.'

'How do you know it was all of Friday night? Maybe he left when everyone else in his house was asleep…'

'We don't feel that Callum had anything to do with what happened. He had some other girls over on Friday night. I think he was just uncomfortable speaking to you. We cannot question him again without a legitimate reason.'

Lydia couldn't believe what she was hearing. 'That can't be…' But she didn't have the energy to continue the conversation. 'Promise me you'll keep looking into this,' she said instead.

'We are still trying to find Xavier. We have our best tech people on it. I promise.'

After she hung up the phone, Lydia realised that the detective had not promised to never give up on figuring out why her daughter had been found in the middle of the bush when she should have been safely in her sleeping bag.

It feels as though the police are losing interest in finding any answers beyond the idea that Zoe is responsible for her own death.

The door to her bedroom opens and Gabriel comes in carrying a mug. The thought of more tea turns Lydia's stomach but she gives him a small smile anyway. He is trying and he is only going into work if people desperately need to see him. She is glad he's here but every day she still wishes for Eli as hard as she wishes that Zoe was still here. Every day, she can't help feeling guilty about that.

'It's not tea,' he says. 'It's hot chocolate with a bit of whisky. I thought you might want to taste something different.'

Lydia accepts the mug from him, sits up and takes a sip. 'Thanks,' she says even though it tastes of nothing to her. Everything tastes like nothing to her these days. 'Has everyone gone?'

'They have. Jessie has gone to her room to study. I took her some lunch but she doesn't seem to be eating. I'm worried about her, Lydia. I think she has real affection for this woman and I don't think she's heard from her. I asked her about deferring the exams again but she doesn't want to and she seems… to not be coping.'

'I want to go to her, Gabriel, believe me I do, but I just don't know how to start the conversation. I'm not sure I even have the energy right now. I just need time.'

Gabriel opens his mouth and she braces herself for his next words. He has no right to criticise her parenting. He has not lost a child and been betrayed by another. What if Jessie could have saved her sister? What if?

She leans back on her pillow as tears trickle down her cheeks. Jessie is in terrible pain. They all are but Lydia cannot bring herself to reach out to her daughter – she is trapped, surrounded by her grief and her anger. The tears come faster as her nose begins to run.

Gabriel leans forward and wraps his arms around her. He holds her until she pushes him a little so she can sit up and get a tissue.

'I'm fine,' she says. 'I'm just so tired.'

He stands up. 'I can only imagine how exhausted you must be.'

'Thanks for the hot chocolate. I think I may just try to sleep a bit,' she says.

'I'll leave you to get some rest. Just shout if you need me.'

Once he's gone and the door to her bedroom is closed, Lydia closes her eyes and sets the scene once more. Jessie is walking towards her car on Friday night when she sees her sister heading away from camp…

CHAPTER TWENTY-TWO

Shayna

You have to tell me what happened.

Becca texted me that because I've been avoiding speaking to her about my conversation with the police last Thursday. But she won't be put off any longer. I don't want to talk about it but then I read a thread on Instagram that said that someone saw the police at my house and that I'd been arrested for killing Zoe, which should be ridiculous enough for me to laugh at, but it's not completely ridiculous and that's the worst thing. It's not completely ridiculous.

It was a really weird experience because I told them some stuff that happened – some stuff that we said we weren't going to talk about.

What? What did you tell them??????

Okay, firstly, you can't get mad at me. I had to tell them the truth, okay? After her funeral I was just so... I don't even know how to describe it. I just wanted to tell them everything because I felt like they were going to find out anyway.

WHAT DID YOU TELL THEM??????

I DIDN'T TELL THEM ABOUT YOU AND CALLUM. OKAY!!!!

I am in my room, sitting at my desk because I was trying to start the English assignment even though I haven't managed to get very far. It's only the first day of the school holidays and we had planned – Zoe, Becca and I – to spend the day shopping and getting lunch in the city. It feels like those plans were made a lifetime ago and like I was a different person then, which I suppose I was.

I hate it when Becca yells at me. She's usually pretty calm and even-tempered but I can feel how angry she is. I don't care. I had to do what was best for me. That's what my mum said to me as we were making tea in the kitchen for the two detectives who came over late on Thursday, after Zoe's funeral.

'What if there's some stuff I haven't told them?' I whispered to her desperately, and I saw this look of, like, shock and fear cross her face.

'What could you not have told them?'

'Just… it wasn't exactly a nice night. We didn't really all just go to sleep.'

Mum ran her hands through her hair. 'Tell them the truth, Shayna.'

'But Becca and I agreed to keep quiet about some stuff that happened.'

'I wish you would have talked to me about this before, but it's too late now. Tell them the truth. You have to do what's best for you. If you're carrying around a lie about what went on that night, you won't survive it. I'm going to be right next to you and I won't leave your side, and whatever happens, Dad and I are here for you.'

So what exactly did you tell them then?

Becca will just have to cope with what I told them and hopefully she'll tell them what she knows. She doesn't know all of it.

The stuff about her and Callum had nothing to do with what happened afterwards. It was the catalyst for everything, yes. Becca's confession did set everything in motion, but it was just this tiny spark that turned into a great flame because of everything that had happened between the three of us.

Two of the detectives came to interview me this time. The woman detective has this way of looking at you, like she can see all your secrets, and the guy – you know the one we both spoke to on Sunday?

Yeah.

Well, he was there too. Mum and I made them tea and then we all sat down on the sofa and, like, just looked at each other in silence for a moment, and I think that maybe they were doing that on purpose so that I would just tell them everything. I wasn't going to, Becca. I swear I wasn't going to say anything about the fight we had and the things we said, but I haven't been able to stop thinking about it, not even for five minutes.

Me too.

The woman detective seemed to know that there was something I had to say because she straight up asked me, 'Is there something else you'd like to tell us about Friday night?'

How would she know anything? Who would have talked? I didn't say anything.

I know you didn't but maybe Leeanne did. I know that you two have been talking and that's good but we don't really know her that well. Maybe she felt she had to say something.

Leeanne wouldn't have said anything. She is 100% trustworthy.

You don't know her that well.

I know her as well as I know you apparently because I thought you would never tell anyone about what happened after we agreed not to talk about it. No more excuses. I need to know what you said to them.

I get up from my desk and look out of my bedroom window into the garden below. It rained last night and this morning, but now the sun has come out, the grass is glinting in the light and I can see little droplets of water on the leaves of the tree that grows near my window. It's all so beautiful that I feel like I want to cry. I have been crying since last Thursday whenever I think about Zoe and everything that happened. I think it's the guilt.

I pick up my phone and lie down on my bed because I have to get this part of the story told.

I told them about the fight, about everything that we said to her and what she said to us and to Leeanne, leaving out the stuff about Callum.

Do you think Leeanne will tell them about the Callum stuff? No, wait – she won't. I think we can trust Leeanne to keep quiet about some stuff. She's really smart.

I hope so. I told them we had an argument with her because she was being really nasty to Leeanne and then things got a little out of control and we, I, told her we weren't going to go travelling with her after year twelve.

So, what did they say? Did they say that it's our fault that she left the cabin? It can't be our fault. She was being nasty and we called her on it. How can we be blamed because she left and killed herself?

I take a deep breath and chew on my bottom lip for a bit until it starts to hurt. Becca is my best friend now. Is Becca my best friend? What will she be to me when she knows what went on between me and Zoe after she left the cabin?

Because I knew she left the cabin.

I heard her get up. I heard her get dressed. And then when she left, I pulled on my parka and I followed her outside.

I stare at my phone for a minute, wishing I could just put it down and do something else, but Becca hasn't left me alone and I know she's not likely to until I tell her everything.

Okay, there's some stuff that you don't know, and I'm going to tell you but you have to promise that you'll keep it to yourself.

I promise. Of course, I promise and I promise like I promise, not like you promise when you promise and then tell everything anyway. My mum is going to be completely pissed at me if she hears what happened. She always tells me to turn the other cheek. But I was really tired of doing that with Zoe, really tired.

Yeah, well, we didn't do that, and after we all went to sleep, I heard her get up. That's the second part that I didn't tell the police at first – that's what I was keeping to myself. I didn't tell anyone until last Thursday after the funeral and now the police know it as well.

You heard her get up??????

Yeah. At first, I thought she was going to the bathroom. I mean, I couldn't see that she was getting dressed. I just heard her moving around, and when she opened the door, I slid out of my sleeping bag and followed her out.

Why??????

I was still really angry at her. I felt like she hadn't really understood how awful she was being. I wanted to, I don't know, just talk to her quietly, I guess, and try and get her to understand because I couldn't sleep because I thought she didn't really care.

What did you say to her?

I caught up with her as she was walking towards the path that leads to that clearing – you know, where we were supposed to have the bonfire on Saturday night? I was walking quickly but she didn't hear me and I touched her on the shoulder and she turned around and said, 'You scared the shit out of me.' I asked her where she was going and she smiled and started to tell me and then it was like she remembered we'd had a fight and she said, 'What do you care? You hate me.'

But we didn't hate her. We were just mad at her.

I told her that. And then I tried to explain why we didn't like it when she attacked other girls. I told her that you and I had been talking about how mean she'd been to everyone else for a long time and that she needed to start thinking about someone other than herself for once.

I don't tell Becca that I was almost grateful that things had flared up. I wanted to yell at Zoe. She didn't just hurt other girls' feelings. She made me feel awful about myself a lot of the time as well. On Friday afternoon when we all went back to our cabins to unpack, I showed her my new top.

'Try it on,' she said and I did. At home I had tried the top on and looked at myself in the mirror and thought, *That looks good.*

But Zoe looked at me for a moment and then she shook her head. 'That makes your arms look fat,' she said.

And just like that, any confidence I had in the way the top looked on me just disappeared. I hated that she could do that to me with just a little comment or a look. I hated that she could make me question myself and feel bad about the way I looked. It's hard enough for me to not hate myself every time I look in the mirror, and Zoe knew that because most of us struggle with not looking like movie stars and models, but she still said stuff like that to me when she should have just been kind.

'No, it doesn't,' Becca said. 'Stop being such a bitch, Zoe.'

'Oh my God, I'm joking. You know I'm joking, right, Shayna?'

I kind of giggled when she said that and nodded like I did know she was joking but I don't really think she was, and I felt ugly and stupid for bringing the top. And I was angry. I was really looking forward to Sunday night and I knew that I would leave the cabin worrying about how I looked and that I wouldn't have the guts to talk to Michael or even look at him, and I hated her then. I really hated her. So, when she attacked Leeanne, I jumped right in. I'd been waiting for a chance to have a go at Zoe. I think I'd been waiting for that for months. But that is not something I will ever share with anyone; that's something I will carry with me forever.

What else did you say, Shayna? What did you do?

I told her again that Callum was no big deal and she could be mad at you for a bit but that she had to understand that you made a mistake. I wanted her to say she understood and that she was going to try and be a better person.

Yeah, I guess I expected too much. She told me that I was a complete wuss and that I was going to die a virgin and she didn't care at all that you and I thought that she was a bitch because we were idiots, and if we wanted to be friends with Leeanne, then we could be. And she said that anyone who would kiss someone else's boyfriend wasn't a real friend and that I wasn't a real friend because I was defending you.

I watch the three little dots at the bottom of the screen as I wait for Becca to reply. Even though I was mad at Zoe, I understood why she was angry at me as well, and of course I understood why she was mad at Becca. When we were twelve, we made a pact with each other to never crush on each other's boyfriends or to even look at a boy that we knew one of us liked. So, I understood why she was so angry at Becca – it had been the wrong thing to do. But it wasn't like she'd never flirted with boys Becca and I liked. She made a habit of it, in fact, so Zoe broke the pact first.

She was really mad at us. You should have left her alone. What did you say to her after that?

I got so mad that I shoved her and I told her she was a bitch and then I turned around and I went back to the cabin.

You shoved her?? Was she hurt? Did you shove her hard? What are you trying to tell me, Shayna???

That's it, that's everything. I shoved her and she fell down but she was fine. We were nowhere near where they found her. Nowhere

*near it. She was absolutely fine even though she was upset. I heard
her start crying but I didn't want to talk to her anymore so I just
went back to bed.*

I did lie awake in my bunk after that because I wanted to see
when she came back but I must have fallen asleep eventually. I
wonder now if I hadn't fallen asleep, if I would have gotten up
again to go and look for her, but I know that I probably wouldn't
have. Zoe has a way – Zoe *had* a way – of going straight for your
insecurities. I was worried that I would never have a serious
boyfriend because I haven't really ever had one. I've only kissed,
like, two boys. It shouldn't matter to me anymore but it still kind
of does, and when Zoe said that stuff, it really, really hurt. And
also, it felt like I was never going to get through to her. Zoe was
going to be Zoe, no matter what we said to her.

After I send this last message, Becca doesn't reply. I lie on my
bed and hold my phone and I wait and wait and wait. I just know
that she hates me now as well. I haven't even told her what the
police said afterwards but I have a feeling she won't want to hear
from me ever again. I bet when I go back to school next term,
I'll have no friends at all. I send another message, desperate to be
heard, to be forgiven.

*It was wrong to go after her and to shove her but that's all that
happened. Please tell me you believe me when I say that's all that
happened.*

My phone is silent. I start to cry, but I try to do it quietly so
my mum, who is downstairs making dinner, doesn't hear me.

Finally, after about twenty minutes, Becca replies. I almost don't
want to read the message. If she says she never wants to speak to
me again, I think I would understand her choice. There's a whole
lot of ugly inside me that made me shove my friend instead of

just talk to her and explain. I wouldn't want to be friends with me either. My finger shakes a little as I go to tap my screen.

Listen, Shayna – you can't feel bad about that. You were angry. I get why you were angry. I think that you and I have kind of been angry with Zoe for a long time now. You probably shouldn't have pushed her and then left her but believe me when I say this: she would have done the same thing to you. She would have happily left you crying. You couldn't have known that she was going to run off into the bush and die. There must have been a whole lot of other stuff going on in her life. We were good friends to her – at least, we tried to be but she could be so nasty sometimes. YOU DON'T HAVE ANYTHING TO FEEL GUILTY FOR. If anyone should feel bad, it's me because of what I did with Callum. And I do feel bad about that. I do and I shouldn't have told her about it but it felt like we were pushed into everything that happened that night. I think we have to just let it go now. There's nothing else to do. You've told the police and I believe that's all you can do. Of course I believe you. I've known you since we were seven years old. I believe you.

I'm so relieved I feel like I might vomit. I couldn't have coped with losing Becca, not at all. I wasn't sure if I was going to tell her about the other stuff the police told me but I assume that when they speak to her again, they'll ask her the same questions they asked me.

The police asked me some other stuff as well, some stuff that they will probably ask you too.

What?

Apparently, Zoe had been messaging some guy – they think it was a guy, like, as in our age but he could have been a man.

No way.

Yeah. He deleted his account but they wanted to know if she had ever talked about someone named Xavier. She didn't, did she? I feel like I might have heard that name before but I don't know where. Does it seem familiar to you?

No, but it would explain something I heard.

What?

After the funeral, Leeanne came back here for a sleepover because we didn't want to be alone and she told me that her brother told her that Zoe and Callum broke up like weeks ago. Apparently, Zoe was talking to some guy on the internet.

But why didn't Zoe tell us? Why was it a secret? How could she have broken up with Callum and not told us? We're her best friends!! I mean we were her best friends.

I don't know Shay, I really don't. She was acting kind of weird in the last few weeks. Maybe she cheated on Callum with whoever this guy was. Maybe there was something sketchy about him.

Why didn't you tell me this before?

I've been texting you every day since the funeral… You haven't replied!!

Fair enough. All this stuff. I feel like we never knew her at all.

Yeah. People are strange. I never thought I would get on with Leeanne but I do. I never thought I would be the kind of person to kiss someone else's boyfriend but I did it – I was drunk but still. Everything that's happened this year has made me feel like I have no idea about anything, no control over anything. My mother says I should see a psychologist.

It might be nice to have someone to talk to. Now that you know she and Callum weren't together… do you think the two of you will…?

No, definitely not! He wasn't exactly a good boyfriend, was he? And I'm not sure how nice he is. I think he gets angry if he feels like no one is paying attention to him.

What do you mean?

When we were together at that party, he said that Zoe would be sorry for just leaving him alone when none of his friends were there. I thought that meant he was going to tell her about us and I begged him not to. He said he wouldn't and he obviously didn't but he seemed more angry than drunk, like he wanted to cause trouble because she had left him alone. Do you know what I mean?

Kind of. It doesn't matter anymore anyway. I have to go now and get some work done. I'll text you tomorrow, okay?

KK.

What I don't tell Becca, and what I didn't say to the detectives, is that I have been playing out this scenario in my head ever since it happened.

I push Zoe down and she calls me a bitch. I walk away but then I turn around again and I say, 'I don't want to fight, Zoe. You're my best friend and I'm sorry I got angry. Can we just pretend it never happened?'

And in my head, she says yes and she comes back to the cabin and we both go to sleep. In the morning, she's a bit bitchy but by the afternoon we're all friends again. Just like it never happened. But no matter how many times I replay the scene, I can't change reality. And that's the thing: it was my fault. I shouted at my best friend and shoved her and left her crying and I didn't stop to think about what she was going through because all I was thinking about was myself.

I could have stopped her from killing herself or from running off into the bush and falling and killing herself. I could have stopped her but I didn't.

I am hungry again; a gnawing, hollow feeling fills me up and I reach under my bed for the box of muesli bars I've taken from the kitchen. I open one up and shove it into my mouth, tasting the honey and the oats and feeling the nuts crunch against my teeth. I could have saved her. I let her die.

I think about the fact that she was messaging some guy – some guy other than Callum. I wonder how mad he would have been that she broke up with him. I wonder what he would have done to make sure she was sorry about it. I wonder why she never said anything to us. She would usually be the first person to tell us.

She told us that when they first started dating, Callum was watching who she talked to on Instagram.

'He's jealous of everyone I speak to,' she said, giggling. 'But I'm not going to let him tell me who I can and cannot talk to.'

'And what if he talks to someone you don't want him talking to?'

'I told him that's not allowed.' She laughed then.

'You can't do that, Zoe,' said Becca, 'it's a double standard.'

'So what?' She shrugged. 'If he wants to be with me, he'll do what I say. It's not like I'm going to cheat on him with some cute boy I meet on Instagram. I hardly know most of the people who comment on my pictures. It's just for fun. And I know he likes me too much to jeopardise what we have.'

But she seems to have done just that. She dumped him for a boy she met on Instagram. He must have been really mad. I realise that I'm just deflecting by thinking about him and how hurt he must have been. What happened to Zoe was my fault and she would have been fine if we hadn't yelled at her, if I hadn't gone after her and if I'd apologised and made her come back to the cabin. She would have been fine but now she's gone and it's no one's fault but mine.

I lie down on my bed and let my head sink into my pillow. I'm so tired. I'm tired of the guilt, of thinking about Zoe and what happened. I'm tired of thinking about anything. I really just want to get on with the rest of my life.

Because I still have a life to get on with. I still have a life.

CHAPTER TWENTY-THREE

Bernadette

I am in shock. That is the only way I can describe my reaction to what just happened.

The school holidays have begun. It's only Monday and the next term starts in two weeks. But I will not be returning to school. I will never be returning to school.

'That's how those who give their all are rewarded,' I tell Oliver. He looks up at me with his beautiful brown eyes. He is sitting on my lap while I brush him. The movement of the brush through his soft, silky hair is soothing for both of us. He is very calm. Usually when I walk in the door there is lots of jumping and running and fetching of toys. But today he just climbed onto my lap and sat there as though he is aware of the utter despair I am in.

I should have taken a union lawyer to the board meeting. I realise I can still call the union but I don't feel it will do any good. Even if I am reinstated, I cannot imagine that I will be able to perform to my full capabilities. I do not want to be teaching at a school where I am not wanted, where sidelong glances and sniggering behind hands occur as I walk by.

I went to the emergency board meeting alone. I thought all I needed to do was to remind them all what a valuable member of the school I was. The whole board was there, all looking serious in their suits. I know they will all have left the meeting to go to their day jobs. I am sure that right now they are all back at their desks in their fancy offices, congratulating themselves on a job well done. They will simply get on with their lives even though they have just devastated mine.

I dressed carefully this morning, choosing a navy-blue dress that George often compliments me on. I only wear it for special occasions like end-of-year assemblies, where I sit onstage as the head of English for the school and the year eleven patron.

At the end of last year, I was gifted with a large bunch of flowers for twenty-five years of service to the school. There was a montage of photographs, beginning with my first year as a year eight English teacher.

I must admit that I laughed along with the girls as I watched myself age from thirty-seven to sixty-two. On my first day I teamed a denim skirt with a denim blouse, thinking I looked smart. It was funny to see my hair, puffed up with hairspray and still its original chestnut-brown colour. As I watched I realised that I had forgotten so many of the activities that I had been involved in with the girls. There I was, directing the end-of-year school play in only my second year at the school and holding up the starter's pistol to begin the cross-country race, visiting a homeless shelter with my year twelve class and dancing with a group of students at the dance marathon they held one year. I have been involved in every aspect of the school. I have never had a family to claim my time and so I have always volunteered for everything. I enjoyed my time with the girls. I loved watching them grow and then seeing who they became after they left the school. I have always believed that there are some teachers who take up the profession because they feel it is an easy job with a lot of holiday time or because they believe they can better take care of their families on school hours or because they simply couldn't get into anything else at university, but that has never been the case for me.

I remember, at seven, visiting my father's sister for a Sunday lunch and finding myself somehow taking care of three younger cousins belonging to my other aunts and uncles. I had no idea what to do with them until I hit on the idea of playing teacher. They had not yet attended school and I was amazed at how well they listened as I sat them all down and told them we were going to learn about shapes and colours. I am sure I didn't conduct the lesson for more than twenty minutes before lunch was ready to be served but I knew from that day that all I wanted to be was a teacher. My father tried to encourage me to study law. 'It may be that you never marry, Bernadette. You need to be able to financially support yourself without the benefit of a husband.'

But my passion was for teaching, and my father understood. 'You'll have to be careful with your money, but you always were a conservative child.'

I have been careful with my money. I have a nice cushion of savings so that I need never work again but that is not the point. The point is that teaching is – or was – my life.

At the end of the presentation to celebrate my twenty-five years of service to the school, the new head girl, Amy Lavelle, made a lovely speech about how I had been part of the formative years of many successful young women. 'There are lawyers, doctors, engineers and teachers today who never gave up on their dreams because Bernadette Fischer never accepted excuses and because by the time they left high school, her mantra had become their mantra: "Now that you know where you went wrong, what are you going to do about it?" Thank you, Ms Fischer, for never letting the young women in your care accept failure.'

It was a beautiful speech, and even as I sat outside the boardroom, I remembered Amy's words and found myself smiling. I wouldn't have smiled if I had known that I was walking into an ambush. That is the only way to describe it. It would have felt no different if the members of the board had been hiding and jumped out to surprise me with guns trained at my head.

They kept me waiting for at least fifteen minutes before they called me in and I let my mind wander as I breathed in the smell of disinfectant and listened to the drone of machines. The school is undergoing a deep clean and tidy-up like it does every holiday. I have always found it soothing to be at school during the holidays with only the cleaners for company. It feels like they are making over the school and I am making over my lesson plans and soon everything will be fresh and new. But I will never have that feeling again.

'We're ready for you, Bernadette,' George said.

I jumped a little. I hadn't realised he had opened the door. My heart began to hammer in my chest but I stood up straight and held my head up high.

I know where I went wrong. I had planned to assure the board that I would never make such a mistake again. I had a whole speech prepared about new procedures I would put in place for the camp next year, and I was also going to suggest moving it to a new location – somewhere with a fence around the property would be ideal.

Inside, all six of them were seated at the large mahogany oval table surrounded by plush, upholstered velvet chairs in sea-green.

George pointed to a chair and I sat down.

'Hello, Annette,' I greeted Dr Annette Patterson, whom I taught in 1997. Annette nodded her hello and the others all nodded as well but I wasn't going to let them forget that I knew them all.

'Hello, Paul,' I said to Paul Wong, a real-estate tycoon whose daughters are in years ten and seven.

'Hello, Elizabeth,' I said to Elizabeth Green, who is a year older than me and a retired circuit court judge.

'Hello, Aaron,' I continued to Aaron Brown, who is in furniture and was, I know, responsible for the gift of the boardroom table five years ago.

'Hello, Lisa,' I said to Lisa Spencer, who is a former Olympic runner. She never won any races but she did compete, and it's my motto to never dissuade someone from trying, even if they are going to fail.

And lastly there was Sofia, who is nearly eighty and hard of hearing. She and I nodded at each other. I don't think Sofia really knows what goes on at these meetings but she does enjoy coming to them, I'm told. They always have tea and biscuits afterwards, and the Hayward Gymnasium that was built twenty years ago is named in honour of her father and her very generous contributions to the school.

I saw the look of irritation that flicked across George's face and then I looked closely at everyone else. Their faces were neutral, no smiles, no sympathy, just blank, and I knew before I even began my little speech that I was doomed, that I had already lost my job.

I gave it anyway. And they listened politely as I listed my achievements, as I accepted that I should have kept a closer eye on a vulnerable student, as I detailed all the changes I would make for future camps.

And then, at the end, they allowed me a moment of silence. I could feel sweat beading on my upper lip. I sat up straighter, raised my chin higher.

'You cannot fire me for this, George. I know my rights. I will go to the union. I have not been charged with anything.'

'Bernadette,' he said sadly, his watery blue eyes filled with sympathy, 'I am aware that this could turn into a protracted legal battle. I am aware that you haven't been charged with anything and even that you could not have anticipated Zoe leaving the cabin.'

'Exactly,' I said, feeling hope flare inside me. I imagined that perhaps they were going to ask me to take long service leave for a couple of terms. I wouldn't have minded that. I would have used the time to visit the Egyptian pyramids, something I have always dreamed of doing.

'But here is the thing, Bernadette. We have had calls – not just from a few parents, but from at least a hundred parents – signalling their lack of faith in you and in the school because of you. It is not a question of whether or not you may be exonerated in the end;

it is that we don't feel the parent body will accept your presence at the school any longer.'

'And what about Paula? She was with me at the camp. We were both responsible for those girls.'

'Paula was not the senior teacher at camp. You were. Paula has, at this stage, requested a leave of absence to decide what to do. I have to say that she has been emotionally affected by this to the extreme. She may very well decide not to come back to teaching. Should she wish to return, we will then decide what to do.'

'I can do the same thing,' I said desperately, hating how eager to please I sounded. 'I can take long service leave for a couple of terms and then come back.'

George sighed and joined his hands together as though he were praying. 'Please, Bernadette, I am begging you not to drag us through what will surely be a long and expensive battle. The parent body has spoken. Many are threatening to pull their students out of the school. We are a private school and we cannot survive the loss of twenty or more students. We need you to resign so that you may leave with your dignity. I know that is important to you. You are so close to retirement anyway. I'm asking you to help us get the school through this tragedy.'

I looked around the table and noted that all the board members were nodding, even Sofia. I wanted to cry, but of course I am not one for public displays of emotion.

I stood up and felt my chin lift even higher as I squeezed my hands into fists, forcing my short nails to push into my palms so that I would maintain a dignified presence.

'I understand what you are saying. I cannot believe that you are allowing the fickleness of parents to dictate who you can and cannot employ. Believe me when I say that if you cave into them on this, more will follow. They will lead you around by the nose, George.' As I said this, I looked at all the board members one by one. I am pleased to say that they, at least, had the grace to drop their heads. I hope they were ashamed.

'I will take early retirement,' I said, making sure to keep my voice strong and forceful, 'but I will only do it to protect the other girls at the school from a difficult and divisive lawsuit. I have no wish to distract students from their studies – especially the girls in their final year – with months of salacious gossip, which will surely come about if I sue the school. But I have to say that I am ashamed of all of you on the board and of you, George. I am one of the best teachers you've ever had and you all know it.'

'Bernadette—' George began, but I did what I have seen the girls at the school do to each other when they have no desire to listen. I lifted my hand. It almost made me laugh to see how he paled. I had said my piece and I walked out of the boardroom, head held high.

The door to my classroom was thankfully open, although it made me realise, once again, that I had had no chance of keeping my job. They knew I would want to collect the things I had left in my desk. Two empty cardboard boxes had been placed helpfully on the floor next to my desk. I nearly lost myself then, but I held on. I held on right until I pulled out of the school parking lot and turned onto the road. And then I let the tears fall.

I allowed myself a strong whisky when I returned home as anger replaced despair but I am back to despair again. There is nothing I can do about this.

And so here I am. Jobless. After forty years of teaching I have been discarded. I am on the scrap heap.

I will not even bother trying to find another job. The spectre of this child's death will follow me for the rest of my existence.

I know that I could spend the rest of my life travelling, taking in the world, enjoying the rest of my years. I have enough money. I own this apartment with no mortgage. I have never lived a very big life and I did inherit a small amount from my parents. I have to confess that last year, on a particularly bad day when none of the girls seemed to be listening and I felt that I was losing the ability to get through to them, I contemplated early retirement. But that would have been on my terms. That would have been my choice. I hate that the choice has been taken from me, that there has not been a fitting goodbye to my decades-long teaching career. I hate it and I am humiliated by it. Deeply, deeply humiliated.

I have no desire to travel now. I have no desire to do anything. I just want this all to be over.

I pick Oliver up and put him in his dog bed. He is fast asleep now and simply curls up tighter, letting out a little snore.

I stand up, filled with a renewed sense of purpose.

The first thing I do is write two notes.

Henry and I have lived next door to each other in this apartment complex for twenty years so I know I can trust him. At first it was him and his wife Ida who were my neighbours, but three years ago, Ida died, leaving just Henry. We don't speak often but I've sometimes thought that he would like more of a chat. But I have always been so busy.

Dear Henry,

Would you mind popping over and feeding Oliver his dinner tonight? I will be out late. His food is on the counter. You know what to do.

Many thanks,
Bernadette

It doesn't take me long to slip the note under Henry's door. He and I exchanged keys many years ago so we could help each other out, and I have, on occasion, asked him to feed Oliver. He took care of him for me when I was on camp. I know they get along. Henry will return from dinner with friends at around seven o'clock. It is three now. Ample time. I know he will have dinner with them tonight because Henry is like me in that way. He is very fond of routine. On a Monday he plays bowls with a group of four other gentlemen and then they have an early dinner at the club.

The second note I will leave on the coffee table.

Dear Henry,

Please forgive me for choosing you to find me. I hope you are not terribly shocked and I feel you will know what to do because of your medical training. I know we spoke about the incident on camp. I can only tell you that none of it was my fault. But in a world ruled by social media and political correctness, it seems that fault is not important. The parents at the school have demanded a sacrifice. And today I was told that I would be the sacrificial lamb. I have lost my job because of what happened. I am aware that you may not understand my choice. But you chose to retire from medicine, and you had Ida and now you still have your daughter and grandchild. I have Oliver but even he is not enough. I need a purpose in my life, a reason to get up in the morning, and that reason has been wrenched from me. Brutally wrenched from me. I see no point in going on. Please don't think me a terrible coward. Please take care of Oliver. I know you two will be great friends.

I pour myself a generous whisky and call the detective who interviewed me.

'Lucas Gold,' he answers.

'Detective Gold, this is Bernadette Fischer.'

'Good afternoon, Ms Fischer.'

'I need to tell you that there was something I left out, something I didn't say because I thought… well, I just didn't tell you.'

'Yes,' he says cautiously.

'I was outside at around midnight. I needed the bathroom.' He doesn't need to know about the cigarette. 'And I saw Zoe. I saw her walking away from her cabin.'

'You did? Why didn't you stop her? Why haven't you mentioned this before?'

'I am not going to get into that, Detective Gold. I am only going to tell you that I saw her friend Shayna come out of the cabin as well. They argued and Shayna pushed Zoe down.'

'What were they arguing about?'

'I have no idea – they were whispering.'

'Yes, I understand. We do have that information, Ms Fischer. We have spoken to Shayna.'

'Fine, but that's not the point. The point is that Zoe got up and walked off after that in the direction of the bush and then someone else… someone else… someone else followed her.'

'Who?'

I tell him my suspicions as to whom the person might be. It was dark, of course, but I do have my suspicions.

This is perhaps my greatest failure of all. This is why some part of me knows that I deserved to lose my job. This is where I should have stepped in but I was tired. I wanted to sleep and forget all about Zoe Bloom, and the truth is that I didn't care what she was doing out at midnight. Girls did leave their cabins after dark. They had done so for years on camp. They left their cabins and went to the clearing and spent time outside in the dark. I knew it happened and I knew that they usually all made it safely back to their beds, excited that they had flouted the rules. But Zoe was different. She wasn't just going to have a little meeting with friends. Something else was going on and I should have stopped her and checked on her, especially after I saw who had followed her towards the clearing. I should have stopped her but I didn't.

And so, the choice I have made is not just because I lost my job. It is also because I believe I could have prevented what happened.

'Okay, Ms Fischer, you need to come back into the police station and give a statement. We need to go over this again so we have the full story.'

'Absolutely. I am with a sick friend at the moment. Would tomorrow morning do?'

'I would prefer it if you came now or I could come to you.'

'No, that won't be possible, I'm afraid. You see, my friend doesn't have long and she needs her peace. I will be there at nine tomorrow morning, Detective. I will be happy to go over what I saw as many times as you need me to.'

'Okay… okay, thanks, I'll see you then.' He sounds unsure but this is not a murder investigation after all. Perhaps it should be but right now it's not.

I should have gone to see if Zoe was okay. I should have taken her back to her cabin and made sure that everything there was fine. I should have… yet I didn't. I was done with Zoe Bloom for the day. And now I have paid for that breach of duty. I have paid for it with everything that mattered to me.

I pour yet another glass of whisky. I take a sip of the amber liquid, enjoying the mellow burn as I swallow it along with the first pill.

I thought these pills would be out of date. My doctor prescribed them last year when I told him I was having trouble sleeping. I never took them, of course. I don't believe in that nonsense. I knew it was mind over matter. But I am glad to have them now. Glad that they are still fine to use. I feel bad about Henry finding me. I feel bad about not going to talk to Zoe. I feel bad about leaving Oliver behind. Dear little Oliver. And I feel terrible about leaving all my girls, some of whom are about to begin their important final exams, but I have been made to leave them anyway – and while they would have been able to contact me, it's not the same as standing in front of them in the classroom.

There is no use in feeling bad.

I take another sip and another pill and I open up my dog-eared copy of *Jane Eyre*. I cannot think of a better author than Charlotte Brontë to see me out.

I turn to the first page. 'There was no possibility of taking a walk that day.' I read the beloved first line and know that, for me, there is no possibility of taking a walk ever again.

CHAPTER TWENTY-FOUR

Tuesday – Ten Days Since the Accident

Jessie

Jessie walks out of the pathology exam drained, exhausted and in complete despair. There is no way she has passed. Even now she can think of at least six mistakes she made in labelling the nervous system, which she's known how to do since first year. She doesn't know how she could have messed up like that – she knows her stuff. She has always known her stuff. She takes out her phone and logs into her university account to book an appointment with the dean of medical science. She should have pulled out of the exams. But somehow, she just didn't, and in truth the thought of having to leave the house, of needing to get to university, was better than the thought of staying home, where her mother's grief hangs heavy in the air. Her mother's grief and her mother's hurt feelings at what she considers Jessie's betrayal.

Jessie doesn't want to but she can't help but think about her father; she can't help wishing he was here. He would have known how to speak to her mother. Gabriel is trying, he really is, but to Jessie, her mother seems on the brink of madness.

Her stepfather came into her room last night. He knocked quietly and then stood in the doorway, looking uncomfortable, and for the first time in the whole messy thing that was now her life, she felt truly sorry for him. Even though he had been married to her mother for the past ten years, Jessie and Zoe had never quite accepted him as a father. And now here he was with his whole life falling apart because of two girls who hadn't wanted him in their mother's life in the first place.

Jessie smiled at him; a small smile but it was all she could manage.

'I just wanted to wish you luck for tomorrow,' he said. 'I know it's going to be really difficult, but even if you don't get what you need, you can always retake the exams – I know I did once or twice and I have a lot of friends who are doctors who also had life get in the way.'

'Huh,' Jessie snorted, 'that's an interesting way to describe it – life getting in the way.'

Gabriel lifted his hands in the air. 'I have no idea what else to say. It's a mess, but things will get better. They always do. It's a case of "this too shall pass".'

'It doesn't feel like it will.'

'I imagine not… but, Jessie, I am here if you need to talk. Your mother will find herself again and find a way forward, but until then, you can lean on me. I'm not your father – I know that – but you can lean on me.'

Jessie nodded. 'Thanks, Gabriel.'

He left then, knowing that there was nothing more to say. No one had anything left to say.

She walks away from the exam hall quickly, not wanting to get caught up in the usual debriefing. In her car she rests her head on the steering wheel, unsure if she has the energy to drive home. A rap on her window startles her and she jumps. When she sees it's Paula, she cannot help smiling even though she is angry, furious, with her because she has ignored her for the last nine days. As her whole life fell apart after her sister's death and her confession, Paula has simply ignored her pleas. And yet Jessie is delighted to see her. She is sure that this is what true love looks like, that this is what it feels like.

She climbs out of the car and opens her arms for a hug because her body needs to touch Paula, to be held by her. But Paula steps back, away from her, looks over her shoulder as though scared of being seen with Jessie.

Jessie feels a stone settle in her stomach.

'Hey,' Paula says softly. She is wearing a long skirt, brown and gold with fringing on the hem. A matching light brown top complements her eyes.

'You look nice,' says Jessie.

Paula smiles. 'Thanks... You look... tired.'

'How did you know where to find me?'

'We discussed your schedule, remember? I was going to take you to a late lunch after the exam because it's school holidays. We were going to eat at that Italian place...'

Jessie looks down at her sneakers, noting that one of her shoelaces is undone. 'Are you still going to take me out?'

'No, love... No, Jess. I came to... to say goodbye and,' she continues quickly, as though she is delivering good news instead of bad, 'I also came to tell you that I've told the police that we met up at the camp that Friday night. It's all getting a bit complicated and I thought it was better to just tell them.'

Jessie feels her lip curl, cannot help the bitterness in her tone. She is still trying to make sense of the news that Paula has come to say goodbye but her resentment at being confronted by the police about her meeting with Paula takes over.

'Yes, I know. They came to the house. My mother freaked out. It was hideous. I've tried to call you. I've left you like fifty messages over the last few days.'

'I know, I know I should have called you back and I should have spoken to you first... but... things have a way of coming out and it's just... I can't do this, Jess. I talked to Ryan, really talked to him, and I think... for the sake of my kids, I think I'm going to give things another shot with him.'

Jessie hears a bark of laughter from across the parking lot. A group of students are cutting through to get to the other side of campus to where the food court is. She registers that the sun is setting and that she is feeling hungry. She didn't eat before the four-hour exam. Her stomach was a churning ball of anxiety. The anxiety comes back now. She has no idea how to process what Paula has just said. It is a betrayal not only of Jessie but of herself as well, of who she fundamentally is.

'But you're gay and you told me that you didn't love him anymore! I don't understand, Paula. Why are you doing this now? My whole life has imploded and you're running away? What happened to supporting each other through this whole thing? I don't get it. I really don't get it.' Jessie slams her hand against her car, attracting curious looks from other students in the parking lot. She feels the sting ripple up her arm but is glad to feel something other than the stone of anxiety inside her.

'Listen, Jessie,' says Paula firmly, raising her hands, 'life is not simple, you know that. I still love Ryan, I do. He's the father of my children and I still have love for him. I know this is difficult for you but you have to understand how difficult this is for me too. I've taken a leave of absence from my job. I need to take some time away, and Ryan can take long service leave from his job. We're going to just try and regroup. They fired Bernadette Fischer. They're saying she resigned but I know they fired her. Her career is over. No one will ever hire her again. I don't want my career to be over but George Bennet says that if I take leave for the rest of the year, then I can come back.'

Jessie brings her thumb to her mouth, pulls at the nail with her teeth and tears a piece off. 'I'm not saying you can't take leave. I just don't understand why you have to take leave from me. I love you, Paula.' As she says these words, she wonders if they are even true anymore. How much betrayal can a person take? How much betrayal will she accept?

'Oh, Jess,' says Paula sadly. 'I think… I think that maybe I just thought… thought I loved you. I need to get my life back together. I need to be there for my kids. I just want to put this year behind me and move on.'

Jessie feels pinpricks of anger up and down her skin. She flushes and feels herself start to sweat despite the cool spring weather. 'Fine,' she says tightly. She opens her car door. 'Put this year behind you, put what we had behind you. Pretend it never happened.'

'Listen, Jessie…' says Paula.

But Jessie is tired of listening. She climbs into the car and slams the door, nearly catching Paula's hand, and then without glancing back, she reverses out of her parking space and drives away, enjoying the way her tyres screech.

Tears cloud her vision. Everything has been taken from her, everything.

She has lost Paula, failed her first exam ever and has to deal with her heartbroken mother, all the while concealing her own heartbreak. She has lost her sister, lost her mother, lost her lover.

She thinks back to that Friday night, pushing past the pain threatening to swallow her whole.

She and Paula met near the toilet block that was only for the use of the teachers. Jessie knew the camp well, having attended once in year eleven and twice more as part of a team-building weekend in medical school.

They didn't kiss or hug, afraid of being seen, but she did grasp Paula's hand tightly, hiding their linked fingers at the side of her puffer jacket.

'I'm so glad you came,' Paula said, her eyes shining.

'Me too. I should be studying.'

'Oh, love. You always think you should be studying. Sometimes a break is a good thing.'

'I know, but I'm worried I won't be able to concentrate as well once I tell Mum and Gabriel.'

'You don't think your mother is going to be too upset, do you?'

'I think she'll be upset that I haven't spoken to her about it before but I'll explain. I'm not sure how she's going to feel about you. You were my teacher after all.'

'Yes, but… God, when you put it like that it sounds strange. We only really started talking about us as an idea six months ago.'

'I know, don't worry about it. I'm sure it will be fine. How's the camp going?'

'Your sister caused a bit of a ruckus. She brought a bottle of vodka.'

Jessie remembers now that she laughed. 'Typical Zoe. She's going to be weird about us, I know it. But she'll get used to it.'

'I know you don't get along.'

'It's not that…'

They went on to talk for another half an hour about university and school and even Paula's children.

It was midnight when Jessie finally left Paula to go back to her car.

Midnight when she saw her sister and Shayna fighting as she crept through the camp.

Midnight when she just ignored what was happening and got back into her car and drove home.

Her phone pings with a notification, which she assumes is confirmation of her meeting with the dean. She hopes he will be understanding. She cannot lose her chance to be a doctor along with everything else. It feels like it's all she has left. She looks around her and realises, all of a sudden, that she has driven all the way home.

Walter sits on the front step, patiently waiting for her, and she remembers her first year of university. After the first week of classes, she had felt overwhelmed by how much work there was. She had come home in tears, weighed down by textbooks and fear.

'I don't think I can do this,' she told her mother, oblivious to Zoe, working on her homework at the kitchen table.

'It's the first week, Jess, you'll get the hang of it,' consoled her mother.

'No, Mum, you don't get it. Everyone is a complete genius. I've never met so many clever people all in one room, and they all seem to have read and learned every textbook already. I felt like I was in a room of qualified doctors.'

'Jessie, you know that you're as smart as any of them. I bet if you give it another week, you'll find that they're all just as scared as you are. Medicine is an enormous undertaking but you have to remember why you wanted to be a doctor in the first place.'

'I'll give it another week,' she grumbled at her mother.

The following Monday she returned home with facts buzzing through her head to find a mug filled with jelly beans sitting on her desk. 'World's Greatest Doctor' was emblazoned in red on the side of the cup. A handwritten note sat next to it.

You're the smartest person I know. You'll be the best doctor in the whole world. I love you. Zoe.

Jessie had laughed and eaten her way through the jelly beans as she completed her first assignment.

In her car she drops her head into her hands. She had loved her little sister even though they didn't get on, and as she sobs, remembering Zoe's smile and her laugh and the way she used to leave treats on her desk whenever Jessie was in the middle of the exams, she wonders, with a wrench in her gut, if she had stepped in and asked Zoe if she was okay, whether she could have saved her. She hasn't allowed this thought to surface before now, too consumed with herself and losing Paula and her spiralling life, but now she lets the guilt flow through her as she admits that she was not a good big sister. She was judgemental and unkind and she could have been so much nicer to her little sister, who was really just a typical teenage girl.

Once her tears have dried, she goes into the house to find her mother. She is in Zoe's room, dusting bookshelves that are stacked with Zoe's collection of porcelain cats.

'Mum,' she says. 'We need to talk. We can't go on like this.'

But her mother just shakes her head. She leaves to go to her own bedroom, where she closes the door on Jessie and locks her out.

CHAPTER TWENTY-FIVE

I was going to end it. That's what I was going to do. There was no reason for me to keep doing what I was doing. I'd had my fun. I'd made my point.

As the days went on and she started getting demanding about meeting me, I had to think about why I had begun my little joke. I began it because of someone else's betrayal. That's the hardest thing for me to accept about what's happened. I started it because of someone else. I didn't like her when I understood who she was, but in the end, she paid for someone else's betrayal. And I know that's not right or fair.

'She's not a good person,' I told him when he started dating her.

'I like her and she's just… I mean, look at her,' he said.

'She's not a loyal person,' I said. 'She's not nice and she's not loyal, and from what I hear she's not even a good friend.'

I knew she would betray him – that's just who she was. I knew it, and so when she turned him against me, I set out to prove it. I wouldn't talk to her because good mates don't do that to each other, but there was no reason why some other guy couldn't prove my point. Some other guy who was also me.

Xavier could prove my point, and he did.

It was a way to show him that he had chosen the wrong person.

'If you really want to meet me, break up with him,' I told her in a message four weeks before she died. And she did. She had never even met me but she just broke his heart and walked away. Proving me entirely, completely right.

I was just going to ghost her again after that, like I'd done before, but then the one person I love with all my heart came home crying as she did most days after she suffered the slings and arrows of Zoe Bloom.

I heard her crying and I looked into her room, through the slightly open door. She didn't know anyone else was home. She was leaning her forehead against the mirror, tears dripping off her face, and she was repeating, 'You're pathetic, you're ugly, no one will ever like you.'

And I understood that, for the first time, I could hand her some power.

I shared what I had done. 'Come to my computer – let me show you something. Let me show you who I've been talking to. Who Xavier has been talking to.'

'Xavier?' she said. 'But that's…'

'I know.' I smiled. 'But no one else knows that.' And she laughed.

'I'm going to ghost her again,' I said. 'She's going to be so pissed. But now you know and you can use the information if you want or whatever.'

'No,' she said as she dried her eyes and sniffed. 'No, don't ghost her, tell her. Tell her so she's humiliated and then share the pictures. Share the video of you telling her and share the pictures. I want her to hurt. I want her to cry.'

'You're angry now and I get it – but are you sure?'

'I'm sure.'

Everyone would know. That's what she wanted. She wanted everyone to know, and everyone would mean my best friend as well. But he would get over it. Maybe he would even find it funny. Maybe.

'I want you to break up with her in front of everyone – tell her who you are and tell her that you've dumped her again and then put the pictures on the internet,' she said. Her brown eyes were dark with hatred and fury. She'd had enough and I didn't blame her. I'd never had to go through the stuff she went through – school was a breeze for me but I knew it was going on. I knew it because everyone knew it, and I should have tried to help more but I didn't know what to do.

I hoped that she would be able to put these years behind her one day, that's what I hoped for her.

'Yeah, but I'll look like a dick then. I'll get her alone and then I'll do it. I'll film it for you and forward you the video and the pictures she sent me. You can do whatever you want with them.' As I said it, I felt a prickle of unease. Callum would be upset when he found out that I had been speaking to Zoe all along, but I would tell him that I knew she was going to break his heart and it was better to have it happen earlier rather than later. We had year twelve exams to think about. I mentally prepared my excuse. I didn't want to do it, not really, but I was caught between my best mate and my sister, and I knew she needed me to make sure Zoe Bloom was publicly, virally humiliated, the same way she had been humiliated by her for years.

'And when will you do it?'

'She asked me to meet her up at the camp, in that clearing where they have the bonfires. I'll meet her there on Friday night, and by Saturday morning, you'll be able to laugh at her.'

'That's what I want,' she said and her face lost some of its redness and she seemed almost happy, and I felt good that I could make her happy. 'I want to be able to laugh at her in front of everyone else. I want them to know she was tricked and stupid. And then stick it up on the net, stick it up there so the whole world can see. That's what I want.'

That was the plan.

Humiliation recorded forever, out there forever. The perfect revenge. She would be in her twenties and thirties and forties and fifties and even older than that, and it would always be there, on the internet for everyone to see. That was the plan and that was the only plan. Everything else that happened was not, and I keep repeating this to myself: it was not part of the plan.

CHAPTER TWENTY-SIX

Wednesday – Eleven Days Since the Accident

Lydia

The house is blissfully silent. Jessie has gone to a meeting at university and Gabriel back to work, and Lydia is washing up the last of the casserole dishes. No one is coming over today. She makes sure she has labelled the dishes as she wraps them – putting thank you notes in each one – so she knows who to return them to. She's glad that most people brought food in disposable containers, and she's not sure how soon she will be able to return the ones that need returning. Gabriel will have to do it for her. She is certain that he will do this for her because right now he will do anything for her. She is aware that perhaps he hopes that he will finally do enough to allow her to resume normal life, and she feels a little like she is perpetuating a lie when she does not let him know that this will never be the case. She will never again be what he considers normal. Never again.

She is going to return to work in a couple of days. It feels too soon but she has a staff and jobs lined up – people who depend on her. How much easier would it be if she wasn't the owner of the business but rather just an employee, so livelihoods didn't depend on her and her reputation? She believes she would stay home for weeks, for months, safely tucked away from the world and the sympathetic looks she feels she has to endure every time she leaves the house.

Zoe's room will have to be packed up but she will leave that for another time, another year perhaps. She likes to go in there and see all her things. She finds moments of peace when she touches her daughter's collection of glass cat figurines and her gold-plated dance trophies sitting next to the silky, gold first-place ribbons she collected from the time she was five years old. Memories jump out at her as though her daughter is standing in front of her, reminding her. In her room, she thinks about Zoe winning a dance competition at age ten and then, as they were leaving, coming upon the second-place winner, standing with her mother and crying.

'Here,' Zoe said immediately, handing her trophy to the young girl, 'I think you actually deserved this more than I did. I loved your dance,' and then she gave the girl a quick hug and skipped away, leaving the child stunned but with a small smile on her face.

'Why did you do that Zoe?' Lydia asked her daughter. 'You won fair and square.'

'I'll win another trophy,' Zoe replied breezily, 'but she's really good and I don't want her to think she should give up. I wanted to, um… encourage her, you know?'

Lydia knows that she is still hoping that her daughter will walk through the door, will return to her. Sometimes she acknowledges her own silliness. Most of the time she is comforted by it.

The police have not come back to her with any more information.

She wonders if the threads of what happened on that Friday night will ever come together. There were people who saw that something else was going on and no one said anything. Zoe's own sister saw and did nothing. Lydia understands that she didn't want to be seen, but still. It was her own sister. Her own flesh and blood.

She doesn't know how she feels about the news about Bernadette Fischer. That has filtered through the Facebook grapevine really quickly. The woman took pills and alcohol. She feels sorry for her, of course, that she was desperate enough to make such a choice, but beyond her sympathy she cannot forget that Zoe is dead because not enough attention was being paid. The different scenarios where Zoe is saved play over and over in her head. Black-and-white movies where everything turns out right. But that too is silliness.

Lydia shakes her head. None of it makes any difference anyhow. Nothing will bring her precious daughter back. Nothing will give Lydia her own life back, her own complicated, frustrating life filled with everyday problems. She doesn't know if she and Jessie will ever recover their relationship, if she will ever be able to watch television and laugh at a joke, if she will ever feel like she is not wearing a necklace of grief that threatens to choke her. In a couple of days, she will meet with the wife of a radiologist who wants to have her house styled for sale. 'She believes that her current house has bad karma, and she has no idea how she will survive living there for another month,' Nathan told her on the phone this morning.

'Why, what happened?'

'She gave a party and things didn't go well,' said Nathan.

If she could, Lydia would refuse to meet her. She knows she won't, of course. She will meet the woman and nod and smile at her little, insignificant problems. She will suggest decluttering and she will suggest the right furniture and subtle tones to make the home appeal to the most people, and she will smile some more. And the world will go on, even if she does not feel as though she is participating.

On impulse she decides to go to the cemetery. As she drives, she keeps the windows open, letting the cold, rushing air fill her mind so that she doesn't have to think about anything else.

She stands by her daughter's graveside that is still waiting for a tombstone and breathes in the damp spring air, inhaling the flowers that are beginning to bud and the earthy smell of the dirt.

She kneels down and looks over at Eli's grave. She had always imagined that this was where she would be buried. She bought the plot after Eli died, needing to know that she would rest next to him forever. She has no idea where she will be buried now – perhaps next to Gabriel. Maybe she will leave that decision to Jessie. She imagines her daughter, one day in the future, organising a funeral for her, and she feels her tears fall for her only remaining child who she is not supporting as she should. She needs to be a better mother to Jessie. She needs to be a better wife to Gabriel, who is working every day to keep their small family functioning. If she doesn't find a way through this, then Jessie will have lost her father, her sister and her mother, even if she is still physically here. Jessie is twenty-two but she is still her child, still her first baby.

She sighs as she reads Eli's headstone for about the thousandth time and thinks about what she will put on Zoe's headstone, what she will say that will do justice to a life cut short. She cannot find the words now and she hopes they will come to her in time. Even though she will not get to lie next to Eli forever, she is glad that he is here, right next to Zoe, right next to his little girl.

'You'll take care of her, won't you?' she says. She closes her eyes and sees Zoe at three years old, sitting next to her father on her bed. He was supposed to be reading her a bedtime story but he had spent the day moving the warehouse around and was exhausted. They didn't know at the time that his body was already fighting something else as well.

'I'll do it,' she knows she told Eli.

'No, it's the best thing about bedtime.' He would read first to Zoe and then to Jessie even though she was already old enough to read to herself.

When Lydia had gone to find out what had happened to him, she found him fast asleep on Zoe's bed as Zoe read *Fox in Socks* to him, her favourite book memorised from many readings, night after night.

'Shush,' Zoe said when she saw her, 'my daddy is sleeping.'

Lydia cannot believe that she can find more tears. Her daughters should have had a father in their lives. Zoe should have grown up and left school and gone on to have her own children. The world should have been a different place but she cannot change it. She cannot change any of it.

'Acceptance,' her mother told her after Eli died. 'Acceptance is the only thing that works.'

'What happened on Friday night, Zoe?' she says in a whisper. 'Why were you outside your cabin? Did you fall? Were you pushed? Were you running from something? Were you running to someone? And who did you love? Xavier? Callum? Did Callum have anything to do with what happened to you? How angry was Callum after you broke up with him?'

Heartbreak hurts as much as any physical pain. How broken was Callum's heart?

All the questions she has been asking herself over the last ten days chase themselves around and around and she cannot find the answer. *If I could find the answer, would that make it better? Would I feel better if I knew exactly what had happened?*

She closes her eyes as she thinks about this final, quintessential question. *Would I feel better if I knew exactly what happened?* She knows exactly what happened to Eli. She watched it happen, week by week, day by day and then finally moment by moment. She knows exactly what happened but she has not missed him any less or mourned him any less because of it. Loss is loss, and the reasons for her loss don't matter. All that matters is that she has lost her daughter. Nothing will ever make that easier to bear. Nothing.

'I miss you both, more than words can say,' she says as her tears dry. 'I hope you're together. I hope you're with your daddy, Zoe.'

A light wind rustles through the trees in the cemetery, a kookaburra laughs in a nearby tree and a feeling of space to breathe, of peace, descends.

Lydia has her answer.

This is the best she can hope for: acceptance that Zoe is with her father, with the only other person in the world who loved her as much as she does. And that will have to be enough.

It will simply have to be enough.

CHAPTER TWENTY-SEVEN

Shayna

My phone has been going nuts since early this morning. Ms Fischer took pills to kill herself after she lost her job because of what happened at camp, and now all her students are going completely crazy because Ms Fischer was one of the best English teachers in, like, the whole state, and even though she got fired they were all going to call her for help.

'I knew she wasn't ready to retire,' says my mum when I talk to her about it. 'I thought that was a rubbish excuse. They fired her and I hope they're sorry. What a thing to do. That poor woman.'

'Yeah, but you've seen Twitter. Parents were really mad.'

Mum shakes her head. 'It feels like Zoe's death has changed the whole world.'

I nod my head and then I grab an apple from the fruit basket. I eat it quickly, taking big bites, stifling my guilt with the crunch and the sweetness of the juice.

'Shayna,' says Mum as she watches me. 'Is there something else? Is there something else you need to tell me?'

I swallow quickly, wondering how I can keep this inside. The only reason I haven't said anything is because I'm not sure. I'm just not sure, and I really don't want to get someone into trouble if I'm not sure. Zoe's death has ruined so many lives already. I don't want it to go wrong for anyone else. I have no proof, only a memory. All the dots I have somehow connected for no reason that I can understand. I could be wrong. I could totally be wrong. I'm not just jumping to conclusions, I'm leaping to them, but I can't let go of the thought.

Despite that, I can't keep it in. I say, 'You know that the police said she was speaking to a boy named Xavier?'

'Yes, do you know something about that?'

'I could be completely, entirely wrong, and I kind of feel like if I get it wrong, then people are going to get mad at me and that I'm going to, like, waste police time or whatever.'

Mum sits down at the kitchen table and lays her hands flat on the wood. I know she's calming herself down so she doesn't yell but I can feel her frustration at me. 'Explain, Shayna. You can talk to me.'

I throw my apple core in the bin, feeling a little sick because the apple is like the tenth thing I've eaten this morning. I sit down as well. 'In year ten we had to do tourist brochures when we did a unit on persuasive language and we were learning about advertising.'

Mum closes her eyes and bites down on her lip.

'We all did travel brochures for Sydney, and lots of them had pictures of people on the beach, and the best one I saw had a picture of this gorgeous guy on a surfboard. Anyway, we were all looking at it and, like, giggling, and Zoe said, "He looks like the perfect boyfriend. And I'm going to name him Xavier. Xavier is the most perfect name for a boy: strong and sexy." I only remembered what she said last night because of the name, because the boy she was talking to was called Xavier. And that seemed like kind of a weird... I don't know – coincidence?'

Mum looks up at the ceiling. 'That could just be... I'm sure it's just a coincidence. Whose brochure was it?'

I tell her as I remember the words 'that's my brother's middle name'. I have no idea why the conversation came back to me. It's like the memory was buried deep, waiting to be unleashed.

Five minutes later, Mum is on the phone to the police. 'Look,' she says to Detective Gold, 'this may be absolutely nothing, but

I thought I would let you know. I don't want to ever feel that we had something and didn't share it.'

After Mum talks to the police she tells me to just go and do whatever it was I was doing today. 'It may be absolutely nothing, but you just never know.'

I don't want to go on with my day because I could be wrong, and I don't want to have to see anyone until I know what's happening. I go back upstairs to my room and I climb back into bed and just lie there, waiting for the hours to pass. I will have to go out tomorrow. Everyone is meeting down at the Chocolate Inn in the afternoon, and someone said that Mrs Fitzsimmons is going to be there as well. She's not coming back to school for the rest of the year, and she said that she wants this to be a kind of informal goodbye to all the year elevens who want to come.

I want to text Becca but I know I shouldn't.

If I'm right about 'Xavier' being the guy she was talking to, then I understand why Zoe was into him. He was just beautiful: blond hair, tanned skin, perfect abs. Perfect for Instagram. She liked a lot of his photos but she liked a lot of photos of cute guys in general –we all do.

The lure of the perfect boyfriend was too much for Zoe; the lure of the perfect Instagram guy meant she stopped thinking properly. She should have questioned 'Xavier' more. There is no way she should have trusted someone she'd never met, and she should have done what we'd agreed – her and Becca and I – to do if we ever wanted to meet up with someone we met online: meet in a group in a public place. We hadn't really had to do it yet because most of the people we spoke to were people who knew people we knew. Last year I was talking to a boy named Shane that I had never met before, except on Facebook. I asked everyone I knew if they knew him, and finally Lilly, who is in the year below, said she knew him. She said he was a complete loser so that was the end of that. But we promised each other, we actually promised each other, that as we got older, we would always make sure we met someone new in public and in a group. It wasn't like we'd never had discussions about being catfished. We'd even laughed at those people on *Catfish* – the television show that catches people who are pretending to be someone else on dating sites and stuff.

'As if anyone would be so stupid,' I remember Becca saying once after we had watched one of the shows.

'There is no way I would fall for something like that,' Zoe said.

'I bet you would if he was good-looking enough,' said Becca.

'No way,' replied Zoe, 'I'm smarter than that.' And she was smarter than that until someone showed up who made her let her guard down.

I feel bad for her, for what happened to her life and for the fact that she broke up with Callum over someone who doesn't exist. Callum must have been so angry. He really liked her. You only give up the other people in your life for someone you really like, and Callum gave up someone really important.

'Have you told Callum that you and his best friend were almost a thing?' Becca asked her after Zoe and Callum decided they were a couple.

'Yeah,' she said, 'I told him what happened. We don't have secrets. But there is no way I'm hanging out with him, so I told Callum it was me or Maddox, and voila… no more Maddox.' She giggled, proud of herself and what she had accomplished.

She made him give up his best friend, and then when her feelings for him were tested, she just dumped him. I wonder if he expected that to happen.

I can kind of understand why 'Xavier' did what he did by pretending to be someone else.

If she was going to meet 'Xavier' and she fell and died, that's hideous. But if 'Xavier' is who I think it is, then I don't know what really happened, and I'm not sure I want to know either. There was a lot of anger and hurt feelings in the cabin that night. But maybe the feelings that were the most hurt belonged to someone outside the cabin.

I shiver a little even though I'm still inside.

If I hadn't walked away from her… If I'd gone with her or convinced her to come back to the cabin, she might still be here.

For the first time since Zoe died, I don't think about our fight or about what really happened to her because I have no idea about that. I don't think about how weird things got between us or anything like that.

Instead, I close my eyes and just think about Zoe.

I think about Zoe at five in her uniform that was too big for her just like mine was too big for me, sitting down next to me at our first school lunch at kindy. 'Your hair is just like mine. We are best friends now.' She was bossy but I was so happy to have a best friend and she made me laugh for the next eleven years. She was there when I kissed a boy for the first time and told her it felt disgusting when he put his tongue in my mouth. She was there when Will Roberts broke up with me when I was fourteen and I cried for a whole week and she came over with ice cream and Oreos and told me that he was a dick. She was there all along, and even though stuff was strained and I was angry with her a lot of the time, she was still my friend, still my best friend, and I start crying and I feel like I will never, ever stop.

I hold my pillow over my face because I don't want anyone to hear me. I just want to think about the girl who used to be my best friend.

I miss her. I realise that since she died, I have been kind of waiting for a text from her, just a message or an emoji like she used to send me every day.

I've been waiting and waiting, and today, a week and a half after she fell off the side of a rock and died, I feel like I finally get it. Zoe isn't going to send me a text. Not today and not ever again.

CHAPTER TWENTY-EIGHT

None of this would have happened if she'd been able to let go of her anger towards me.

I get that she was upset about me going cold on her at the beginning of the year. No one likes to be ghosted. I understand that, but I couldn't be with someone who did the stuff she did to other people. I couldn't be with someone who treated my sister the way she did.

She'd been liking my posts, commenting on my Instagram and generally trying to get my attention for a while before I started replying to her. I knew who she was. But I didn't know much about her. After a few days I asked my sister – I asked Leeanne, 'Do you know Zoe Bloom?'

'Of course,' she said, 'everyone knows Zoe Bloom.'

'I'm kind of talking to her. We're meeting up this weekend. What do you think of her?'

Leeanne's face flushed red and she blinked rapidly as though trying to stop tears. 'I hate her,' she said. 'I absolutely hate her.'

'Why?'

'She calls me names. She makes fun of me all the time just because I'm smarter than she is. She's made the last couple of years at school just awful. I dread seeing her every single day. If you go out with her, I'll stop talking to you. I swear I will stop talking to you.'

'Whoa, don't get all dramatic about it. It won't be like you're dating her.'

'Please, please… I'm begging you. She's a terrible person. Please don't go out with her.' Tears dripped off her chin and her nose began to run.

I hate to see her cry. Absolutely hate it. She's only two years younger than me but ten years smarter. She was sent to school early and it has never been easy for her.

'Okay, okay. I won't. I won't date her. Don't worry, sis, I won't date her.'
She hugged me hard. 'Thanks, you're the best.'

It was easier to just go quiet on her. Easier than all the discussions and explanations that would have had to take place.

But she was angry about that. Most girls are. And so, she turned to him, to Callum. And that would have been fine. I'm a big boy. It would have been fine. But Zoe had her own agenda. It wasn't enough for her to just be dating my best mate. She needed more.

And Callum was completely in love with her, and so he gave her what she wanted. What she wanted, what she needed, was for him to betray me, for him to dump me the way I had dumped her.

He should have been strong enough to tell her no. But he wasn't and now she's paid for that betrayal. And he doesn't even know that's what happened. I feel bad about that but he should have been a better friend. He will be from now on. I know he will be.

I understood why she hooked up with my best friend. She was showing me, punishing me, and I was fine with that – not happy, but fine. I resolved to always be polite, to act like there had never been a chance for her and me, and I thought that she would do the same thing. But it was never about her liking him. It was only about her getting back at me, and once he was completely taken in by her, she made sure that I paid for what I had done to her.

After I first tried to convince him not to go out with her, I just accepted it. 'Hey, man, if you're happy, I'm happy. I'm not the one dating her, and I won't say anything else about her,' I told him and he was good with that.

And then he called me a couple of weeks later. 'Look,' he said, 'she's kind of got a thing about you because you ghosted her, and I don't care – I'm happy you didn't want to be with her – but she doesn't want us to hang out.'

'What do you mean she doesn't want us to hang out? I don't have to see you when you're with her. We go to school together. We can see each other when she's with her friends. What difference does it make?'

'I… She's still mad at you. She says you're talking shit about her and I told her that you're not but she doesn't believe me. She wants us to stop talking. She says it's her or you, and I love you, buddy, but she's amazing. We'll catch up at school, you know, in between classes, but not on the weekends, and that camping trip has to be cancelled. She wants to go away with me instead. She says it'll be wild.'

We used to go camping once or twice a year. We'd spend a couple of days in the bush, just drinking and talking. It was a way to start the holidays and it had been for ten years already. First, we went with our fathers – they drank the beer and we had junk food – but once we turned fifteen, we'd be dropped off and left to ourselves. It was the best part of the holidays, and this year we would have been able to drive ourselves up to the mountains for the first time. It was going to be momentous. Just us and some beers and a fire and the stars and that kind of talking about nothing much that goes nowhere but somehow manages to keep going for hours. In the middle of the chaos of year twelve, I was looking forward to that pause, to those two days where we didn't have to think about the life-changing exams that were racing towards us.

'You can't do that… How can you do that? I won't say anything about her, I promise.'

'Geez, Mad, just leave it. I want to spend as much time with her as I can. I think I'm in, like, love or something. Just leave it, okay?'

'You know she would dump you if I started talking to her.'

'You wouldn't do that,' he said softly, and he was right. He was my best friend. Of course I wouldn't do that.

'You can't be throwing away our friendship over some bitch,' I argued.

'Yeah, I really don't want to hear anything else from you,' he said, and then he just ended the call. We had been friends for twelve years and he just ended the call and stopped speaking to me. He wouldn't even fucking look at me at school, not even a look. Hatred for her burned in my throat. I stopped talking to her when I found out what a bitch she was. I didn't want to get into a whole thing so I just stopped talking to her. But she was more of a bitch than I'd imagined. She went out with him to get at me – it was so obvious and I didn't know why he couldn't see it.

I couldn't let it go. I couldn't just lose my best friend over a girl. And so I created Xavier.

And Xavier showed him the truth. How awful she really was.

Just one day after she dumped him, he called me. 'Thanks for picking up,' he said when I answered.

'Obviously I was going to pick up.'

'Yeah, well, I just called to tell you, you were right. She is exactly who you said she is. She dumped me.'

'Why?'

'She wouldn't say, but there's some guy on the internet whose pictures she keeps liking. I don't know, maybe it's him, maybe it's one of a hundred other guys who like everything she puts on Instagram. It doesn't matter. You were right.'

'I'm sorry, man.'

'Yeah, well, I'm sorry I was such a dick to you and all for her. I won't let that happen again.'

'You won't?'

'I won't, believe me. Now let's talk about that camping trip.'

I was done then. I had achieved what I needed to, and I knew that she would be fine and so would Callum and life would go on.

The important thing was that Maddox hadn't betrayed his friend by talking to the girl he was going out with. But Xavier wasn't going to accept his friend's betrayal in dumping him for some girl.

But it's all gone wrong and now Maddox Xavier Donaldson can't sleep or eat or think straight.

I should have gone up to the camp to break up with her like I said I would, but I had my best mate back, and a night with him and some pretty girls was way more appealing. So I texted my sister to let her know.

Look, I'm not coming. Spending the night at Callum's house. Best if we leave it now. She'll stand out there in the cold, all alone, and then tomorrow you'll be able to take a few digs at her. Hope camp is good, sis. Xx

What? No! You promised!

Sorry. Holly and Matilda from year 12 coming over. His parents are away for the night. You have the pictures. Show them around and just chill. She got what she deserved. Serves her right. Got to go. Xx

CHAPTER TWENTY-NINE

I wanted to scream when I got that text. All I had been holding onto was the thought of him telling her the truth as she stood in the cold waiting for the 'love of her life' – pathetic. I couldn't wait to see the video he promised to take. And then he just decided there was something better to do. He didn't understand. He didn't understand at all because he had always had everything go his way. Losing Callum made him angry. Losing Callum to a girl like Zoe made him furious. But his fury faded quickly as his life just got back to normal. It wasn't the same for me. It could never be the same for me. He hadn't been through what I'd been through, so I had to see it through. I had to wait until the end.

I hadn't counted on the argument before she left the cabin. I hadn't imagined the things that would be said. If I had known, then perhaps it would have been enough for me, but once it happened, I still needed more. I was greedy for her pain and humiliation.

Once the lights had been turned off, I was quiet while I waited for her to move. Tension filled the air even though we had all descended into silence. So many ugly things had been said.

I heard her move and then I heard someone else move. That wasn't the plan. But I had to do it. I had to see her and so I crept out quietly and then there was only one person left in the cabin. One person, curled up in her sleeping bag, unaware of what was going on.

I stood out of sight and watched the fight between her and Shayna, watched Shayna push her down. I heard her tears. That should have been enough but it wasn't. It still wasn't.

When Shayna stalked back to the cabin, I waited until she was inside and then I followed Zoe to the spot where she had told him to meet her. As I walked, I thought about what I would say and I realised that it would make things even worse if she thought she had been talking to me, to a girl, to a nerd she took pleasure in tormenting.

She was shining her phone on the ground, using it as a torch to light her way. And she was swearing and talking.

'Oh my God. What the hell was that? Oh no, what was that? I hate him for making me do this. He knows I hate things that crawl and bite. He better be there. I swear he better be there!'

And finally, she was there, right in the middle of the clearing. There were no trees to hide the stars and I looked up briefly to see them scattered across the sky in their millions. They looked close enough to touch. I realised that I'd been holding my breath and so I breathed out a white cloud into the ice-tasting air. I didn't have time to think about what might be rustling in the low dark bushes around the clearing. I had a plan to follow through on.

She had been banging and crashing and talking so much she hadn't heard me behind her.

She shone her phone torch around at the bushes and I could see her shiver when something ran across the ground.

I took my phone and pressed record, the anticipation sweet in my mouth, and I walked out to her, shining the light in her face so she couldn't see it was me.

When I was a few feet away from her, I dropped the light to the ground and I opened my mouth to tell her everything but she jumped in before I could speak and I realised that I hated her more than ever.

'Who's there?' she said and then I lifted my phone so she could see me.

'What? What are you doing here? Did you follow me? I don't need any more crap from anyone. I've had enough for tonight. Just go back to the cabin.'

'I didn't follow you,' I replied. 'You came to meet me.'

'What? Stop talking crap. I didn't come to meet you. Are you insane?'

'Yes, you did. It's me you came to meet. I'm Xavier.'

I watched her eyes widen and she bit down on her lip.

'No, you're not. Why would you say something like that? How do you know Xavier? Did he send you to meet me?'

I wanted her to go further into the bush, further into the thick, dark places where she might trip over a rabbit hopping away from a fox or step on a poisonous snake. In the distance I could see the floodlit Three Sisters looming over the whole valley, guarding the mountains. I liked how much the unknown scared her. 'Maybe he did. Follow me. I'll take you to him.'

I started walking and she just followed me, like a little dog, making tiny sounds of fear and surprise at the wind and scuttling creatures that seemed to be everywhere.

When I stopped, it was because I felt the edge of something. My foot slipped just a little and I realised that even though there seemed to just be darkness ahead of me, I was standing on the edge of something. I didn't know what. But I knew I couldn't go any further.

'Why would he come here? What is going on?' she asked.

I turned around to face her. 'No one else is coming. You followed me like the idiot you are but no one else is coming. I'm Xavier. I'll say it slowly so you understand. I'm Xavier. It's me you've been talking to all this time. It's me you like, me you sent the photos to. All this time, it's been me.' I couldn't help giggling. It was even better than I had anticipated, even better to see the look of confusion and distress on her face.

'You're lying.'

'No, I'm not. I'm the one you've been speaking to. How else would I have known to meet you tonight?'

'But where's Xavier?'

'I'm Xavier, you idiot,' I snarled. I was really enjoying myself.

'But… but the pictures, the pictures of Xavier… I saw…'

'Pity you weren't smart enough to do an image search. That would have saved you a lot of trouble. All you had to do was type in "teenage boy on surfboard" and there he would have been.' I had seen the pictures my brother had used. They were just standard images, cliched and ordinary. Similar to the ones I had used on my tourist brochure in year ten. I have no idea how she fell for it.

'Who is he?' she asked in a small voice as all her illusions crumbled.

I felt a bit bad for her then because I know she'd really fallen for Xavier. She broke up with Callum to be with him. She wouldn't have minded so much if it was my brother pretending to be Xavier. She might have even liked that idea, liked how obsessed he had gotten with her. As I stood there, I was glad he'd let me down. She didn't deserve an ounce of compassion from me or anyone else, and Maddox might have been swayed by her distress.

Everything that she was getting, she deserved. Zoe Bloom spent her whole life stepping on and using and hurting people, and I was pleased to be the one person who made sure she understood that everyone, even she, was fallible. How ironic that I was the person to bring her down.

'Who knows? He's an image on the internet. He's a boy who likes to put up pictures of himself. I don't know.'

She sniffed and I realised she was crying but I didn't know if they were real tears or just for effect. That's the kind of person Zoe is. Was.

'I can't believe... I can't believe you would do that,' she said.

'You deserved it,' I replied. 'You deserved it because you're mean to everyone around you, even your very best friends. You've been a bitch to me for years. You can't go on treating people badly, Zoe, no matter how pretty you are or how popular you are. You can't treat people the way you do. I made Xavier to show you that, and now I've got this recorded and it's going all over the internet. By tomorrow everyone will know and everyone will see the pictures. Can you imagine how people will laugh at you, Zoe? Can you just imagine?'

She sniffed again and then she turned, like she was going to go. I stepped forward and she turned around again. 'You utter, utter bitch,' she spat. 'You complete fucking cow.'

She ran at me and shoved me hard so I fell over. 'Ow!' I yelled because I felt my butt hit some sharp stones on the ground.

'Cow,' she laughed. 'Go on, post it, let it go viral. I hope it does. I'm going to tell everyone that you're in love with me and that you've been in love with me for years. I'm going to tell them you made up a fake profile to get me to send you pictures in my underwear. Did you enjoy those, you pervert? Did you touch yourself when you looked at me in my panties and bra? I bet you did. I bet you've wanted to get a photo of me in my underwear forever. You are completely pathetic. Go on, post it! Post it! I can't wait to see what happens. You'll be the laughing stock of the whole school, of the whole country.'

She laughed this terrible, sneering laugh and I knew that, somehow, I hadn't won. Somehow, she was going to turn this around and I would be laughed at and scorned for the rest of my life, and I wasn't going to let that happen. I didn't understand how it had happened. She had turned the tables on me without a second thought, and the hatred I felt for her burned inside me.

I jumped up and ran towards her, anger pounding through my veins. 'You're evil!' I shouted, my words echoing, and I pushed her. She stumbled backwards, one step, two steps. I knew there was a drop-off but I assumed it was just a small one – just enough so she would be hurt if she fell. I wanted her to be hurt.

Behind her there was just black. I saw that she was close to the edge. She moved back a bit more and I took another small step forward. I wasn't thinking about anything except how much I hated her, how much I had loathed her for all the years I had known her, for all the years she'd made my life hell.

And then her foot came to the very edge and it slipped. Her body tilted and her eyes widened and she reached out her arm for me to take.

'I'm going to fall. Please,' she begged.

I reached out my arm as if to grab her but instead I said, 'Then fall,' and I gave her a small shove, just a little one.

I had already raised my other hand because it was my intention to grab her to save her. I wanted her to believe she was going to fall and then I was *going to save her, but as she fell backwards and I reached forward to take her hand, my foot slipped on the moss and I reared back to save myself.*

I heard the thump of her body hitting the ground, her small cry of pain.

I stood in the cold air, hearing only my own breathing, my own pounding heart. There were no sounds coming from her. Zoe was silent.

And then I was afraid. I knew she was going to be really angry with me.

I contemplated waking Ms Fischer and telling her what had happened. I even prepared an excuse for her. I was going to tell her I had seen Zoe sneak out and had followed her for her own protection. I rehearsed the things I would say until they felt real and right.

But then I knew I couldn't do it. I imagined her being helped up. I imagined her spitting and snarling at me and telling everyone what I'd done. I couldn't deal with that. Not after everything I had done to get my revenge, not after everything my brother had done to help me. I couldn't deal with it at all.

I didn't go and look at her. I didn't want to see. I turned around and left, running through the bush, feeling leaves and sticks scratch against my face, sweating in the cold air. I almost screamed as my foot stepped on something that slithered away. I heard the trees rustle their leaves in the wind and I felt like I was being watched. Like I was being judged. I ran faster.

I slowed as I got back to camp, let my heart rate settle, and then just for the look of it, I went to the bathroom. We were allowed to leave the cabin to go to the bathroom. No one else was there. The camp was silent.

I went back to bed because I thought she was hurt but fine and I knew I needed a plan for the morning so I could counter all the terrible things she was going to say about me. I lay in bed, awake and thinking and worrying, until the sun rose and then I walked around with one of the searchers, still planning, thinking that I would take them to her and I would be a hero and maybe, just maybe, I could convince her to keep quiet and I would keep quiet and it would all be over. I could tell her it had all been a joke.

But the person I was walking with wanted to go in a different direction. And when we did circle back to where I'd first met her, I realised that the bush looks different during the day. I didn't know where we'd gone.

And I couldn't think how to tell the searcher what had happened, how to point her in the right direction or where the right direction was. All of Saturday I kept hoping and waiting for them to find her because it was so close to camp. How could they not have found her? But the hours passed and then I began to think that she had gotten up and run away because she was humiliated. That thought kept me quiet. Kept me from saying anything at all.

But then they found her.

And the reality of what I'd done, what I'd actually done, has destroyed me.

Everything has changed because she's not here. People are hurt. Lives are ruined and hearts are broken.

The whole school will forever be different because I did something completely against my own moral code, against the moral code my brother and I have been brought up with. I have done something I never thought I'd be capable of. I have taken a life. Guilt weighs me down, slows my steps, steals my sleep and my appetite. Guilt is the only emotion I deserve to feel. It's the only emotion that goes well with another word: murderer. That's what I feel. That's what I am.

That's what I feel. That's what I am.

CHAPTER THIRTY

I didn't go because he'd texted me to come over, and any time I spent with him was always good.

And he had invited pretty girls. Holly and Matilda were not interested in anything except a night off from studying. It would be easy and fun, and suddenly the heated need for revenge I felt just went cold.

I had my mate back. I had a Friday night with two cute girls to look forward to. I was over Zoe Bloom. Completely over her. So, I bailed on our plan. I bailed and everything went wrong.

I did a shitty thing to Zoe but she deserved it. I didn't understand that my anger at her had been mild at best compared to my sister's anger at her. I didn't understand her deep-down hurt that dogged her every move as she dragged herself through high school. I didn't understand it and I couldn't understand that while my need for revenge had gone cold, hers only heated up until it flamed and set everything on fire.

I have helped someone take a life. I encouraged her to give in to her hatred and anger, stoking the fire. I let it happen and it makes me feel sick, completely sick.

She won't tell me exactly what happened.

'It was an accident,' she told me. 'I didn't mean for it to happen.'

I want to just let it go, just leave it, but I can't. I cannot live with this and I know she can't either.

It wasn't the plan, but now when I think about it, I feel like an idiot for thinking that there was ever a plan at all. I got pissed and I did something in my anger and then I shared what I had done. But I didn't think about who I shared it with. No matter how well

I know my own sister, there are some secrets she keeps from me. Her deep-rooted anger, bubbling under the surface, is a secret she has kept. Her terrible pain, pain that won't just go away when she leaves school, is something she has kept from me. I didn't think she would really do anything with the pictures. I thought she might share them but I also thought she would probably just keep them. I never imagined that she would follow through and go and meet her.

I feel like I don't know her at all. I didn't really know Zoe, not until I was Xavier, and when I think about what I've done, I realise that I don't know what I'm completely capable of either. That arsehole twelve-year-old who shoved a ten-year-old onto the stage during assembly is still there. He's still there and I need to deal with him.

When I look at Leeanne, I can see. I can see the churning inside her. I can see that she can't eat or sleep, just like me. I can see what she's done.

She has taken a life. I helped her take that life. I have committed no less of a crime than she has. We both deserve the guilt we feel. We are both murderers.

CHAPTER THIRTY-ONE

Bernadette

The snow-white ceiling of the hospital room is unexpected. It is instantly frustrating and makes me want to cry.

I know I am in a hospital because the first thing I hear are the tings and beeps of machines and the first thing I smell is the astringent odour of antiseptic.

I took the whole box. How could I have failed?

'You're awake,' says a voice beside me.

I turn my head to see Henry, his green eyes filled with concern.

'I…' I begin but realise that for the first time in my life I am speechless. I was not meant to be on this earth anymore. I have no idea what words to use now that I find myself still here.

'Why would you do something like that?' he asks. There is no anger in his voice. No pity either – only confusion.

I take refuge in silence and shrug my shoulders.

'It was a terrible thing, a terrible thing to find you on that sofa. You were lying on your side. I thought you'd had a heart attack.'

I stare at him.

'Oliver is fine,' he says, reading my thoughts. 'He and I are, as predicted, great friends. But I am angry at you, Bernadette. I read the note and I understand – I do. It is a terrible thing to feel like you've lost everything. I know this because when Ida died, I thought that I wouldn't survive it.'

'I'm sorry,' I whisper. My throat is dry and my voice scratches. He picks up a glass of water with a plastic straw inside it and holds it to me. I take it and drink gratefully. My arms feel heavy and I want only to return to sleep. But I need to do Henry the courtesy of listening to him. It was unfair of me to involve him. But there was no one else.

'I appreciate that,' he says, his voice stern, 'but I'm not finished. I wanted to die with Ida, but do you know what saved me?'

I shake my head.

'A week after she died, you came to my door – do you remember?'

I nod my head. I do remember because I felt so awful about it. I went to ask him to feed Oliver for me because I would be at a parent–teacher conference and I knew I would be home very late. I had been to Ida's funeral and dropped off a casserole that I knew Henry would enjoy, but we hadn't spoken much. He had his daughter there and I almost didn't ask him but then I thought about poor little Oliver, confused and hungry, and asked him to please feed him.

'Of course,' he said.

I thanked him profusely.

'When you asked me to feed him,' he continues, and I notice that he is wearing a green cardigan that matches his eyes and that he still has a full head of silver hair, 'it gave my day, that day, purpose. I knew that at five I would go next door and feed him and perhaps chat with him a bit, pat him and reassure him that you would be home soon. He is a lovely dog.' He smiles for the first time and I can see that Oliver, blessed little Oliver, has made his way into Henry's heart.

'I understand why you wanted to do… this dreadful thing, Bernadette. You have lost your purpose or what you thought was your purpose. But I want to tell you this: after I fed Oliver it occurred to me that the next day would be easier if I had something that I needed to do. And so, I told Matt that I would take care of his orchid while he was away.'

Matt lives on the floor below us and he travels a lot for business. His girlfriend bought him a vivid blue-dyed orchid and then they broke up but he kept the orchid. I know because he frequently asked me to take care of it. I did it a few times and then I thought the plant had died but he must have asked Henry to do it after that.

'That orchid is long dead,' says Henry. 'I think Matt overwatered it, but it gave me purpose for a week and then I joined the bowling club and I made a few new friends who only knew me as a widower.'

I stifle a yawn, not wanting to seem rude.

'Anyway, I am not going on and on but I wanted to explain to you that even though you think you've lost your purpose, you still have a life to live and time to find something else. This is not the end, Bernadette. It does not have to be the end. Even when you are dealing with what feels like insurmountable grief, it is not the end until you leave this earth. There must be something you have always wanted to do.'

'I wanted to see the pyramids,' I say, my voice croaky and dry.

He laughs. 'The pyramids, what a thing, what a thing. I have never been anywhere like Egypt. Ida hated to travel but I have always wanted to have an adventure. You have a purpose, Bernadette, and you have Oliver, and I would like to think I'm your friend. You are not just your job. You are more than that and you have years ahead of you to find joy in something else.'

I nod my head, noting that I am crying.

'Now, now,' he says, standing up and patting my hand, 'I didn't mean to upset you.'

'No, no, it's not that, Henry. It's that you're right. It was so... I don't know what I was thinking.'

'Some days,' he says quietly, 'are harder than others. But now I will go and give Oliver his dinner. He likes a little walk afterwards but that works because I like a little walk too.'

'Henry,' I say as he makes his way to the door of my hospital room. He stops and turns back. 'Thank you.'

'I came back for a jumper. It was warm in the afternoon but Ronald said that it would get cold after dinner so I came back for a jumper. I saw the note and thought I may as well feed Oliver early.'

'I'm… glad,' I say.

'Me too.'

'Henry?'

'Yes?'

'Will you come back tomorrow?'

'I will, Bernadette, I surely will, and maybe I will bring some travel brochures.'

'That would be lovely,' I whisper because I am crying again. A nurse comes into the room and Henry lifts his hand in a wave and leaves.

'You're awake,' she says to me.

'I'm awake.'

CHAPTER THIRTY-TWO

Thursday – Twelve Days Since the Accident

Jessie

Jessie drags herself out of bed. It's after seven. She calculates she has slept for at least twelve hours. She had no idea she could sleep that much. The dean of medicine agreed not to count her exams for this semester, but he was angry that she had not come to him before. 'Why on earth would you think you could handle exams after something like that?' he asked her. 'Physician, heal thyself,' he said when she shrugged her shoulders. It was an enormous relief, and last night her sleep was deep and still. She feels as though she has taken a sleeping pill that has yet to wear off.

The house is silent, the air still and a little chilly. Summer seems far away.

She wonders where her mother and Gabriel are but assumes they are sleeping. Her mother returns to work tomorrow and Jessie knows she is absolutely dreading it. Mourning is exhausting, made worse by the fact that she and her mother aren't speaking.

Jessie is glad of the quiet. She cannot nod her head and thank one more person for telling her how sorry they are about her little sister. She realises now that she was shielded from a lot of things when her father died. When she thinks about the time after his death, she believes that she was in agony for weeks, that she was constantly being hugged by people who came over to sympathise and that she was never given a moment to herself. But now she knows that her mother sent her to her room a lot, telling her to lie down even though she wasn't tired so that she could get a break from all the mournful faces, from the soft whispers of condolence that she knows are now starting to make her feel crazy.

Everything feels worse because of the tense silence between her and her mother. She doesn't know what to say to make her understand why she concealed so much from her.

In the kitchen she fills up the kettle and then she changes Walter's water and leans down to give him a good morning pat. It is only when she touches him that she realises that the silence in the house is heavier than usual, and why this is so. Usually Walter rolls onto his back as soon as he sees her, ready for her to scratch his stomach, but today she missed the fact that he has not moved. He is still in his bed, his paws resting on his favourite raggedy teddy bear. His body is stiff, his eyes closed.

Jessie touches him gently. 'Walter,' she says and she shakes him a little but she knows that he's gone. He was twelve years old.

She lies down next to his bed and rests her head near his paws as she strokes his fur. 'Oh, Walter,' she says softly. 'You were such a good boy.' And suddenly it is too much, everything is too much. She cannot be strong for one more moment, for one more second.

She gets up off the floor and races up the stairs to her mother's room, flinging open the door – not something she has done since her mother and Gabriel married.

Her mother opens her eyes immediately and sits up. 'Jessie?'

'It's Walter,' says Jessie and she turns and runs down the stairs again.

Her mother follows her without speaking.

In the kitchen her mother drops to her knees and covers her mouth with her hands. 'Is he?' she says, dropping her hands to her lap as though she is afraid to touch Walter.

'He's gone, Mum,' says Jessie. She bites down on her lip as her eyes burn with tears.

'Oh, Jessie,' says her mother. 'I am so sorry, baby. I'm so sorry, sweetheart.'

Her mother reaches out a tentative hand and then strokes Walter's golden fur, tears coursing down her cheeks. Jessie moves her hand along with her mother's, their fingers touching as they smooth the soft fur.

'Oh, Jessie,' she repeats, 'oh, Jessie.' She looks up at her and Jessie feels her own tears on her cheeks. How can they lose someone else? How can they possibly lose one more thing? From deep inside her a howl emerges. A howl of despair and grief for everything she has lost.

Jessie pulls her knees up and drops her head, sobbing as she hugs herself. And then she feels her mother next to her, feels her arms around her shoulders growing tighter and tighter, holding on stronger and stronger. She leans sideways and turns her head to her mother's chest, seeking comfort and warmth. Her mother doesn't let go. She doesn't let go at all.

Together they cry for Eli, for Zoe, for Walter, for all those they have lost. For the love they had for those who made up their family, for all they have suffered together and for how terrible life can be.

When Jessie feels as though she cannot cry anymore, she lets go of her mother and stands up, grabs tissues from the box off the counter for both of them.

They sit in silence, occasionally stroking Walter.

Finally, her mother says, 'Can you tell me… Can you explain why you didn't come to me, why you didn't tell me when you realised? It must have been so hard for you to be questioning things. Why didn't you come to me?'

Jessie wraps her arms around her legs and stares at her grey and black sneakers. She has asked herself this very question over and over again. She knew from the moment she understood that she was gay that there was no question of her mother's absolute support, and yet she had kept it to herself. It's more than just that she needed to get used to the idea herself, and as her mother waits for her reply, a memory surfaces and she finally realises what had held her back, what has been holding her back all these years.

'When I was eight years old,' she says, 'Dad fetched me from school one day and I was crying. I'd gotten into trouble for pulling a boy's hair. He'd tried to grab my book away from me when I was showing a friend that I got an A. He went for the book and I yanked his hair and he cried. I got into trouble and I had never gotten into trouble before. I was horrified and scared about what you and Dad would say. In the car on the way home, Dad kept asking me what was wrong and I kept telling him it was a secret because I was ashamed and worried about what would happen if I told and then he got worried and told me I really needed to explain. I think he thought it was more than what it was. So, I finally explained and he pulled over the car and hugged me until I stopped crying. And then he told me that pulling hair wasn't an ideal reaction. I agreed and he started driving again and then he said, "You can always tell me your secrets because you are part of me and so telling me is like telling yourself. I will keep all your secrets safe – as safe as you keep them."'

Jessie doesn't look up because she can hear her mother sniffing and she doesn't want to cry again as well. 'I guess… I guess I've been waiting to tell him this secret first. I've been waiting and waiting and logically I understand that he's not here, but I've still been waiting to tell him first.'

'Oh, sweetheart,' says her mother, 'you are part of me too, and I promise that I will always keep your secrets as safe as your dad did.'

'I know, Mum,' says Jessie because she does know. 'I know and I'm sorry I didn't say anything sooner and that I didn't tell you about Paula and then about seeing Zoe at the camp. I'm sorry I didn't stop her or help her. I'm just so sorry.'

Her mother reaches over to her and lifts her chin. 'I know, love. But I don't want to be angry about that anymore. I'm sorry I shut you out. I couldn't find a way through the pain and it was easier to shut everyone out. But I know that's not how I survive this. It's not how we survive this. I don't want to fight with you. I just want us to be here for each other. Can we just be here for each other? We've lost so much; can we hold onto each other?'

'Yes,' agrees Jessie, 'yes, but I wanted you to know how sorry I was, how sorry I am, about all of it.'

Her mother nods. They hear the high-pitched calls from the lorikeets outside the kitchen window and they look at each other and understand that there has been forgiveness on both sides.

'What will we do about Walter?' Jessie asks.

'Gabriel and I will take care of him. You go on your run. Take your time. Let this all go. It's time to let it go.'

Jessie stands up. Her legs feel stiff as though she has been sitting still for days. 'Okay,' she says because she knows that when she runs, she will breathe in the spring air and breathe out some of her pain.

She opens the back door that leads from the kitchen to the garden and steps out into the weak morning sunshine.

'Oh, and Jessie,' says her mother.

'Yes?'

'Forgive yourself, sweetheart. That's the most important thing. Forgive yourself.'

Jessie bites down on her lip as a hundred thoughts crowd her head and then she nods. She starts walking and then she is running, and then she is almost sprinting as she listens to the beat of her heart, her broken but still held together heart, she runs.

CHAPTER THIRTY-THREE

I smile at everyone as we slide into the booth in the Chocolate Inn.

I never imagined I would get to hang out here with everyone else. I never imagined I would be able to walk through the door, into the wide-open space with slick white marble tables and sandy-brown leather seats, and not feel that everyone was looking at me and wondering how I had the audacity to enter this sacred place, where only the cool people, the beautiful people, anyone who isn't me really got to be. I could never have imagined being able to stare at the walls where giant framed posters of their chocolate desserts tempt diners or that I would sit, looking at the menu, and not worry that all anyone could think was, 'she shouldn't be here'.

I am under the protection of the prettiest, the most popular, the queen bees of the school.

In conversation with friends online, friends who live everywhere in the world but here, friends who have suffered the indignities of their teenage years because they don't look like they should or dress like they should or act like they should, I have always professed to hate the idea of fitting in. 'No one wants to be the girl who peaks in high school,' we have all agreed as we look forward to distinguished university careers and jobs where we are CEOs and MDs and successes, not defined by our teenage years. But we're all lying. We are. Everyone wants to fit in and feel part of something, and the sly looks and snide comments and sometimes outright bullying can make you want to hide away for the rest of your life.

Zoe was the worst of them. She was mean and she was nasty and I was her favourite target. I don't think people knew how much of a target

I was. Most people only saw what was going on at school but Zoe was smarter than that, more vicious than that.

She used to send me pictures over Instagram of flies and crickets and moths and caterpillars. I replied once that stick insects only eat leaves and then she sent me twenty laughing emojis in a row. I realised that I'd just accepted her horrible nickname by correcting her. I played right into her hands. In the classes we shared, she would sigh loudly whenever I put my hand up, as though to say, 'Here we go again.' And after Maddox just stopped speaking to her, she made an effort to bump into me, to trip me up. I think she knew I was the one who told him to stop speaking to her. I could have blocked her and ignored her. That's what my mother said I should do. That's what Maddox said I should do. That's what everyone said I should do but I reasoned that at least she was paying me some attention. It's pathetic. I'm pathetic. She accused me of being in love with her. I was in love with the idea of being her, of being the girl that looked like that. Of being someone who got to go through the world skipping lightly over obstacles and skating on her smile.

It seemed only fair that Instagram was used to get back at her. Only fair but it went too far. I swallow as I look around at the posters on the wall. Once I could have eaten everything in this store, relishing the cold sweetness of the ice cream, the sticky chewiness of the toffee and the glorious, heavy, dark taste of chocolate. But now I realise that I will not be able to swallow a thing. I can only exist on guilt now.

'Why aren't you eating?' my mother asked me this morning. 'Are you ill?'

I shook my head but I wanted to scream the truth at her. I kept quiet. My mother has never tolerated melodrama.

'Eat up, Maddox,' she said in the same breath as he stared at his food. We are, both of us, eating our guilt to sustain us.

'What did you do?' he finally asked me last night. 'What exactly did you do?'

The question has been in his eyes for eleven days. He has been waiting for a confession for eleven days. And finally, last night, I gave him one. I thought it would help if he understood it was an accident. He'd started it as a joke. I ended it by mistake.

I was terrified when I learned I would have to share a cabin with her and Shayna and Becca. Terrified, horrified, nervous.

I had expected her to attack me. I knew it would happen. But what I didn't expect, what I could never have expected, was that Shayna and Becca would stand up for me.

'I'll just have a diet Coke,' I say now, pushing away the memory.

'Come on, Lee, share a waffle mountain with us,' says Becca.

'Maybe a bite or two,' I reply.

Maybe this can be my life now. If I can just find a way to move forward, if Maddox can do the same, then maybe this can be my life now. Not teasing and torment and lonely Saturday nights and a time you just want to forget; but friends and parties and memories you want to hold onto forever.

The bell over the door jingles and I look up to see who has just arrived.

It's the detective, the woman who's been asking everyone questions, and her partner.

And standing next to them is Maddox, his face red, his hands clasped together as though he is praying. He looks at me, and as I gaze back at him, he mouths the words, 'I'm sorry.'

And I want to hate him. I want to shake my head at him so he knows I cannot forgive this breach, this betrayal, but I nod instead. He has done the only thing he could do, and I think when I told him the truth last night, I knew he was going to do it. This was never going to be my life.

The detectives head over to our table. They walk purposefully and with complete confidence. They have got their man/woman/girl.

I should feel fear but as I take a deep breath, I understand that what I mostly feel is relief.

'Leeanne Donaldson,' says the female detective and I nod. 'We need you to come with us. We've spoken to your mother and she's meeting us at the station, but you need to come with us, please.'

The male detective stops Maddox from walking over to me, and as I watch, he moves him towards the door. Outside, through the window, the red and blue circling lights of a police car are finally noticed by everyone inside.

'Why?' asks Shayna, glancing fearfully at the car outside, at Maddox and at the detectives.

'We have some questions for Leeanne,' she says, looking at me as she answers Shayna's question.

I nod my head. I know they must have a lot of questions for me. I know it's over.

I didn't start it but I ended it, and once I decided to get involved, I think I knew. I think I knew that at the end of it, hearts would be broken and lives would be changed. I think I knew.

Becca stands up to let me out of the booth. I can feel her and Shayna staring at me. I can feel everyone staring at me but I won't lift my eyes. I look down at my feet as I move, and when I am standing next to the detective, she takes my arm gently. I look at her and I can see nothing but judgement in her eyes. I wonder if they know everything. I was going to catch her before she fell. I didn't know she would land on a rock.

It was an accident.

Was it an accident?

They say high school is brutal, that the years you spend sharing a space with the same people day in and day out can be the making of you or the undoing of you.

I wish I was a better person, a stronger person. I wish I hadn't been so bent on revenge and filled with hate.

I wish Zoe and those like her had not forced me to become the person I have become.

But here I am and the word 'guilt' hangs around my neck.

As I am guided to the car by the detectives, I look back at the Chocolate Inn, where the faces of my classmates are pressed up against the glass, and I watch as their heads go down and their fingers begin to type and my crime goes viral – all over the Internet.

EPILOGUE

Six Months Later

Lydia

Lydia stands back, looking over the room with a critical eye. 'I think we need a brighter rug for the floor,' she says to Nathan, who is standing next to her.

'I have the sea-green one in the back of the truck. I can go get it,' he replies and he walks out of the room.

Lydia knows that this will be the final touch for the house they are styling. The real-estate agent will be pleased and she hopes the owners are as well. A house like this should sell quickly, making everyone happy. The happiness has not reached her though. It will be a long time, she thinks, before the simple joy of helping someone sell a house makes her happy.

While she waits for Nathan to return, she checks her phone to see if Jessie has texted her. She is sitting her final exam of the semester today and Lydia is waiting to see how it went. But there is nothing from her daughter and so she moves on to her emails.

There is another one from Leeanne. She writes them at least once a week. Lydia reads them sometimes if she feels strong enough, but other times, she simply deletes them. They are all long apology emails, full of emotion and angst and guilt.

I never meant for it to happen. I was depressed about my life. I just wanted her to like me. I am so, so sorry. I will be sorry forever. Please forgive me. Forgive my brother. He had no idea.

She is serving her time in a juvenile prison for the first two years and then she will be moved to an adult women's prison.

Her brother was charged with stalking and harassment but given a suspended sentence. Even though Lydia was angry about the light sentence, she does have moments where she feels that the right thing was done. Leeanne will be in prison for six years, and her mother could not have survived the loss of two children to prison, Lydia is sure. As a mother she feels for another mother, for her shock at not knowing exactly who her children were and what they were capable of. She has felt the same shock about some of the things she has learned about Zoe.

At least her son is home but her life will never be the same, just like Lydia's life. Just like the lives of everyone who knew and loved Zoe. The whole community has been shocked by the story, and she knows that at the school they are bringing in cybersecurity experts to talk to the students about catfishing and they are giving endless seminars on bullying.

Maybe it will stop something like this from ever happening again. Maybe not.

Lydia was not able to go to the trial and the sentencing. She did not want to listen to the details of how and why Leeanne chose to end her daughter's life. She has heard enough and read enough just from the reports on television and articles on the internet.

There are moments that she feels sorry for Leeanne, for how desperately sad she was, for how Zoe's treatment of her affected her. But it's no excuse. And she has moments of raging anger at Maddox, at a now eighteen-year-old boy, who set out to break up Zoe and Callum and then to break her heart. But a broken heart doesn't end your life, and Zoe would have chalked the whole thing up to experience eventually if not for Leeanne's need to take things further.

She understands that what happened in the Blue Mountains was a mistake, an accident, and she knows that Leeanne never meant for Zoe to die, but murder is not always premeditated.

She cannot forgive her, will not forgive her. Gabriel attended the trial. He went every day and reported back to Lydia and Jessie, as much or as little as they could bear to hear.

'You don't have to do this,' Lydia said but he insisted.

'I am your husband and I was her stepfather. I am there to represent our family.'

When Lydia reflects on how things are, it seems strange that they do feel more like a family now. She supposes they are clinging to each other. Jessie and her stepfather seem to spend more time together because Gabriel has begun getting up early every morning to run with Jessie. He struggled at first but now he keeps up quite well.

'I thought you hated running,' she said to him when he told her what he was going to do.

'I do,' he replied, 'but she needs… I don't know how to explain it. She doesn't have to talk to me or wait for me, but if she needs to, if she wants to, then I will be there.'

'Maybe I should come too.'

'No, Liddy, you're there all day and sometimes she wants to say things that she cannot say to you because your heart is as broken as hers is. Please, just let me do this for her, for you.'

Lydia had realised as she agreed to leave him to it that what she felt was relief. Relief that Jessie would have someone else to turn to if she needed it, relief that they both have Gabriel, who is patient and kind and simply here.

She looks at her watch. This afternoon she will visit Zoe's grave and she will place the small striped stone she found on a bushwalk last week on top of her grave. She likes to find Zoe different-coloured stones, different shapes and different kinds. Every time she looks at the stones, she sees something else and it reminds her of the juxtaposition her daughter was.

Zoe was funny and kind and could be mean and angry and defiant. She was beautiful and intelligent and maddening. She was Zoe, and Zoe is gone, but just like Eli, she will never be forgotten.

'Here you go,' says Nathan, and Lydia deletes the email from Leeanne and looks at the rug.

'Perfect,' she says. 'That will do nicely.'

Shayna

'So, do you want another spoon?' asks Michael, and I start to shake my head but then I open my mouth and he puts the ice cream and whipped cream on my tongue. I swallow the bitter dark chocolate, chewing on a piece of brownie and savouring the sweet taste of the cream. I watch Michael smile at me.

'Oh, that is so good,' I say and he laughs, his brown eyes dancing in the light from the café. He is so beautiful that sometimes I can't believe I'm going out with him.

'Rubbish,' says Becca when I say this, 'you're the catch.'

'I should go soon,' I say to my boyfriend. 'I have so much work to do.' It's Friday afternoon and my mum and I have agreed that I get a couple of hours off on a Friday afternoon despite this being year twelve. I'm working really hard at school, and so far, it's going okay. I want to study psychology next year.

'Makes sense,' my mother said when I told her, 'after everything that's happened.'

I would like to be a school psychologist. I want to get to people before they become Leeanne, before they feel so awful about their lives that they need to ruin someone else's.

Maddox is doing year twelve again because he couldn't finish the school year last year. He moved down to Melbourne to stay with his grandparents and finish up there.

When we talk about it, Becca and I, we are still trying to figure out how it all went so wrong. Maddox did a terrible thing but he thought he had his reasons. I know that Callum will never speak to him again. It's so sad that he started the whole thing because he was angry about losing his friend, and now he's lost him forever. He's lost a whole year of his life and his sister is in prison. He didn't understand how bad things were for Leeanne. None of us did.

So much is gone from Maddox's life. Lots of people thought he should go to prison as well but I think he's paid a big enough price. He'll have to live with this forever.

'What a strange world you children are growing up in,' my mum keeps saying. She's right but it's all we know. We just have to learn how to figure out who and what to trust and who and what to question when we meet people in cyberspace.

Leeanne writes to me and Becca, and even though Becca doesn't email her back, I do. I don't think she wanted Zoe to die. I know she didn't. It just got all tangled up in her head. She thought pretending to be Xavier at camp would make things better and she thought humiliating Zoe and recording it would make things better. But you can't lift yourself up by hurting someone else. You just can't and now her whole life is ruined. She will never be a lawyer like she wanted to be. Everything has stopped for Leeanne. Not the way it did for Zoe but I think she's being punished enough. She'll be in prison for six years, and while she will still have a life when she gets out, it will be very different to the kind of life she wanted for herself. And she will come back to a very different family. Her brother was the one who called the police and told them what she'd done. I don't know if she'll ever be able to forgive him. I might ask her when I send her my next email, but I might not. I can feel, from the way she writes, that she's fragile and broken.

'Yeah, I should go soon too,' says Michael, bringing me back to the present, 'but not long now and then it will all be over. I can't wait. I can't believe that less than six months from now we'll be on a tour of Europe.'

'I know and it's so great that Becca is coming as well. It will be fun.'

He sighs and runs his hands through his dark hair. 'But until then there is so much work, it might kill me.'

'Don't say that,' I say quickly because I can't hear those words. I still can't hear those words.

'Sorry… sorry, babe,' he says quietly.

He stands up and reaches out his hand for mine, and I hold on tight. He is taller than me and he pulls me close as we walk out of the door to whatever awaits us.

Bernadette

'Are you all right?' I ask Henry as he pushes his hands into the small of his back, bending a little to stretch.

'I'm fine,' he says. 'We sat at that café a bit too long.'

'True, but the coffee and pastries were divine.' Even though we have just finished eating, my mouth waters at the thought of the crunchy *kunafa* filled with sweet whipped cream and the delicious foamy coffee from the café just on the edge of the market. It is a balmy twenty-five degrees so we can stay out all day long if we want, but I know Henry likes an afternoon nap before we head out to dinner. Egypt has been a revelation for both of us. Every day I think that I cannot be more amazed and every day I am. The pyramids took my breath away.

I turn and begin walking past stalls, knowing that Henry is behind me.

'Look,' he says when he catches up to me as I examine a colourful sequinned bag, 'I got a message from Sarah.'

I look down at his phone to see Sarah's three-year-old daughter in their garden with Oliver at her side. 'She says Mia wants Granny Bernie to know that she is taking good care of Oliver.'

I smile as I look at the picture. 'She's such a serious little thing. I knew she and Oliver would be fine.'

It is not just Egypt that has been a revelation to me; it is everything that has happened since the afternoon I decided that I could no longer go on living.

It is Henry and his endless kindness. It is the way his daughter and her husband and child have accepted me. It is how easily Henry and I spend a day together with Oliver. It is how happy I am, after all these years alone, after being sure that I knew what the course of my life would be. After everything.

I was a very different person six months ago. Zoe's death changed everything, not just for me but for her family and friends as well. I still find myself saddened and stuck in a guilty spiral over everything that I missed with Leeanne. I thought we were kindred spirits but I somehow missed how much pain she was in. I didn't think she was following Zoe to hurt her. I really didn't. I knew that she struggled with bullying but I could never have dreamed what she was capable of. I had no idea of the ruse perpetrated by her brother or of how far she would go to use what he'd done. I thought that, like me, she was looking forward to being out of school. But fitting in is even more important these days than when I was a child. When I was at school, I went home to the shelter and peace of my bedroom. Teenagers these days have nowhere to find peace. The bullies follow you home, into your bedroom. Leeanne should have been helped before she did something so terrible and drastic. I will never forgive myself for failing in this.

'You were not her parent, you were her teacher,' Henry says and he's right, but I should have been a better teacher. I should have been a better human being.

I write to Leeanne once a month, encouraging her to keep up with her studies and to not give up on a career when she gets out of prison.

She is, strangely enough, tolerating her situation quite well.

We're all misfits in here. The other girls come to me for help with their homework – some of them never got the chance to have a proper education. I enjoy working with them. It's nothing like I thought it would be.

She tells me that they are very short of English teachers in the prison system, and when we get back to Australia, I might look into doing some volunteering.

Paula sent me a short email a couple of months ago. She was one of the few people I hadn't heard from. Most of the teachers at St Anne's contacted me via email, expressing concern and wishing me well. A lot of the students have contacted me as well, and I have replied to each of them, telling them that I made the wrong choice but that I was fortunate enough to have been saved so I could learn to live my life in a more productive and positive way. I have said that I am available to talk any time of the day or night. No one should feel so alone as I did.

Paula's email was short and to the point, but I appreciate it must have been difficult to send.

I bear as much responsibility for what happened as you do. I should not have allowed Jessie to visit. I should have been concentrating on the girls. I will always feel terrible grief over the loss of such a young life.

Ryan and I have settled in Queensland and the children are happy at their new school. I am working in a bookshop and I don't think I will ever go back to teaching.

I hope you're well and I wish you all the best.

I wrote back that I wished her all the best as well. I hope she manages to move forward with her life.

'All right, this way I think,' calls Henry, and I see that he is ahead of me now.

I smile at the stall holder and follow Henry, happy to let him lead us home.

Jessie

'I can't do it, Val. I don't have the time and my mother will go nuts if I do,' says Jessie but her friend Valerie only laughs. They are both in a jubilant mood, having completed the last exam of the semester. She texted her mother to let her know it went well and received a smiling emoji in reply.

She and Val only have a few days off before work at the hospital begins, but a few days feels like a lifetime to both of them.

'For the tenth time, I have cleared this with your mother. And you will find the time. You're up early and your mum goes in later and she gets home early and she says she'll hire a dog walker. Any puppy will be lucky to have you. Even Gabriel is on board.'

Jessie slumps down in her seat and crosses her arms. She can't help but feel she is being pushed into a puppy, but at the same time, her heart races with excitement.

'But what if there's something wrong with it? It's from a shelter, and you never know, do you?'

'Ah, now there I have an answer for you. You know my cousin Candess?'

'Yes, because you talk about her all the time. She's studying to be a vet.'

'Yes, and she volunteers at this shelter on Sundays. So, she knows that this puppy is in very good health even though she's not sure what he's crossed with. She knows that he has some golden retriever in him, but as for the rest – well, it's a bit of a mystery.'

'And won't it be adopted already? I know that puppies move really quickly in shelters.'

'I asked her to keep him for us. She came in specially today to show him to you. Just look at him, Jess, and if you don't like him, you don't have to take him and I will stop bugging you about it.'

'No one can replace Walter,' says Jessie and she slides down further in her seat, wiping a stray tear from her cheek. She knows that it's more than just Walter she is crying for but she's trying to do what her mother says she does, which is to think of three good memories of Zoe and three good memories of Walter whenever it all starts to feel overwhelming.

She thinks about Zoe reading Walter a story when he was a puppy and she insisted that he couldn't go to bed without one because all the children in the family got a bedtime story and Walter was now one of the children, and she smiles.

And then she remembers Zoe climbing into the bath with Walter when he was a puppy and her mother's despairing laugh as the two of them played. 'Walter got mud on his feet, Mum, and he didn't like it. I'm gonna use all the bubbles to make him nice and clean.'

An image of her sister sharing a bag of chips with the old dog, one for her and one for him, emerges and Jessie feels her smile grow wider.

She misses her sister more than she thought possible. She misses what they could have been to each other and what they might have become as they got older. She aches for all that Zoe will never get to experience. Walter lived a full life, and even her father got to have a family before he died. Zoe will forever be sixteen, and the unfairness of that sometimes takes her breath away.

A few days ago, after an exam, as the sun was setting, she went to visit her sister's grave. She stood reading the white-and-pink marble headstone, mouthing the words as her brain relaxed.

Zoe Bloom
Beloved daughter of Lydia and Eli Bloom
Darling sister to Jessie
Forever sixteen, forever in our hearts

She and her mother had chosen the words together. Simple words, simply true.

'I'm sorry, Zoe,' she whispered. 'I should have been a better sister. I should have been there for you. Can you forgive me?'

She waited as the sun dropped and warmth faded from the air, and she watched the gravestones of her sister and father. In the last moment before darkness fell over the cemetery, a slice of sun lit up the words 'forever in our hearts', and she understood that to be what Zoe would have hoped for. Her little sister doesn't have to worry. She will never be forgotten.

She has not heard from Paula, and when she thinks about that time, Paula's face has faded and the moments they had together don't seem real. It was something that never should have happened, and Jessie has been guarding her heart closely since then.

'Here we are,' says Valerie, and Jessie sits up straight to see a large, open piece of land dotted with what look like small houses, surrounded by a metal fence.

Valerie rings the bell and announces herself and the gate buzzes open. As Jessie and Valerie walk towards what appears to be the front office, Jessie looks around at the dogs in their pens. There are a lot of them but they all look like they have comfortable beds and toys to play with. Some of them get up and come over to inspect them as they walk past; some ignore them.

'There you are,' calls a voice. 'I was afraid you wouldn't get here before we closed.'

Jessie turns to see a young woman carrying a ball of golden fluff. She looks first at the puppy, who is snuggled up against the girl, and then at the girl, who has short red hair and a small gold hoop in her nose. Her green eyes light up her face. 'You must be Jessie. I'm Candess and this is… well, whoever you want him to be, I guess.'

She hands the puppy to Jessie and he cries a little but then settles against her chest, going back to sleep as though he is perfectly happy to stay in her arms forever. Jessie feels his warm fur and his little heart beating against her chest and knows that she is taking home a puppy.

'He's just…' she says.

'I know,' says Candess, stroking his little head. 'He's got such a sweet personality but he's a bit of a baby and you'll need to keep him close.'

'He can sleep on my bed,' says Jessie, 'right next to me.'

Candess laughs. 'Your girlfriend might have something to say about that.'

'I don't have a girlfriend, and anyway, I couldn't date someone who didn't like dogs.'

'Me neither,' says Candess.

In the car on the way home she strokes the sleeping puppy, who is wrapped in a blanket, making little snuffling noises.

'That was a set-up, wasn't it?' she says to Valerie.

Valerie is silent for a moment. 'Yes,' she says finally. 'I thought… I know you've been through… well… so much, but it's time to start living again, Jess, not just studying and sleeping. Candess is wonderful and I've been waiting for the right time to introduce you two. If you want, I can ask her over to dinner next Saturday night and you can bring this little guy and we can just chill together.'

Jessie looks out of the window at the cars they are passing, at everyone going on with their lives, knowing that in each car there could be someone who is suffering, who is in pain. She feels like she has been suffering and in pain forever, like she has been stuck in the quicksand of her grief and she will never get out.

OMG, Jess, what is wrong with you? She's so cute, she hears her little sister say, and she allows herself a small smile.

'Okay,' she says quietly.

'Okay?' asks Valerie.

'Okay.'

A LETTER FROM NICOLE

Hello,

I would like to thank you for taking the time to read *The Girl Who Never Came Home*. If you did enjoy it, and want to keep up to date with all my latest releases, just sign up at the following link. Your email address will never be shared and you can unsubscribe at any time.

www.bookouture.com/nicole-trope

For a long time, I was told to 'write what you know', but that never really worked for me. Instead I write what I fear.

I write about families in crisis and about lives changing in the blink of an eye.

This was a particularly scary concept for me to write about because it is always frightening to entrust others with your child's care. A school camp should be a safe place but no one could predict what would happen between the girls in that cabin or what Leeanne had planned.

Having and raising children seems to become more complicated with each passing decade. The intrusion of social media into the lives of the next generations means that those of us who raise them are never entirely sure what they may be reading or seeing or who they may be speaking to.

If you have children, you know that who they become and who you think they will become are often very different things. I hope you understood Lydia's distress at realising that she didn't know her two daughters as well as she thought she did. I do believe that she was doing the very best she could in a difficult situation. Losing a partner is something no one wants to go through, but having to raise two young children after the loss of someone you thought would be there to help you makes it more difficult. My heart broke for Lydia and all that she had lost, but I hope that readers will see that at the end of the novel she also found acceptance and a way forward. I want that for all of my characters, even Leeanne and Maddox, who made such dangerous and disastrous choices in their lives.

I really enjoyed writing the characters in this novel and I was especially fond of Bernadette. I'm so glad she got to visit Egypt and that she has Henry to share it with her.

And, in case you're wondering, Jessie and Candess are very happy together, and the new puppy has been named Buddy because from the moment Jessie brought him home, he was her little buddy, following her everywhere and sleeping on her bed.

If you have enjoyed this novel, it would be lovely if you could take the time to leave a review. I read them all and find it inspiring when readers connect with the characters I write about.

I would also love to hear from you. You can find me on Facebook and Twitter and I'm always happy to connect with readers.

Thanks again for reading.
Nicole x

🐦 @nicoletrope
📘 NicoleTrope

ACKNOWLEDGEMENTS

I would like to, once again, thank Christina Demosthenous for being an excellent editor and an all-round fabulous person who doesn't mind reassuring worried authors about the same things over and over again. As always, she has pushed me to do my best work, and I have absolute faith in her judgement and opinions about each novel.

I would also like to thank Kim Nash, Noelle Holten and Sarah Hardy, publicity and social media gurus, for helping my novels into the world. Thanks to the whole team at Bookouture, including Alexandra Holmes, Martina Arzu and Lauren Finger. Thanks to DeAndra Lupu for another brilliant copyedit and Liz Hatherell for proofreading.

Thanks to my mother, Hilary, for being my first reader and then for casting a close eye over the final version of the novel.

Thanks also to David, Mikhayla, Isabella and Jacob.

And once again thank you to those who read, review and blog about my work. Every review is appreciated and I do read them all.

CPSIA information can be obtained
at www.ICGtesting.com
Printed in the USA
LVHW091448010921
696688LV00012B/108